Death's Favorite Child

Frankie Y. Bailey

This book is a work of fiction. All names, characters, places, and events are the product of the author's imagination. Any resemblance to actual events or persons, living or dead, is entirely coincidental and beyond the intent of either the author or the publisher.

Hardcover ISBN 1-57072-145-9
Trade Paper ISBN 1-57072-146-7
Copyright © 2000 by Frankie Y. Bailey
All Rights Reserved
Printed in the United States of America
1 2 3 4 5 6 7 8 9 0

"It is perhaps natural that around the three great mysteries—birth, love and death—a crowd of superstitions cling, the children of those unnamed fears which accompany so many of us from the cradle to the grave, and which certainly dominated the lives of less enlightened generations."

Bertram S. Puckle

Funeral Customs, their origin and development (1926)

ACKNOWLEDGMENTS

My gratitude:

To the Wolf Road Irregulars—Joanne Barker, Audrey Friend, Christopher Myers, and Caroline Young Petrequin—who have provided years of support, stability, and humor during our Sunday evening meetings and elsewhere.

To Betsy and Scott Blaustein, former proprietors of Haven't Got A Clue and early friends in the Albany mystery community.

To Alice Green (and husband Charles Touhey) for concocting (and taste-testing) my "yummy ball" recipe. Alice, I also thank you for the cover photo.

To Joy Pollock and son Gregory—who stopped to vacation in Cornwall, England, en route to a Fulbright semester in Finland and invited me to join them. Joy, your suggestions were invaluable. Gregory, you're my favorite kid.

To Gray Cavender, fellow academic and mystery writer. Thanks, Gray, for telling me about Silver Dagger.

To Carolyn Smith, colleague and friend, who read a draft of this book and who did what she could over lunch to educate me about things British.

To Mom, for being Mom. To Donna Hale and Hans Toch for words of encouragement. Donna, don't forget those devious plots we've been hatching. Hans, I hope this mystery is full of people you'll enjoy analyzing.

To the good folks at The Overmountain Press, particularly Beth Wright, Sherry Lewis, and Ben Kneisley. Thank you too, Deborah Adams.

To everyone who contributed in any way to this book—including kind strangers I stopped on the street or e-mailed to ask odd questions.

Thank you all.

Chapter One

Rituals for the Dead and Dying. I'd scrawled those words across the yellow page of a legal pad one robins-chirping, tulips-blooming afternoon in May. That day, moving my hand across the page had been the only thing that had kept me from toppling over. The paperback thriller in my tote bag had stayed there, too intricate for my brain even if my eyes hadn't been filled with grit.

Rituals. During slavery, blacks on plantations often wrapped their dead in "winding sheets" and buried them at night. Laboring from sunup to sundown, the slaves spent their daylight hours performing their masters' tasks. Night was the only portion of the day that they could call their own. So that was when they buried their dead. Singing, carrying torches to light the way, they delivered the body to its grave.

Such processions puzzled, even frightened, the whites who observed them. Prone to their own superstitions, whites in the antebellum South understood better the "death watch" for the departing loved one and the "laying out" of the corpse.

They, white people, died of diseases and in childbirth. Black slaves died of the same causes and of hard work and abuse. Death was a constant presence in the lives of both groups. Death required rituals.

It still does. My grandmother, a descendant of field slaves, did her dying in a hospital room under medical supervision. But each day I drove back and forth to Lexington to keep my vigil at her bedside.

On the night that she died, I had lost my battle with exhaustion and fallen asleep in an armchair. Her voice jolted me awake. She had pushed herself upright in the bed. "Becca? Don't you play your games with me. I see you there."

I twisted around in my chair. For a moment, in that dimly lit room, I expected to see something there in the shadows.

"Becca, you stop your laughing!"

I had never heard Becca laugh. Neither one of us had laid eyes on Becca, my mother, in the thirty-eight years since my birth. But to the best of my knowledge she was still alive. Not a ghost to haunt her mother's passing.

I staggered to my feet. "Grandma? Shh, it's all right. Let me help you lie back down."

She turned her head and looked up at me. "Becca? What you come back here for?"

"Grandma, it's me. It's Lizzie. Here, let me—"

She grabbed my hand in an urgent grip. "It would kill your daddy if he knew. We can't never let him find out. We can't let nobody find out."

"What . . . find out what?"

She groaned, rocking herself. "How could you do it, Becca? That man—" Her voice sunk to a whisper. "Oh, lord, baby. Becca, get on your knees and pray . . . pray for you and that child growing inside you."

"Grandma, what—?"

She slumped against my arm. I held her for several heartbeats, then eased her back down onto the pillow.

She was dead. I knew that even before I pressed the button for assistance, even before a nurse rushed into the room to check her vital signs. Hester Rose Stuart was dead.

As for Becca—Rebecca, headstrong by all accounts, had been a few weeks short of eighteen when I was born. Five days after my birth, still without revealing the identity of my father, she had boarded a Greyhound bus and left town. Or so my grandmother had always told me.

In the days since my grandmother's death, I had been adjusting to living alone in the house that was now mine. Adjusting to silences filled with voices from my childhood. At around three that afternoon, I came to rest there in the kitchen doorway.

Silver-edged thunderheads loomed. I considered getting in my car and driving down to the Sheraton Hotel. I thought of sitting there in the lobby cafe sipping mint tea while the pianist played and the fountain tinkled, drowning out the storm raging outside. I thought of leaving home before the storm broke, but I kept on standing there in the doorway with that photograph in my hand.

It had been taken out by the old oak tree. My grandfather, Walter Lee, grinning that grin that people still mentioned when they spoke of him, faced the camera. He was ebony-skinned and lanky. Hester Rose, petite and pecan-colored, peeped around his shoulder. That afternoon, touched by some fleeting joy, she had dared risk one of her rare full-mouthed smiles. A hand had snapped the photograph and then it had been forgotten.

I had found the camera when I was searching the attic. After two hours of dust and spider webs, after finding nothing more significant about my mother than the paperback novels—*Moby Dick*, *Jane Eyre*, and *The Scarlet Letter*—that she must have been assigned in a high school English class, I had been about to give up. Then I'd opened a dented steamer truck. The camera was buried beneath a pile of moldy sheets. When I realized it contained film, I ran downstairs to change. Half an hour later, I was walking into a camera store in Lexington. There among the prints of house, flower beds, and vegetable garden had been that single photograph of my grandparents, the proud homeowners.

Both dead now. He of a heart attack, years ago when I was at graduate school. She at a little after midnight on June 1, the combined effects of hip surgery, diabetes, and a virulent strain of pneumonia—and perhaps whatever it was that had kept her mouth tight and her eyes wary.

Lightning zigzagged across the sky. I stepped back into the kitchen and let the screen door bang shut.

When I was a child, I had been sure God was Zeus, with lightning bolts that he flung down at people who had been bad. I shared this with my grandfather during one of our tramps through the woods, and he laughed until tears streaked his cheeks.

Seeing my chagrin, he hugged me to his side. "Lizzie, if that was the way of it, child, you wouldn't be able to walk after a storm for all the dead folks you'd be stumbling over." That might be true, but all these years later I could still have gone for a very long time between colliding weather fronts.

Lightning flashed. Thunder cracked and boomed, shaking the house. I clutched my grandparents' photograph and scrunched myself tighter into a corner of the flowered sofa. The shutter on one of the upstairs windows was loose and banging. Rain slashed against the picture window in the living room. I huddled there on the sofa, mumbling an apology for being ungrateful for what I had. An apology for being angry because I was without kin.

God did not strike one dead for having wicked thoughts. If that were the case, I'd already be dead.

I was astraphobic, brontophobic. Scared of storms. One of those silly childhood fears I intended to outgrow someday soon. The upstairs shutter banged like a gavel in the hand of an irate judge.

"All right, you're being ridiculous. One hundred, ninety-nine, ninety-eight. First thing tomorrow, find a repairman to fix the shutter. Ninety-seven, ninety-six. I am calm and relaxed. I am—"

White light exploded into the room. I screamed. I thought I was dead. But it was the tree. The old oak tree in the backyard had been struck by lightning. Blasted to its roots. Hester Rose, my grandmother, would have said it was an omen. A "sign." But a sign is only useful if you know how to read it. At any rate, it was a moment of transition. Not dying was amazingly therapeutic.

Chapter Two

The sunlight was deceptive. At well past six in the evening, it looked warm enough so that it was not surprising to see people still down on the beach. But while I was waiting at the train station for a taxi, I had tugged my jacket from my tote bag and put it on. Before I left the hotel, I would have been equally well-advised to take off the shorts I was wearing and put on slacks. But I had been eager to get out and see St. Regis.

The first official day of this, my vacation, had begun less than an hour ago when I arrived in St. Regis on the afternoon train from London. The taxi I had called when I found the tiny train station unattended had brought me up the hill to my hotel. If I had known where to look, I would have been able to see the hotel from the train station. I might have even walked up the hill, climbing the path up from the beach, except the path included the steep steps I had come down. Those steps would have been difficult with luggage in hand.

Anyway, I hadn't known where I was going. And the taxi driver had charged almost nothing for the short trip through town and to the front door of the private hotel Tess had chosen.

Now I was strolling into town—the center of town—along the pedestrian walk that overlooked the beach. There was to be a children's parade. The two sisters who ran the hotel had said I must come out and see it.

What I also should have done before I left the hotel was ask for something to drink, for a glass of ice water or a tall orange juice to soothe my parched throat. But I would undoubtedly find a place to get a cup of tea. England was overflowing with tea.

Tea and wives. How did that nursery rhyme go? Not about St. Regis, but about a trip to the market town of St. Ives. "As I was going to St. Ives, I met a man with seven wives—" And each wife was carrying something. Cats? No, sacks. "Every wife had seven sacks. Every sack had seven cats—"

A head full of rhymes, riddles, and other useless information. That was me. A grown woman should have something better to think about. I did have something better to think about. I just didn't want to think about it.

I focused on the panoramic view. It was the kind that made one take a deep breath and reach for a camera. Mine was in my tote bag back at the hotel, but there would be other chances for picture taking during the week. For the moment, I was content to look.

Down the hill, on the access road above the beach, a car and a truck had met. The car was backing up to let the truck pass. Several people weaved their way around the vehicles en route to the white concrete building with tiled roof that must be the public rest rooms.

On the other side of the road, a line had formed in front of what looked like an ice cream stand. Parked adjacent to the stand was a black van with white letters on its side and a satellite dish attached to its roof. A radio station broadcasting live? Late in the day for that.

But, of course, the sun was still bright. And a good number of vividly clad sunbathers were still holding down the patches of sand they had claimed with umbrellas, towels, and what appeared to be windbreaks.

Toddlers played in a tide pool while farther out, adults and older children dashed in and out of the surf, laughing, calling to each other. Beyond them, stretching to the horizon, shimmering blue ocean merged with cloudless blue sky. Wonderful. Picture perfect.

But even after reading the tourist guides to Cornwall and everything I could find on the Internet, I was still not prepared to find a resort town on this rugged coast of England. Put it down to the lingering effects of adolescent exposure to Daphne du Maurier's fiction. In spite of what I had read to the contrary, I had been expecting more shadows than sunlight. A shy young bride haunted by the ghost of first wife Rebecca.

Or shipwrecks, smugglers, and Revenue men. Tin mines and tenant farmers with work-worn wives. And the brooding hero of the series, Ross Poldark, married to feisty Demelza and still in love with his former fiancée, now his cousin's wife. Those were my images of Cornwall.

In my mind's eye, Cornwall was a place of storm-swept coasts, dark secrets, destructive passions, and medieval lore. Tristan and Isolde country. The begetting of King Arthur at Tintagel Castle by the lustful Uther. Instead Merlin might have conjured up this summer day for his lady's pleasure.

At the Merrimont Theatre, *Macbeth* was on the schedule for the month of August. The Merrimont was described in the tourist guides as a stone amphitheater with the Atlantic Ocean as its spectacular backdrop. That would be the same ocean over which the sun was now shining. How on earth did they manage to create the gloom necessary to do a matinee performance of a play like *Macbeth*? I needed to see that. But meanwhile, it was time to shake off my gloom and get with the program.

Time to get a move-on or I would miss the children's parade. The Sisters Crump had insisted that it was ridiculous for me to waste my evening sitting about waiting for my friend Tess to return from her travels. "Nonsense," Edith had said. And Sarah—the younger sister by at least a decade—had nodded her head in agreement. It was obvious that they thought Tess had behaved rather badly by not being present to greet me when I arrived on the train from London.

I, on the other hand, appreciated having some time to myself to depressurize before I slipped into my role of holiday companion. I had expected to have that time on the flight from Newark, during my day in London, and, of course, on the five-hour train trip to the West Country. So far, nothing had gone quite as I had planned. I rubbed at the stiffness in my neck, a souvenir from yesterday's near brush with a London bus.

I turned for another glance up the hill. The Crump sisters' private hotel had disappeared into the greenery, anonymous up there among the white and gray houses on terraced streets. Maybe I should have waited there for Tess to come back. I needed to tell her about Michael. I needed to give her the package that I had almost gotten myself killed trying to hold on to.

I stood there weighing the wisdom of climbing back up the hill and sitting in my room to await Tess's eventual return against the growling of my stomach. I had not eaten since breakfast. I had intended to have lunch on the train. That was before I found that my reserved seat was in the smoking car. The dapper old gentleman occupying the aisle seat beside me had a dog—a sad-eyed hound who had settled himself at his master's feet with a tired sigh. A few minutes later, both man and dog were asleep, and it had seemed cruel to bother them to get out into the aisle. So I had sat breathing the smoke and nursing a dull headache while the hound's snores whiffled across my bare legs.

Well, I was here now, and I was hungry. Tess would probably have eaten when she returned, so I might as well have something to eat. I would be in a better mood after some food. Pasta to soothe anxiety. It worked every time. Well, some of the time.

A seagull soared out over the beach below and then swooped downward with a raucous cry. That cry was echoed by another.

I held my breath, listening. Hidden by the next bend in the path, an argument was going on—a man and a woman, their words carried away on the breeze. Well, it was probably just a minor disagreement. It was either go on along the path or climb back up the steps and go the long way into town.

Two people were confronting each other. He held her by her arm, snarling angry words into her face. I thought of retreating. But I hadn't lied to my students when I explained the theory of bystander intervention. As the only bystander present, I felt compelled to do something. There was no one else there to whom I could diffuse the responsibility. Worse luck.

"Is there a problem?"

Both heads swung toward me. Eighteen or nineteen, she had tears running down her cheeks and blood dripping from her split lip onto her bright yellow sleeveless blouse. He held on to her while he glared at me. "This ain't none of your business," he said. Black jacket, boots, jeans, white T-shirt. Only missing a black leather-brimmed cap to cover his tousled blond hair. Did the British have their own version of the Marlon Brando biker?

Quaking in my walking shoes, I moved closer. "I'm sorry, I really can't pretend I don't see what you're doing. I don't think you should hit her again." The girl brushed back her long black hair, baring her swan neck and slender arms. Her eyes were sapphire blue. "You work at the Gull's Nest Hotel, don't you?" I asked. "Remember, you were coming out through the garden gate as I arrived."

She nodded her head. "Yes, I remember."

"And where were you going?" he demanded in his coarser accent. He was not much older than she was. There was a trace of acne on the chin that he was thrusting forward. "Where were you going, then, Dee? Weren't you standing here telling me you had no plans at all to meet your—"

"Shut up, Sean!" Blood sprayed from her cut lip. "Just shut up."

"Shut up? Don't you go telling me to—"

I sprang forward, grabbing at his upraised arm. The sleeve of his black leather jacket was butter soft. I noted that fact as he turned in my grasp, bringing me up against his T-shirt-covered chest and within smelling distance of the beer on his breath.

"I told you to sodding well stay out of this! It ain't your business." In his brown eyes, pain warred with anger. Both were in the hands that had me by the shoulders. I grabbed at his wrists.

"Let the lady go, mate." The quiet command was sufficient to freeze us all in mid-action. The newcomer to our gathering stood with his hands at his sides, stance relaxed, expression neutral. His gray Philadelphia 76ers sweatshirt, faded jeans, and running shoes matched what had sounded like an American accent. Tall, five or six inches taller than my five-seven. Not as brawny as Sean and certainly older, but with the lean, muscled look of someone who kept himself in shape. Dark auburn hair, gone forty-something gray at the temples but showing no sign of thinning.

Where had I seen—

The Army base. I had been eight or nine that year. Polished buckles glistening in the sun. Precision drills as the band played. And afterwards, another visit with Sergeant Barnes. Sergeant Russell "RJ" Barnes, my grandfather's friend, with whom he talked of the old days when they had come up together in rural Mississippi. With whom he talked, his grin gone, about Vietnam and all the young black men dying over there.

I had been eating an apple. Sergeant Barnes and my grandfather had gotten to the pouring-whiskey, telling-lies part of their visit. "You can always spot one, Walt. Take off that uniform and put on anything he want, but once a man got soldier in him, ain't no use at all trying to pretend he no civilian."

This man, standing relaxed and at his ease, had the look of years of uniforms and discipline about him. Right down to the creases in his faded jeans. But his face was weary. As if he were recovering from an illness. Dark circles under eyes as silver-gray as his sweatshirt. High cheekbones stark under pale skin.

And while I was standing there staring at his face, I might give some thought to protecting my own. I took a giant step away from Sean, out of his slackened grasp.

Silence. Sean was sizing up the newcomer, who was examining him with equal interest. Dee—with a studied lack of interest—was looking off into the distance, dabbing at her cut lip with a tissue that she must have found in the red leather backpack dangling from her shoulder.

So there we stood, four slightly wounded souls on a footpath in St. Regis. What nursery rhyme should we do? Well, someone had to say something.

"Thank you," I said to the man who had come to my rescue. After all, I might not have remembered how to execute any of the escape moves I had learned in the self-defense course I took several years ago and hadn't practiced since. Sean would probably have made mincemeat of me and then continued his two-fisted discussion with Dee.

"Sodding busybodies," Sean mumbled, offering his assessment of the situation. "Come on," he said to Dee.

She continued to dab at her lip.

"Come on," he said.

She turned her head. Her sapphire blue gaze flickered over him.

"Go away," she said.

"Dee—" There was a note of pleading in the way he said her name.

"Go away," she said again. This was no cowering battered woman. Sean might have struck her, but she—at least for the moment—held the balance of power.

Sean's gaze fell from hers. Then he glanced in my direction. "It ain't what you think," he said. "Ask her why. Ask her!" He shot an angry, defiant look at the other, older man, who was observing him in silence, then he charged off up the path toward town, head down, walking fast.

Dee watched him go. She nodded her head at us. "Thank you for your help." She departed in a whirl of ankle-length black and yellow flowered cotton skirt, gliding off in the direction from which I had come. Was she going back to the hotel? What would the Sisters Crump say about her split lip? Or perhaps they knew about this. About Sean.

"Care to make a sporting wager?"

I turned to look at the man with whom I had been left standing. "On what?" That was what I was trying to ask when I sneezed. A loud eruption of a sneeze, followed by another, and then a third as I scrambled through the contents of my shoulder bag for my tissues. "Oh, dear, I'm sorry. Excuse me."

"Catching a cold?" Amusement in the cool eyes.

"I don't think so. Something tickled my nose. A sporting wager on what?"

"The survivor."

He meant Dee and Sean. "That's a grim way to look at it."

"Did that look like happily ever after?"

"No, but—"

"But they might have the good sense to stay away from each other? Don't count on it." He glanced down at the flat, no-frills watch on his wrist. "I'm about five minutes away from being late. So long, Yank. Try to stay out of trouble."

"I always stay out of trouble," I called after him. "And you're the one with the Northern accent."

"Wrong war," he called back.

Wrong war? Oh, of course—in England, World War II would be the operative war. Yank, as in generic American.

I watched as my countryman took the steps to the street above with long-legged ease, a man departing the scene of an incident that had delayed him in going about his business, whatever that business was. I somehow doubted he was a member of the famed artist colony that gathered at St. Regis, drawn there by the luminous light that was the trademark of the town. And, from what I understood, Cornwall and the West Country had yet to catch on as a red hot vacation spot for American tourists. The area attracted mainly Brits, who came to enjoy their own "English Riviera."

Of course, I was there. But only because of Tess, my college-roommate-turned-travel-writer, and because of my need to get out of Drucilla, Kentucky, for a while. What I was not there to do was to wonder why other people were there. "Having established that, Lizabeth, shall we move on?"

A man and woman in matching white shorts and stripped summer sweaters came around the bend in the path just in time to hear my question. I smiled to indicate I was harmless and followed in their wake.

By the time I got to the town square, the children's parade, scheduled to began at seven, would be over. I would have to content myself with finding a cozy restaurant and ordering a large pot of hot tea and a decent meal. And if I were lucky, nothing else would happen.

Not that I could expect any good to come of sneezing on Sunday.

"You gonna spend the whole week trying to keep one step ahead of the devil, Walter Stuart."

He had nodded his head as he tucked his white handkerchief back into his suit coat pocket. "Now, that's one of your sayings that makes some sense, Hester Rose. Sneezing probably do mean you're gonna spend the whole week trying to keep ahead of the devil—that devil of a cold you trying not to get."

A rational man, my grandfather. I had always been grateful for the balance he brought to our lives. And I was his rational granddaughter. So go have some tea with honey and lemon and start fighting off my budding cold.

Of course, the truth of the matter was that whether I caught a cold or not, so far this vacation was not going well. In fact, the past two days had left a great deal to be desired.

It had started in London. True, the overnight flight from Newark had been turbulent, and I had arrived at Gatwick Airport with jet lag and a fluttering stomach. But it was on Saturday afternoon that my vacation had begun its downward spiral. Having walked until my legs were speaking their mind, I was sitting in a restaurant near Piccadilly Circus having a proper British lunch of fish and chips. I was shaking on more vinegar when my waiter came over to my table.

He nodded his head in a little bow. "The gentleman asked me to give you this." He held out a folded paper napkin. I stared at it. "There is something written on it," the waiter said.

I took the napkin. "What gentleman?"

The waiter gestured toward the open doors leading out onto the terrace. "He was over there. He is gone now."

"This man—what did he look like, please?"

The waiter shrugged his thin shoulders. "An American, I would say. Light hair—blond—and he was wearing dark glasses." The waiter held his hand above his own head. "A little taller and slender."

The waiter left, and I unfolded the napkin. "Lizzie, meet me Madame Tussaud's. Inside. 3 o'clock."

Lizzie? How did this man know my name? I picked up my glass of what the British called lemonade and took a sip. I choked and coughed. Because of the note, not the beverage.

Lizzie? Well, I was certainly not going. But how did he know my name? I didn't know anyone in London. There was no one here who knew me. If he were an acquaintance—someone I had met at a professional conference in the States, for example—why wouldn't he have come over and said hello? Why this cloak and dagger? Meet him at a wax museum?

I was not going, that much was certain. I crumpled the napkin into a ball and dropped it beside my plate. Meet him—when turkeys fly.

But in the end I did go. I was reaching into my shoulder bag for my camera to take a picture of a street mime when the balled up napkin (snatched up from the table as I was leaving) fell out. Not that I had forgotten it was there; I was choosing to ignore it. As I plucked the paper from the sidewalk, I accepted the fact that I was going to go to Madame Tussaud's. If I didn't, I would never know what this was about. What could happen in a public place?

A lot. I could rattle off a list of unpleasant things that could happen during and after a rendezvous with a strange man in a public place. But if he already knew my name, he might very well know where I was staying. So I should find out who he was and what he wanted. Maybe it was someone I knew who hadn't had time to come in and say hello. But he'd had time to write the note. And why Madame Tussaud's?

I took the tube and then walked along Marylebone Road. When I saw the line winding around the corner in front of the wax museum, I almost said to heck with it and turned back. Almost. But not quite.

The truth was that I was no more capable of resisting the lure of that note than a shopoholic was of resisting a sale. I had passed my teen years in Drucilla, Kentucky, longing for an escape from my occasionally humiliating, but generally humdrum, everyday life. I had gone away to college and to graduate school and then returned to Drucilla. But once—as the beneficiary of a doctoral fellowship award—I had spent a week in London, attending a conference. And now I was back again, and I'd just received a note from a mystery man. The lure of adventure trumped the voice of caution. I had watched too many movies to be able to pass this up.

The sign above the front entrance of the wax museum informed those in the queue that the waiting time was approximately twenty minutes. It was a hot day. As we waited in the sun, people in line ate ice cream and sipped on soft drinks purchased from the two vendors who had set up carts on the sidewalk. I spent the time thinking about the sunscreen I should have put on that morning and taking frequent glances at my watch. Behind me in the queue was a group of Indian tourists, the women in lovely, cool-looking saris, the men in European slacks and shirts. One of the men, recounting his experiences of a Colorado winter, watched a British postman remove the mail from the bright red box on the curb, then explained that in Colorado that mail box would have been buried under a snowdrift. Buried under a snowdrift? At least, if you were a mail box you could survive until spring.

When we reached the entrance to the museum, the uniformed attendant waved me in; I was the last person in the group she was admitting. Upstairs, I purchased my ticket and then squeezed into one of the elevators. The question now was, where in this hall of rooms was I supposed to meet my note writer?

On my first trip to London as a grad student, I had visited Madame Tussaud's, and as I recalled, one exhibition room opened into another. Some were well lighted, others not. The Chamber of Horrors, definitely not.

The first room was jammed because the crowd had to move down steps and around an upper landing before entering an area in which wax figures were grouped around a small pond, a baby grand piano, and some potted trees. There was an air of halt, dodge, and shuffle as people paused to "aah" and "oh" as they recognized the wax celebrities. Elton John, for example, was sitting at the piano. Some people were having their photographs taken as they stood beside a personal favorite. Feeling claustrophobic, I edged my way through and out into the corridor leading to the main rooms.

In display cases along the corridor, there was an exhibit that showed how the masks were made. Madame Tussaud, wearing a mobcap over her black hair, focused her sharp eyes on the mask she was shaping. The streaks of red on the mask were a reminder that Madame had perfected her craft during the French Revolution. She had been forced to prove her allegiance to the Revolution by fashioning death masks of executed nobles, including that of Marie Antoinette.

In the grand hall, I glanced around but saw no likely blond man in sight. Or at least no one who seemed to be unattached and looking for me. With nothing better to do, I joined the other tourists who were edging their way from exhibit to exhibit. London in August was crowded, especially at Madame Tussaud's.

But the exhibits were worth the jockeying for a view. British royals, writers, scientists, generals, African presidents, Martin Luther King, and Bishop Tutu. An exhibit of American presidents featured Bill Clinton at the podium, Kennedy, Bush, and Reagan standing behind him. Fascinated, people leaned closer to the wax figures to study a wrinkle in a cheek or stroke a wiry mustache. But it was the perfectly rendered eyes of the figures that drew me to them. Their eyes seemed to be looking back. I almost expected to see them blink.

In one exhibit, an elegant woman's diamond-drop earring seemed to move with her heartbeat. It took me a moment to realize the movement was being created by a current of air. I had watched Vincent Price as the mad proprietor of a wax museum one time too many. The thought of being locked in this place at night made me shiver.

Shivers not withstanding, it took me at least half an hour to look my fill and make my way out of the grand hall. In the smaller exhibit rooms—the "sound stages"—the legends of Hollywood films were on display, among them Marilyn Monroe in her billowing white dress and John Wayne in his cowboy hat and sheriff's badge. Alfred Hitchcock was there too, although he must have posed for his wax figure when he was less rotund than he had been in his later years. I moved through with no more than a pause here and there, impatient with myself for forgetting why I had come.

At the bottom of the stairs was the entrance to the Chamber of Horrors. The words over the doorway that led into the shadowed chamber beyond said, YE WHO ENTER HERE ABANDON HOPE. It was dusk inside. I glanced up at the shadowy wax figures dangling in cages from the ceiling and peered at the plaques describing the methods of execution employed in dispatching pirates, highwaymen, and other felons.

A corridor connected the anteroom to the main chamber. In her exhibit, Joan of Arc burned at the stake. A studious-looking father was trying to relate the saga of her life to his teenage son, who was more interested in discussing the technology involved in producing the flames and smoke.

I followed an older couple along the corridor, past other figures of the damned and the suffering, and into the main chamber. In a window display—a replica of a cobbled Whitechapel alley—one of Jack the Ripper's victims lay sprawled in her bloodied gown and petticoats, her intestines spilling from her abdomen. I had read a book not too long ago in which the author made the argument that Jack the Ripper had ushered in the age of the "sex killer."

Jack the Ripper had gotten away with his murders. John Christie, on the other hand, had not. Depicted in his flat at No. 10 Rillington Place, Christie was unaware that his crimes were about to be discovered and that he would be tried, convicted, and executed. In Madame Tussaud's Chamber of Horrors, Christie's fate was on full display. In a spotlighted window, a grim-faced judge in black robe, his voice coming from a tape, read out the serial killer's sentence of death. That window darkened. In the next, the condemned man stood on the scaffold, a rope around his neck, a black hood over his head. The seconds ticked off on a clock as the sound of his harsh breathing escalated. Then darkness and the sound of a body dropping.

It was *Punch* magazine that had given the name "The Chamber of Horrors" to the "separate room" at Madame Tussaud's which was devoted to the macabre. Such things were not for the eyes of delicate nineteenth-century ladies who were given to swooning.

But I was made of heartier stuff.

"Lizzie?"

I jerked back and away from the fingers that had touched my upper arm. The man standing behind me was slender and blond. I blinked at him in the dim light.

He laughed. "Hold on, Lizzie, don't scream. It's me, Michael Donovan . . . Tess's Michael."

The last time I had seen Michael was five years ago when he had shown up uninvited at a wedding Tess and I were attending. No one except Tess had thought of asking him to leave. Michael in a tuxedo added a touch of class even when he was gate-crashing.

I let out my breath. "Michael, were you the one who . . .did you send me that note?"

"I knew you'd come. No Hitchcock fan could pass on a note like that."

We'd had a conversation once about Hitchcock's superb handling of suspense. It was one of the few times I could say I had enjoyed a conversation with Michael. "What are you doing here? I thought Tess told me you were in South America or Australia or somewhere."

"I'm always somewhere," he said. "Last month I was in Paris. Didn't Tess mention seeing me there?"

"No, she didn't mention that. What I would like to know is why you wanted me to come here."

"I came by your hotel this morning. My taxi was rounding the corner when I saw you striding off with a determined expression on your face and what looked like a map in your hand."

"How did you know where I was staying?"

"I happened to see the note Tess wrote to herself about your flight and hotel, and since I was going to be in London, I thought I'd look you up."

"You—" I stepped back to let two women get closer to the Christie exhibit. "Wait a minute, you said I was leaving the hotel as you arrived."

"So I decided to do a bit of sleuthing."

"You what?"

Michael's whiter-than-white teeth flashed in a grin. "I was curious about where you were going, about how you'd spend a day all on your own in London."

I glanced around me and caught back the salty response that had sprung to my lips. "Are you saying that you've been following me?"

"And I did a damn fine job of it, didn't I? You didn't even notice me."

"I was too tired to notice. I'm still tired, and I don't appreciate your juvenile game. I would have thought with a company to run you'd have more important things to do with your time."

"I am properly put in my place, ma'am." He leaned toward me. "But just between the two of us, didn't my note give you a wicked little thrill?"

"I'm leaving now, Michael."

"Lizzie, come on, wait. You're right, it was a juvenile game. I apologize. I need your help with something."

"With what?"

"I want you to do something for me. Look, I know you've never approved of Tess and me as a couple—"

"What makes you think that?"

"Ouch. When I saw your snazzy new haircut, I was hoping I might get a little sympathy."

I touched my hand to my brand new, inch-long haircut, a haircut that had probably made my grandmother wish she could rise from her grave.

"It is new, isn't it? Tess didn't mention it."

"Do you and Tess often discuss my hair?" I asked.

"No, but she keeps me up-to-date on you. You're her best friend, so she talks about you now and then."

"When the two of you are on speaking terms?"

"We speak quite often, Lizzie. Sorry to hear about your grandmother, by the way."

"Thank you."

"May I have a few more minutes of your time?"

"Since you've already gotten me here, I might as well hear what you have to say."

"You have loosened it just a bit, haven't you?"

"Loosened what?" I said.

"Your whalebone corset."

"You really don't want me to listen to you, do you?"

He caught my arm and tucked it into his. "Lizzie, it would take a saint to resist teasing you a little, but I am now on my best behavior. Promise. I also promise not to keep you long."

There was a uniformed guard standing over by the wall, probably already wondering what Michael and I were up to, and I didn't care to treat him to a wrestling match. "Good, because I don't intend to stay long."

"Let's find a place to sit down. How about the cafe? I'll buy you a cup of tea."

As we passed the silent guard, I met his gaze. He was a wax figure. "Oh, wonderful!"

"What?" Michael asked.

"Nothing. Nothing at all."

He gave me an uneasy look. It served him right.

We stepped out of the shadows into the well-lighted cafe area. Michael glanced around the room.

"There's a table over there," I said. "Those people are leaving."

"I have a better idea. Let's do the 'Spirit of London' ride."

"If you'd like." I had planned to do the ride anyway.

We joined the people queued up to climb into one of the miniature replicas of a London taxi cab. The cabs moved along a conveyor belt through an exhibit of four hundred years of the city's history.

As we waited in line, I noticed Michael was carrying a white shopping bag. He had found a moment to buy another toy while he was following me around London.

"All right, Michael, out with it. What do you want me to do? And, if it's something about Tess—"

"Tess and I ran into each other in Paris."

"You've said that already."

"We spent the evening together. It was almost like when we first met. But then she was off to Rome the next morning on an assignment. Just when we were having fun"—a comic little boy pout—"and believe it or not, she wouldn't invite me along."

I believed it. Tess had never explained why she had divorced Michael after less than a year of marriage. On the surface, he seemed an excellent catch—attractive, well-bred, scion of an old New England family, an executive in the family pharmaceuticals business. And, although not given to true confession, Tess had once told me that her toes curled every time Michael kissed her.

Not that she'd had to tell me about how he affected her. I had been there when they met. It was one of those weekends when Tess had swooped in to "liberate" me from my word processor and my dissertation-in-progress, insisting we drive to Boston for the day. As we were leaving the restaurant where we'd had dinner, Tess and Michael had literally bumped into each other. Enough sparks had been in the air to singe an innocent bystander.

"What are your plans for the evening?" Michael asked now.

I cast him a sidelong glance. Surely he was not going to suggest we do something together. "An early bed and a good night's sleep," I said.

"That's no fun. You're in London. Live a little. You like to walk. Why don't you do one of the evening walking tours? Do one of the Jack the Ripper tours of Whitechapel. You'd love that."

"Really?" I said. "Why?"

"Because in spite of all the modern changes in the neighborhood, there are still places where you can imagine Jack lurking in the darkness, waiting for his next victim. I did it on a cold, rainy night. Wind blowing. Everything but the fog. You would have loved it." He flashed me another grin. Michael at his most charming.

Within five minutes after he'd met Tess, he invited her to go dancing. She explained she had to get her hardworking friend back to Albany, New York. He said he'd drive over to Albany the next day. She said she was on her way to an assignment in Montreal. He said he loved Montreal and asked where she was staying. Three days later, she called to tell me he was there and taking her to dinner.

Four months later—as I was packing my belongings and my brand new Ph.D. to head home to Drucilla—she had called, sounding stunned, to say Michael had proposed and she had accepted. On their wedding day, she had been radiant. He had been the picture of a man in love.

Less than a year later, she had started divorce proceedings. That was almost seven years ago. Since then he had been engaged in a sustained effort to win her back. I had never decided whether it was love or ego.

Whatever Michael's motivation for his pursuit of her, I was surprised to hear Tess had spent an evening with him. He must have caught her at a weak moment, or maybe it had been Paris weaving its spell. They had honeymooned there.

At the moment, Michael and I were next in line for our taxi ride through London history. An attendant motioned for us to climb in as a cab moved toward us. Michael settled into the seat beside me, holding his shopping bag out of the way as the safety bar came down in front of us. Our cab moved down an incline and around a turn, and we were surrounded by the narration coming from the loudspeaker. I settled back to enjoy the animation and special effects. It was Michael's conversation. Let him get on with it.

I twisted my head for another look at the bird-beaked costume that physicians had worn to protect themselves during the plague. I had seen that in a television documentary on the Black Death. We were passing the replica of the Tower of London with a red uniformed Beefeater in front when Michael gestured at the bag in his lap. "Will you take this to Tess for me?"

"What is it?"

"A gift."

"Do you think Tess will want it?"

"It's nothing expensive or extravagant. Just something I saw in a shop window and thought she'd enjoy."

I grabbed for the safety bar as our taxi cab twisted sideways and began its uphill climb past the displays of recent London history. "I don't think so, Michael."

"Why not?"

"You know why not. Tess won't want it."

"It is possible that she might have had a change of heart."

"If you want her to have it, mail it."

"The mail's too slow."

"Is it something perishable?

"No, but it is something that I want her to have as soon as possible."

To my relief, we were coming to the end of the ride. "Why don't you send it by—"

"I knew I could count on you, Lizzie." He shoved the bag into my lap and jumped out of the miniature taxi cab as the safety bar came up.

"Michael! Michael, I'm not taking this!"

He ignored me. But everyone else turned to see what the fuss was about and to watch me stumbling over my own feet in my haste to follow him. He was gone—leaving me holding his bag. I looked inside and saw a square box wrapped in shiny blue foil paper with a big pink bow on top.

Mumbling some unladylike words, I turned toward the exit. The sun was shining, the day was hot, and Michael was nowhere in sight.

I had put the plastic handles of the shopping bag over my wrist. As I stood at the curb waiting for the light to change, I felt a sharp tug. On pure instinct, I clasped the bag to me as I turned. The hand that had fastened on my wrist belonged to a man with pale blue eyes. Mean eyes. One of them was ravaged by a thin, zigzagging scar that slashed through his sandy brow and down across his cheek. He shoved me backward with a thrust to the chest.

I held on to the bag even as I was falling in what seemed to be slow motion. It was a stupid thing to do. If I had been thinking, I would have known better. When I looked up, I was staring at the front end of a London bus. I closed my own eyes.

"Is she hurt? Are you hurt, dear? That was a near thing, wasn't it? Dear, are you hurt?" I was still holding on to Michael's bag as people picked me up and brushed me off.

"He tried to snatch her bag," a woman in pearls was explaining to the bobby who had appeared on the scene with commendable speed. "He ran off down the street." She pointed to indicate his direction.

"Is that right, miss?" the bobby asked me. He had a police radio in his hand. I nodded, I had no idea which way he'd run, and at that moment, too many thoughts were going through my head at once for me to be able to form coherent sentences.

That was how it had begun yesterday in London. And continued today in Cornwall. And there was still the matter of Tess's reaction when I gave her the gift from Michael.

I poured what was left of my tea into my cup and signaled to my waitress as she passed. "Could I have another pot, please?"

"Sure you can."

I broke off a piece of the multigrain bread and buttered it. I had discovered this cafe in one of St. Regis's narrow, maze-like streets. The dining room had five other tables, all occupied by people who seemed to be enjoying their meals as much as I was enjoying mine. The bonus was that the cafe's menu would have gotten a seal of approval from the American Heart Association. Herbal teas, hearty vegetable soups, healthy pasta dishes, and homemade desserts. So I was satisfying my hunger without undue guilt. And wallowing in more guilt than I should have felt because I had opened the package Michael had given me.

At the time, it had seemed the sensible thing to do. The driver of the bus that had almost run over me had been as rattled as I was. It had taken me several minutes to make him believe that I was all right and that, no, I did not need medical attention. Then I had to explain to the bobby that I really would rather not file a police report because I was leaving London the next day and I lived in Kentucky. Finally, with a big smile pasted on my face, I had backed away and made my escape.

I was in the tube station, waiting on the platform for the train, when I started to shake and realized that I was standing as far from the edge as I could get with my back pressed against the wall.

I walked from Victoria Station to the moderately priced hotel that Tess had recommended. The clerk at the desk greeted me and gave me my room key. I climbed the stairs and unlocked my door. I put Michael's shopping bag down on the bed and stood there looking at it. I stood there feeling sweaty and grimy, with little tremors going through my insides, thinking I should go take a hot shower because I was beginning to feel the aftereffects of my fall.

I sat down on the bed and took the gift-wrapped box out of the shopping bag. I shook it, held it up to my ear, then shook it again, but nothing rattled. I slid the pink ribbon off and turned the box on its side. I would have to find some tape to rewrap it. Maybe I had some in one of the side pockets of my tote bag. You never knew when you would need tape or paper clips.

Or a bodyguard because you were carrying around a package that someone wanted. Although why anyone would want a Winnie the Pooh figurine. . . .

That was what it was. A little woodland scene with Winnie the Pooh holding a jar labeled HONEY. Michael had enclosed a card, "All my love, Christopher Robin." I slid the card back into the envelope and put Winnie the Pooh back into his nest of white tissue paper.

"Afters, love?" the waitress asked, bringing me back to the present.

"Dessert?" I translated. "Yes, please."

"They're there on the board. All made fresh today."

I read the list again and decided to have the blackberry pie with clotted Cornish cream.

I hoped that Tess would be fooled by my rewrapping of the gift her ex-husband had sent her. Because what it came down to was that I had opened the package because I didn't trust Michael. Not for any concrete reason I could point to, but simply because I had never felt at ease around him.

I might have attributed that to the fact that, having grown up in a small town in Kentucky, I felt gauche around old money and urbane sophistication. I did think that at first. But then I realized he knew I was uncomfortable around him. And he seemed to like that, which made me like him a lot less than I might have.

I had tried to like him because Tess loved him. And although she might have divorced him, might swear she would never go back to him, she did still care for him. So if I should ever come right out and tell her how I felt about him, she would probably give me one of her "haughty Latina" looks and inform me that when it came to that, distrust was my instinctive reaction to any attractive man.

Not quite true, but it would be enough to get us into an argument that I didn't want to have and had managed to avoid having all these years. I wanted to keep it that way.

I wanted the rest of this vacation to be peaceful. I wanted to relax and enjoy myself. So I would deliver Michael's gift with as little commentary as possible.

Chapter Three

HAVING MADE MY DECISION about what to tell—and not tell—Tess, I was much more relaxed. I lingered over my tea until a trio of hungry-looking people appeared in the doorway of the cafe. Signaling to the waitress, I yielded my table.

The streets were crowded. Like any good resort town, St. Regis did not pull in its carpets at dusk. Feeling no compulsion now to rush back to the hotel, I joined the throng of holiday makers who were drifting from one shop to another in the winding streets looking for a bargain or that perfect gift.

I was not ready to buy gifts yet, but it was fun to look. The only problem I had was to keep reminding myself of the conversion rate from pounds to dollars. What at first looked like a good buy, sometimes wasn't in U.S. dollars. Still, now that I was finally tenured, I could be a little less frugal. Or I could have been if not for thirty-eight years of training at my grandmother's knee. She had believed in saving for rainy days. As she said, they always came.

With that bit of philosophy in mind, I shook my head and handed back the silver and ruby Celtic cross I had asked the woman behind the jewelry counter to show me.

I was sidetracked on my way out the door by the glint of the charms in a display case. As I was packing I had tucked my bracelet into my tote bag. Not that I expected to wear it. In the eight years since I'd bought it I had worn it no more than twice. It was gold, it jangled, and bracelets bothered me. But I had bought a charm, and I'd needed a bracelet to put it on. There were four charms now—a baseball bat, a boxing glove, a train caboose, and a magician's hat with a rabbit inside. Small gold charms symbolizing Walter Stuart's legacy to his granddaughter. But there was nothing there in the display case that said Hester Rose. She was a more difficult matter. I turned and walked out of the store.

It was late, almost ten o'clock. Time I headed back. It took me another twenty minutes to find my way back to High Street, the main street in St. Regis which, according to my taxi driver, would take one from the bustling waterfront to the outskirts of the town. It climbed up the hill, past the street on which the Crump sisters had their hotel.

I had started back along the pedestrian path overlooking the beach, but even with people about, it had looked a little too dark. I hadn't thought to ask how cautious one had to be in St. Regis when walking about at night. The Crump sisters hadn't seemed concerned when they sent me out alone to see the children's parade. Maybe they had assumed a woman who was a criminologist (Tess had mentioned that to them) would know how to defend herself or have the good sense not to get into dangerous spots in the first place. In the past two days, I had been doing a little too much of that, first by resisting my London mugger and then charging right into a quarrel between two strangers.

Speaking of whom, had Dee gone back to the hotel? If she had, what had she told them about her split lip? What was I supposed to say?

The woman passing me grabbed my arm. "Lizzie? I thought you'd been kidnapped."

"Tess! Hi! I was thinking so hard . . . and it's dark out here."

"Why do you think I came looking for you? I thought you'd gotten lost." We were hugging as we spoke. Then Tess stepped back and subjected me to closer examination. She started grinning. "I can't believe it. You've cut your hair! We will now break out the champagne and rumba in the streets of St. Regis."

I touched my nape. "Was it that awful before?"

"Not if you happen to think Olivia Walton's bun was sexy."

"You never can remember the difference between Virginia and Kentucky, can you, Theresa?"

"I wasn't referring to location. I was referring to the fact that somewhere around the time you left graduate school, you decided you ought to look like a spinster schoolteacher."

"I wasn't trying to look like— I just wanted to have a little dignity—"

"By looking like someone's maiden aunt? Those long skirts were the worst."

"You never told me you thought I looked that awful," I said.

"Yes, I did. You weren't listening. At least, you got over the long skirt stage. But I've been wanting to get my hands on that hair for years."

"Well, you must be pleased now that I've cut it all off."

"I am," Tess said. "It looks great and it suits you."

"Thank you."

"You're welcome."

We were walking as we talked, climbing the hill, moving in and out of shadow and light. Off in the distance, the sea was a dark presence, shimmering in the moonlight. I shivered in my lightweight jacket.

"So now that we've finished dissecting my appearance, how are you? Everything okay?"

"That depends on which portion of my life you're asking about."

"Tell me about the good part first."

"The good part is that I have a shot at a travel show on one of the cable channels."

"On TV? Tess, that's wonderful!"

"At any other time, it would be."

"What does that mean?"

"I'll tell you about it later."

"Why can't you tell me about it now?"

"Because you need to be sitting down. How was London? You should have given yourself more time there."

"I know. I really wanted to see a play. Are you all right? You're not ill or anything?"

"Nope. I'm in tip-top health. So what's new besides your haircut? What about your book?"

"The book I'm doing on folk culture and violent death? Actually, that's coming along quite well. I found this really fascinating manuscript in the archives at—"

Tess groaned. "Spare me, please. I meant your mystery."

"Oh, that."

"Yes, that. What happened with the agent? The one your friend in the English department had you contact?"

"He read the synopsis and wanted to see more, so I sent him the first three chapters. But I'm not holding my breath."

"And you're not the least bit excited."

"Okay, a little. But I wrote it for fun." I paused as I uttered that lie. "No, that's not true. I wrote it because the whole thing was so frustrating. I spent months tracking down everything I could find about Claire Everton and Matthew Ashford and the people around them, and I was still no closer to knowing how she ended up in the river."

A young man passed us, striding down the hill toward town, carrying a guitar case and whistling a tune under his breath. Something sweet and haunting. Was it "Greensleeves"?

"Maybe she really did kill herself because he called off their engagement," Tess said.

"No. Claire wasn't that kind of woman. She was practical and sensible. And the question was why he called the engagement off in the first place. He'd courted her for almost three years. Why would he suddenly change his mind about marrying her?"

"He was going off to war."

— 24—

"That doesn't make sense. Thousands of men were going off to war. The country was at war."

Tess laughed. "You're the only person I know who can get this worked up about something that happened almost a century and a half ago."

"I just don't like not knowing. That's why I wrote the thing. I couldn't write it as nonfiction because I didn't have enough solid evidence. And anyway, I was supposed to use my release time to work on the paper I'd been selected to present at the conference. A paper about pre-Civil War lynchings in Kentucky—not about a drowning death that I'd stumbled across and become fascinated by." I shoved my cold hands into my jacket pockets. "But I couldn't let it go. I was even dreaming about it. I needed to get it sorted out in my mind."

"So being the conscientious soul that you are," Tess said, "first you finished your lynching paper, and then you did what you really wanted to do—"

"And wrote a historical murder mystery. Spent two years of my life using up my limited supply of spare moments to write a novel. And it's not as if anyone will view it as a scholarly work."

"Why not? You're a scholar. It's your work."

"If it's ever published. And fiction only counts as a publication toward promotion if you're in the English Department. My dean happens to hate mysteries."

"She's a social worker."

"She's 'nonviolent' and objects to what she calls 'violence for entertainment purposes.'"

"Never read Shakespeare, has she?"

"Shakespeare's 'art.' Anyway, aside from what she's likely to think about it—I'm not really comfortable with the fact that I finally ended up just using the solution to Claire's drowning that seemed to make sense. It might still be the wrong one."

"Lizzie, you wrote a novel. Fiction. And after all the research you did, your solution can't be that farfetched."

"No, but it certainly isn't the official version of what happened. I did my research and then I chose my own solution."

"Too bad we can't do that in real life."

"Do what?"

"Choose the solutions we find most satisfying to life's little dilemmas."

"Isn't it, though? I'd be the first to sign up." With that the mood had shifted and I took a deep breath that had nothing to do with the incline of the hill we were climbing. "By the way, Theresa, I ran into someone when I was in London."

"Someone? As in someone tall, dark, and handsome?"

"Try blond and charming. Your ex-husband as a matter of fact."

Tess stopped walking. "Michael?"

"We ran into each other at— We both ended up at Madame Tussaud's." I paused and took another breath. "And he asked me to bring you something."

"What?"

There was wariness in her voice. But something else too.

"A gift. He said he saw it in a shop window, and thought you'd find it amusing."

Actually, he'd said he thought she would "enjoy it."

Before I could correct myself, Tess said, "Amusing? That's one thing I can always count on with Michael."

"Yes, he is entertaining. Correction—what he said was he thought you'd enjoy the gift. And while you're thinking about that, could we keep moving. You might be warm enough in that nice, bulky sweater, but I'm freezing."

We were almost there. As I recalled from my earlier arrival by taxi, our street was a few steps past the large white hotel with the enclosed outdoor swimming pool. I had a feeling that the people staying there were paying somewhat more than we were at the Gull's Nest, but our view was every bit as good as theirs. In fact, I had a room with a small (albeit bird-spattered) balcony and a view of the sea.

"Where did you go today?" I asked to break the silence. "I hope you didn't go anywhere interesting without me."

"No, today was a scouting expedition."

"Scouting? You make exploring the West Country sound like a trek into the Australian outback."

"I like to know where I am."

I had the feeling she was talking about more than her preference as a travel writer. But maybe I was reading things into her mood. "I've always wanted to go to Australia, especially since you sent me those photographs. If you happen to come across any travel bargains—"

"I'll keep you in mind."

We turned onto our street. It ran downhill toward the beach with the steps leading down to the pedestrian walk about halfway along. Cars were parked on each side of the narrow side street with as much economy of space as possible.

"You rented a car?" I asked Tess.

"Hired a car," she said. "And while we're on the subject of 'Britspeak,' remember to ask for the w.c., lavatory, or toilet—not the ladies' room."

"Thank you. I've already been reminded of that one. Which car is yours?"

"The little black one right there. I don't intend to use it a lot. I want to emphasize 'getting there by bus and train' in my article."

"Good. With vivid memories of your driving—"

"I have yet to have an accident."

"You've come close a few times. We won't even mention speeding tickets."

"No, we won't, because I never deserve those. The cops have it in for me."

A man edged past us on the sidewalk, carrying two whiskered gray terriers—one in each arm. "Splendid evening," he said, nodding his head in his checked cap.

"Yes, it is," I said.

Tess reached out to stroke the ear of one of the dogs. She was a sucker for animals and would have enjoyed that snoring hound on the train.

Two broad white steps led up to the alcoved door of the Gull's Nest Private Hotel. "Do you have your key, Tess? Mine's buried somewhere in my shoulder bag."

"It always is."

The door opened as Tess was about to insert the key she'd taken from her pocket.

"Bang! You're dead!"

"Benjy, my boy, that's not nice. Apologize to the two young ladies." The man was in his late seventies, perhaps. Bearded and bespectacled, with a sparkle deep in his dark eyes and a warm smile on his face. He patted the little boy's head, ruffling his blond curls.

The little boy tilted his head to peep up at his grandfather, then he grinned at Tess and me, revealing a dimple in each cheek and a missing front tooth. He was adorable, a child who could have stepped straight into a television commercial. "Sorry, I didn't mean to be not nice."

"Don't worry about it, pardner," Tess said. "That's a fine looking six-shooter you've got there."

His grandfather shook his head. "Guns. Everywhere guns. But his father says that all the other little boys have them. What a ridiculous argument, huh?" He smiled at me. "I already know Miss Tess. And you must be her friend. Miss Elizabeth, is it?"

"Lizabeth without the E," I said, extending my hand. His grip was firm for a man of his years. "But please call me Lizzie."

"I am Benjamin Stillman and this is my grandson, Benjamin Joseph, age six next Friday."

"But everyone calls me Benjy," his grandson said.

"Hello, Benjy." We shook hands. "Nice to meet you."

"Come inside," Benjamin said. "We are keeping you here in the doorway. Come into the lounge. The sisters are serving tea." He made an elaborate show of looking over his shoulder, then back at us. Then he winked. "Or perhaps a nightcap for those of us who wish to sleep well."

I liked Benjamin Stillman.

I had seen the lounge when I arrived, a large room with Victorian furniture and a bay window. Now it also contained several people. A woman, blonde and fragile, perched on the edge of a burgundy velvet armchair. Dressed in a stylish rainbow-colored silk pantsuit, she looked rather like a woodland fairy about to take wing. If Dee was exotic, this woman was ethereal.

Sturdy little Benjy ran over to her. "Mummy, can I have a hot chocolate?"

She looked from her son to the tall, unsmiling man sitting on the sofa beside another woman. The woman on the sofa was not young, but she was aging with an elegance that bespoke salons, spas, and iron willpower when it came to diet and exercise. Her blonde hair shimmered with silver highlights. Her face was made up to draw attention to the clarity of her skin and eyes and away from her crow's-feet and the wrinkles about her mouth. The resemblance between the two on the sofa was evident. The man was in his thirties, but he had the woman's haughty nose and mouth, her blonde hair. She wore a simple blue shirtdress, he an open-necked white shirt and khaki slacks. They both looked out of place sitting on a sofa in the Crump sisters' homey parlor.

"May I, Mummy?" Benjy asked again.

His mother's wide green eyes returned to his face. "Darling, I really don't think you should. You've had so many sweets today—"

"But the chocolate has milk," his grandfather objected. "Milk is what he needs to grow up big and strong."

"On the contrary, Benjamin. Rosalind is right," the woman on the sofa said. "The child has had enough sugar for one day." She looked at me and stood up. "How do you do? I'm Pamela Stillman."

"Hello, I'm Lizabeth Stuart."

"But she prefers to be called Lizzie," Benjamin said.

The man who had been sitting beside her on the sofa stepped forward and held out his hand too. "I'm Jeremy Stillman. You've met my father and son, and this is my wife, Rosalind."

"It's a pleasure to meet all of you."

As I was speaking, the door at the far end of the room swung open and Edith Crump came in carrying a tray. "Tarts," she announced, a smile struggling with the perpetual worry lines on her face. "Fresh from Sarah's oven."

"Tarts, did you say?" The high-pitched voice came from behind the Chinese screen by the bay window.

I shot a look at Tess. She was biting her lower lip to keep from laughing.

The woman who stepped from behind the screen wore hiking boots and Army camouflage pants with a green knit tunic. She had blue eyes that were alive with interest, and her gray-blonde hair dangled in a braid down her back. "Tarts. Lovely!" She paused in her sniffing of the air and smiled at me. "Hildegard Martin. Pleasure to meet you."

"A pleasure to meet you too. I'm Lizzie Stuart."

My hand was shaken firmly and released, as Hildegard's blue glance swept over my face. "And did you see the sign in the hall, Lizzie Stuart, about peanuts being forbidden?"

"About—? Yes, I— Miss Crump—Edith—explained about Dee's allergy."

"Allergies are such a nuisance for everyone, aren't they? I do love peanuts so much. Dreadfully miss having them when I'm here. In fact, I was thinking a moment ago of a peanut butter and banana butty."

"Butty?"

"Sandwich," Tess said.

"Lovely with a cup of tea," Hildegard said. "Do you have them?"

"I . . . not since I was a child."

"Oh, then you must try one again. But not while you're here." Hildegard Martin smiled at Edith Crump. "Not that we mind, Edith, dear. Dee is such a sweet child. A minor sacrifice, isn't it?"

Edith smiled back at her. "Tomorrow Sarah's baking a chocolate torte, Hildy."

"Tarts tonight and torte tomorrow," Hildegard beamed. "Sarah's earning her stars this year." Her glance swept back to me. "You're probably wondering what I was doing behind the screen."

I was catching on to her rapid change of subject. "Yes, actually I was."

"Meditation. Clears the brain of cobwebs. I try to do it several times a day, but it is rather rude to drift off in front of people, isn't it? And I didn't feel like climbing the stairs and coming back down again, so I just popped behind the screen."

"Oh, I see."

"Lovely, so glad you do. Now," Hildegard Martin rubbed her hands together. "Shall we get to the tarts?"

"I have the clotted cream," Sarah Crump, a smaller, softer edition of her older sister, announced as she came through the far door. She limped slightly and walked with the aid of a slender mahogany cane. "I do hope the tarts are all right."

"Of course, they're all right," Edith said. "You make the best tarts in the district."

"Indeed, you do, dear Sarah," Benjamin said with a small bow.

"Right they are," Hildegard said as she helped herself to one.

We followed her example, helping ourselves to the warm, flaky tarts while Edith poured our tea. Benjamin patted his grandson on the head again and asked permission to pour himself a brandy from the decanter on the side table.

As for his wife—she was willing to relax the "no more sugar tonight" decree when it came to Sarah's tarts. It was she who broke off a piece of the pastry on her plate and held it out to her grandson.

Rosalind's green eyes widened for a moment as if she were about to protest. Then her lashes fluttered down to conceal her expression. She turned to her husband and began to chatter. "Jeremy— do you think I should ring tomorrow to check on the preparations for the dinner party? I'm not sure . . . do you think the Auslanders would prefer fish or fowl?" Her hand smoothed at a fold of her jacket. "Oh, darling, did you remember to bring in Benjy's new monkey from the car? He'll want it if he wakes, and you know how much you'll hate having to get up and go outside to—"

Jeremy paused in the act of sipping his tea. As their eyes met, his wife fell silent. He took another sip of his tea and slumped back against the sofa cushion. He looked tired and preoccupied, undoubtedly with things on his mind. And Rosalind's fluting voice was not soothing. But that was no excuse for the look he had given her.

God, please, preserve me from brooding men. Very attractive in the pages of romance novels, but more bother than a woman needed in real life. That also applied to vacationing soldiers encountered on beach paths. Best to forget them as quickly as they forgot you.

But where was Dee? Should I ask about her or just mind my own business?

Across the room, Tess had recovered her Michael-disturbed equilibrium and was busy questioning Edith and Sarah about the abandoned tin mine she had visited that day. Hildegard Martin, seated cross-legged on the worn Oriental carpet, was chatting with Benjamin, who had made himself comfortable in an armchair, brandy snifter in hand. Their topic of conversation seemed to be bird-watching.

Pamela Stillman placed her teacup in her saucer. "I understand you're from Kentucky," she said. "We go there quite often for Derby."

"To Louisville? I live in Drucilla—about fifty miles away."

Benjy had settled himself in her lap and, after finishing the pastry she was feeding him, had fallen asleep. It was the loving arm she had tucked around him that made me bear with her as she began to cross-examine me about my background.

"So you've spent most of your life—except for the time you were away at university—in Drucilla?"

"Yes," I said.

"Don't you find it rather restricting?"

"Sometimes. And you, Mrs. Stillman, where were you born and reared?"

She frowned as if she didn't consider turnabout fair play. But she answered my question. "In Oxford. My father was a professor of inorganic chemistry."

"Really? I did a bus tour to Oxford during my first trip to London as a grad student. I was so impressed by the university. What was it like to grow up in that environment surrounded by—"

The crash from the rear of the house came at about the same moment that I realized Pamela was not interested in discussing what it had been like growing up in Oxford. A second crash brought us all to our feet.

"Come, Jeremy, " Benjamin said. "Ladies, please remain here." He might have saved his breath. The ladies were hard on the men's heels as we hurried through the dining room to discover Dee sprawled on the kitchen floor amidst broken pottery.

"Sorry," she said, giggling. "I slipped." She was drunk.

Edith made a clucking sound. Sarah said, "Oh, Dee, love." Jeremy stepped forward and hauled Dee to her feet.

"She's cut her lip," Edith said. "Sarah, get the first-aid kit from the pantry."

As Jeremy sat her down in a chair at the kitchen table, Dee's semi-focused eyes met mine.

"Can we do anything to help?" I asked.

"No," Edith said. "Thank you . . . we'll care for her."

"Good night," Tess said and took my arm, pulling me toward the door.

The others had followed us out of the kitchen. Tess and I said good night to them on the stairs. The elder Stillmans, Benjamin and Pamela, went into the room next door to mine, Hildegard Martin went down the hall to the room next to the full bathroom (with a second toilet adjacent to it). And with Rosalind trailing behind him, Jeremy carried his son up the stairs to the third floor that they were sharing with Tess.

Tess followed me into my room. "I couldn't get a look at this room yesterday when I arrived because the couple that was in here hadn't left yet."

"It isn't bad," I said. "I even have a balcony."

"All I have is a window." Tess studied her reflection in the mirror above the sink. She twitched at her bangs, flipped her fingers through her chin-length cap of black hair. "I found another gray hair yesterday."

"Get used to it. I've been finding them for months. We're both two birthdays short of forty."

Tess turned away from the mirror. "Don't remind me."

"What did you make of that?"

"By *that* I assume you mean the housekeeper of this establishment stumbling in as drunk as a sailor on shore leave."

"The Crump sisters seemed to take it rather calmly. A drunk employee disturbs the guests, and they—"

"She's their niece."

"Their niece? Oh, horse hockey."

"What?"

"This evening on my way into town, I came upon Dee having a fight with her boyfriend. That's how she got that cut lip."

"You saw him hit her?"

"I got there after the fact. But he was still manhandling her when I turned the corner."

"And don't tell me . . . let me guess. You went charging in."

"I just told him I didn't think he should hit her again. Luckily, before he could register his resentment at the suggestion, another man—an American—arrived. And Dee's boyfriend scowled a few times and left." I stood up and tugged the pillow from beneath the pale blue comforter. "Dee started back in this direction, so I thought she might be coming back here. Apparently not."

"She did come back here. She just made a stop or two along the way." Tess dropped into the chair by the balcony doors and stretched out her blue-jeaned legs. "Where is it?"

"What?"

"Michael's gift. I might as well have a look at it." She was being too casual. That meant she wasn't feeling casual at all.

I stepped over her feet and opened the closet doors where I had stored the blue foil-wrapped box on the shelf inside. I took it out and handed to her. If she noticed the gift had been rewrapped, she didn't say anything. In fact, her long silence finally made me look up from the tourist guide to Cornwall that I was pretending to read.

She had her hand pressed hard to her mouth, tears running down her cheeks. I dropped the guidebook on the bed. "Tess?" I squatted down beside her chair. "I knew I shouldn't have brought it."

"I'm pregnant. I'm going to have a baby."

That landed me hard on my bottom. "A baby? A diapers and bottles baby?"

"Yeah, that kind."

"Is it—? Michael said the two of you ran into each other in Paris."

Tess scrubbed at her eyes with the back of her hand. "Dinner by candlelight, champagne, dancing. We even went for a walk in the rain." Her throat moved as she swallowed hard. "And then we stopped at his hotel for a nightcap in the bar. The next morning, I woke up in his bed."

"You woke up there? You don't remember how you got there?"

"I got there on a wave of stupidity."

Not a drug Michael had dropped in her drink.

"Are you sure you're pregnant? Maybe you're just late."

"I did a home pregnancy test, then this afternoon I saw a doctor. That was where I was when you arrived. I drove to Truro to see a doctor and she confirmed it. I'm pregnant."

"So now what? Are you going to tell Michael?"

"Not now. Maybe not ever."

As I got to my feet, I plucked up the ribbon from the gift Michael had sent. "Are you considering an abortion then?"

"Lizzie, I know you have mixed feelings about—"

I dropped the ribbon onto the dressing table. "What I think or feel doesn't matter. You have your career to think about. You're up for that television job."

"A television job is a wonderful reason to have an abortion."

I shook my head. "You have the right to choose not to have this baby."

"As long as I never mention it to my mother or my grandmother or all the other good Catholic women in my family." Tess swiped at her eyes again and stood up, still clutching the box containing Michael's gift. "I'm off to bed, pal. See you in the morning."

"Are you okay?"

"Fine. Breakfast at seven-thirty. We have to catch a bus at nine."

"Catch a bus? Where are we going?"

Tess paused with her hand on the doorknob. "I booked us on a day tour to Tintagel Castle. You said you wanted to go there. There are stops along the way at Jamaica Inn and the town of Boscastle."

"Are you sure you're up to it? Maybe we should just hang out on the beach—"

"I'm on assignment. I have an article to write, and I'm not going to get the work done sitting on the beach." Tess pointed at the clock radio on my bedside table. "Set it."

"I'll wake up," I said. "If I don't, come get me."

"With pitcher of water in hand."

Tess closed the door behind her, and I flopped down on my bed and gave the pillow a thump. Tess was pregnant. Michael would love that. It would give him leverage.

"Dammit, Tess, haven't you ever heard of a condom? If you were going to be swept away by lust, couldn't you at least have—"

But Michael had been there too. Maybe he had been hoping this would happen.

What Tess had implied was true. I couldn't be objective about this. I couldn't think about a woman making a decision about whether or not to have a baby without thinking of my own mother. I had good reason to suspect that if she'd had a choice—money and someone to do the procedure—I would never have seen daylight.

Lucky for me, the man who'd fathered me either had not known or not bothered to open his wallet.

Chapter Four

Around dawn I woke to the sound of birds. Not the gentle coos of doves or the haunting calls of nightingales, but screeches. Loud ones. No wonder Daphne du Maurier had written a horror story about birds set in Cornwall.

"Shut up! Go back to sleep." They didn't. I put the pillow over my head and tried.

I woke up next in full daylight as the clock radio came on. I fumbled with the buttons until the music—classical—stopped. A seagull was sitting on the balcony rail, staring at me through the French doors. I sat up. He kept staring, then he tilted his head back and called out. As I got out of bed, he settled down to grooming himself, lifting a wing to pull at the feathers underneath.

I pulled on my robe and gathered up my shower gear. There was no sound from my floor when I opened the door, but I could hear Benjy in the hall above. I scooted toward the bathroom, hoping it was empty.

But then Edith Crump had said two of the rooms were en suite. The ones occupied by the Stillmans, of course. Why were they staying in a private hotel anyway? They looked more like resort hotel people. Or at least Pamela, Rosalind, and Jeremy did. So it was probably Benjamin's decision to stay here.

I closed and locked the bathroom door as I heard Benjy and his parents coming down the stairs from the third floor. I was not ready to meet and greet the public.

As a child, I had been fascinated by my grandparents' ability to get out of bed talking as if it were four in the afternoon. God help me if I ever married a man who wanted to talk in the morning. Not that I was likely to have to worry about that.

Douglas Conroy was the closest I had come in recent memory to being pursued by a man. We had met over his price list for coffins. He had assured me that he would do his best to provide the kind of funeral my grandmother would have wanted, and he had handled the service with consummate professionalism.

He presented himself for courtship with the same fine style— bouquets of summer flowers and Godiva chocolates, dinner and dancing. He was easy on the eyes, funnier than you'd expect a mortician to be. A really nice man.

Maybe I was one of those women who couldn't appreciate a nice man, because I couldn't imagine loving him anytime between now and the grave. I had enjoyed the chocolates. But it was cheaper in all kinds of ways to buy my own.

When I got downstairs, everyone else was already in the dining room. I offered my "Good morning" with an attempt at enthusiasm and sat down at the table Tess and I were sharing.

Hildegard Martin paused in stuffing what looked like sausage into her mouth. "And a splendid one it is. A perfect day for sightings."

"Sightings?" I said.

"Birds," Tess said, grinning.

Benjamin Stillman inquired about how I had slept and advised me to try the plum jam. Pamela nodded and gave me a stiff smile. At the table across from ours, the younger Stillmans and their son were discussing their plans for the day. Benjy had his heart set on a day at the beach. His father was informing him that they had spent the past two days at the beach and today they were going to do something else.

"But I want to go to the beach."

Rosalind shot a wary glance at her husband. "We're going to see monkeys, darling. Your father says we can stop at the monkey preserve."

"And you can bring along the monkey I gave you," Benjamin said from his table, "so he can see his real live cousins swing from trees."

"From trees?" Benjy said. "We're going to see real monkeys swing from trees?"

"Yes," Rosalind said, "at an animal preserve. Won't that be more fun than another day on the beach?"

Benjy started to ask questions about the monkeys, and I turned my attention to Tess. She had been listening to the family chatter too. She smiled as our eyes met, shrugged. "So . . . are you awake yet?"

"Almost."

The kitchen door swung open, and Dee came through carrying a loaded tray. The only sign of her adventures yesterday and last night was the cut and slight swelling on her bottom lip.

As she put his orange juice down in front of him, Benjy said, "I saw you this morning real early. I woke up 'cause I heard this noise. And when I looked out the window, you were going somewhere."

"For my walk along the trail. I go every morning."

"What's a trail?"

"The Coastal Path," Rosalind said. "The walking path that goes all the way around Cornwall along the cliffs. Remember when we were on the beach yesterday and we looked up and saw the hikers walking along it?"

Benjy looked back up at Dee. "You went all by yourself?"

Dee smiled. "It just looks high from the beach. It's easy to get to and not at all scary. I don't go far. Only far enough to get my blood flowing."

"What does that mean?"

"To get some exercise."

"Oh. My mummy goes to a gym place to do that. She gets all sweaty and then she sits in this room with heat—"

"A sauna," Rosalind said. "Now, drink your juice, darling."

Jeremy gave Rosalind an impatient look, then turned his gaze on Dee. "How long before our breakfasts are ready?"

"In just a few minutes," Dee said.

She turned to Tess and me to take our breakfast requests. I wanted to ask how she was feeling; instead I asked for the continental breakfast.

"As you can see, ladies and gents, the streets of St. Regis were not laid out with motor coaches in mind." This wry observation from our tour bus driver drew chuckles from the sixteen of us who had signed up for the day tour to Jamaica Inn, Boscastle, and Tintagel Castle.

We peered through the windows as a line of cars backed up so that the bus could navigate its way around a corner. Pedestrians, strolling two and three deep farther down the street, shifted to single file and clung to the narrow sidewalk as they eyed the large blue and white bus.

"Used for tours in the South of France, this luxury coach is," the driver, whose name was Jack, informed us. "But definitely an unwieldy vehicle in downtown St. Regis." But he was in control of the situation. And the drivers of the cars were tolerant.

"Can you imagine a whole line of American drivers backing up?" I said to Tess.

"Only with horns blowing and curses."

Another twist or two of the steering wheel and Jack had us on High Street, headed out of town. He began to inform us in his chatty fashion about our itinerary for the day.

The Jamaica Inn was a tourist spot because of Daphne du Maurier's historical novel about the smuggling trade. The metal plaque in the floor of the tavern marking the spot where a murder had occurred was perhaps its most interesting feature.

Boscastle, our next stop, was a village buttressed by cliffs. Shops and houses lined the street, with a car park—Brit for parking lot—in front of the restaurant. As in St. Regis, flowers bloomed in profusion. Jack said we would be there for a couple of hours, long enough to look around and have lunch.

Tess and I decided to visit the Witch Museum before we did anything else. The museum offered a serious collection of artifacts on the lore, history, and practice of witchcraft—ancient and modern-day—but the volume of people moving through limited the amount of time one could linger over each item on display.

When we emerged from the building, Tess paused to photograph the rocky cliff path that overlooked the town. "Let's go up there." She was pointing toward the summit where a number of people had gathered for the view.

"Are you sure you should? I mean—"

"I'm pregnant, not an invalid."

We crossed the small bridge spanning a narrow stream and started our ascent up the path. I tried to savor the crisp, clear day. Halfway up, we met several people from the bus on their way back down. We exchanged smiles and greetings. Tess and I kept climbing.

"I'm hungry," I said. "We do need to leave enough time for lunch."

"We have enough time."

My foot slipped on a stone and I stopped walking. "Tess, I am not going up there. I'm not a mountain goat."

"Okay, already. Let's go eat."

"Thank you." True, I didn't like heights. But I had also read somewhere, that babies were at their most fragile during the first trimester.

Tess trudged back down the hill in silence. At the bridge she said, "It's not that easy, Lizzie."

"No, I guess it wouldn't be. Want to talk about it?"

"Not yet. I need to think some more."

She was still thinking when we reached Tintagel Castle later that afternoon. I had spent the time glancing out the window and enjoying the farmland of the West Country, interspersed with villages and woodland and hedges and stone walls that ran along each side of the road.

As we navigated our way down the bustling main street of Tintagel Village, Jack pointed out the Old Post Office that was held by the National Trust. It was actually a small fourteenth century manor house, but during the Victorian era it had served as a post office. It was "worth a look-see," he said.

The shops along the street were also attracting their share of attention. My mouth watered when I spotted one selling fudge. Tess pulled out her notebook and started scribbling.

Jack drove into a gigantic parking lot that shared space with an outdoor market, offering everything from baked goods and fruits to racks of clothing and novelty items. As he sent us on our way with a reminder about our departure time, Jack added that we could either walk to the castle or take one of the cars that carried passengers back and forth. Tess had her camera out, taking photographs of the outdoor market.

"Want to ride?" I asked.

"No, I don't."

"Just asking."

She lowered the camera. "Lizzie, someday you are going to make someone a wonderful mother."

I held up my hands. "For the rest of the afternoon, I will cease and desist."

"And we'll both have more fun."

The way to the castle was a wide, dusty, unpaved road where the sun beat down. Vendors, anticipating the needs of parched-throat pilgrims, had set up stands on the grassy knolls to offer ice cream and soft drinks.

The walk was at least a couple of miles, but it was worth it. The castle ruins stood atop a cliff, among the green grass, reached by climbing what seemed to be hundreds of steps that clung to the side of the cliff. But other people—including small children and senior citizens—were doing it, and I was damn well not going to miss this. At the ticket booth we paid our entry fee and bought a map showing the layout of the castle.

"*Excalibur*," I heard a woman behind us telling her companion. "A really lovely film, wonderfully dark and passionate."

"Was it?" he asked, clearly less enthusiastic about popular culture manifestations of Arthurian legend than she was.

I had liked that movie a lot too. I could still see in my mind the scene in which the lecherous Uther Pendragon, transformed by Merlin, the magician, into the likeness of the Duke, galloped into the stronghold. Igraine, believing the man to be her husband, had welcomed him into her bed, made love with him as her true husband fell in the battle that was raging between the two opposing forces. And Arthur, the once and future king, was conceived.

According to the guidebook to the castle, the moat bridge across which an intruder would have galloped to gain access to the castle keep no longer existed. The steps we were climbing had been constructed later to provide access to the ruins.

Of course, it was all legend, not to be mistaken for fact. The matter was still the subject of debate. But the authors of the books I had read seemed to be of the opinion that although there was archaeological evidence of earlier occupation of these grounds, the castle itself had probably been constructed in the thirteenth century. That would make it a bit too late to have served as the site of Arthur's conception, assuming he had actually existed. And if he had been a real person, he was more likely to have been rugged soldier of fortune than noble king.

Still, it was fascinating to stand there amidst the ruins of Tintagel Castle and look outward toward the sea, to stand there on the cliff side and look down at the small stretch of beach and the entrance to "Merlin's Cave."

As my grandfather had once said, there was no harm in believing in magic for an hour or two. "*Just don't buy none of them magic beans and expect them to grow.*"

In the museum gift shop I read the information in the exhibit about the castle. It seemed the geological forces of nature were still at work. One day, what was left of the ruins would fall into the sea and be swept away. So much for legend.

By the time we got back to St. Regis, Tess, who had spent the return trip scribbling in her notebook, had worked herself into a better mood, so I agreed when she suggested we have some dinner before walking back up the hill to the hotel.

We opted for pasties, the Cornish version of fast food. The workers in the tin mines had found having a hearty meal sealed inside a flaky baked dough both convenient and tasty, but they had always left a bite of their meal for the malevolent imps that lived in the mines. I intended to eat all of my huge steak and onion pasty. From the way Tess was eyeing hers, I had no doubt she intended to do the same.

The shop we had bought them in had only a few tables and they were all in use, so we went back outside and found a place to sit on the harbor wall. Lots of other people were sitting or strolling along the boardwalk as they nibbled. Seagulls swooped down, grabbing any dropped scraps. Laughter and chatter filled the air.

I swallowed a savory bit of beef and wished for my camera, buried in the denim backpack Tess had talked me into buying. Hands full of Cornish pasty, I couldn't get to it. But I would remember this scene, pull it out on some dull rainy day back home: Sea and people and sunshine and boats.

"It must be such fun," I said to Tess, "traveling, seeing so many things."

She took a swallow of her orange juice before she spoke. "Sometimes. A lot of times. But other times, it's plain hard work. And then there are all the annoyances and inconveniences—I've told you about all that."

"But you wouldn't trade it for a desk job."

"No, I wouldn't. So tell me: what am I going to do with a baby?"

"Give it to Michael."

"Great idea. Thanks for the suggestion."

"If you want suggestions—"

"Not yet."

When we walked through the door of the Gull's Nest Hotel, Michael was there. Dee—standing on the stairs, holding a stack of towels—was giggling at whatever he was saying to her. Michael straightened from his leaning position against the banister and gave Tess a dazzling smile. "Tess—"

"What are you doing here?"

He sobered. "I came to see you. We need to talk."

Tess pushed back a lock of hair from her face, glanced at Dee. "You're right, we do need to talk."

"How about I take you to dinner?"

"All right."

I caught back the reminder that we had just finished dinner.

Michael turned his smile on me. "Lizzie, I'd ask you to join us but—"

"Thanks, but I've already eaten."

"Then we'll see you later," Michael said as he took Tess's arm.

I moved aside to let them pass. "See you later."

Tess said, "I won't be late." I almost reminded her that I wasn't her mother.

The door closed behind them. When I turned, Dee was watching me. "How are you today?" I asked.

"Better than yesterday, thanks." She nodded her head toward the door. "He is such a lovely gentleman, isn't he? It's a shame he won't be staying with us this time."

"This time? Are you saying he has stayed here before?"

"Last spring. Early . . . before the season began. He was the only guest that week, but he was so pleasant to have about." Dee's glance became inquisitive. "But he said he was the one who recommended the hotel to Ms. Alvarez. Didn't she tell you?"

"No." And why hadn't she?

"It must have slipped her mind," Dee said. "Will you be needing anything?"

"No. Thanks, I have everything I need. I think I'll go up to my room and read for a while."

The historical romance, set during one of my favorite eras, was not quite riveting enough to hold my attention. The battle of wills between a Norman knight and a Saxon lady failed to keep my eyes from wandering to the digital time display on my clock radio. I could hear laughter coming from the parlor downstairs. I considered going down and being sociable, but my heart wasn't in it.

But I did have to go to the bathroom. As I came out on the landing, I heard a sound. Poised midway on the stairs leading down to the foyer, Benjy was looking up at me, his expression pure "caught in the act."

"Hi, there," I said. "Are you supposed to be in bed?"

"I forgot about Chester."

"Chester?"

"My monkey that my grandpa gave me. I have to go get him." He started down the stairs in his bare feet and pj's.

"See you later," I called after him.

Sneaking out of bed to listen to the adults was something every child did now and then. But a few minutes after I got back to my room, I heard Benjy being escorted back up the stairs by one of the adults. He was protesting. "Why do I have to? I'm not sleepy. Will you tell me a story?"

I picked up my novel again, tried reading, and then tried pacing.

At eleven o'clock, I got undressed and made one more trip to the bathroom so that I wouldn't have to get up in the middle of the night.

At around twelve-thirty, hearing a car stop outside, I jumped up and ran over to the balcony doors in time to see Tess get out of a burgundy sedan.

I opened my door and stepped out into the hallway. The lights were so low Tess had reached the top stair before I could see her expression. "You don't look happy."

She gestured toward my open door.

"Did you tell him?" I asked when we were inside.

"I told him."

"And?"

"He wants to get married again, thinks it's the only practical solution. He says if we're married, I'll have a nanny to take care of the baby while I'm working."

"You can hire a nanny on your own, Tess. You could even hire someone to travel with you—"

"I don't make that kind of money."

"If you get the cable travel show job—"

"*If* I get it. They have at least two other top-notch candidates. And even then, traveling— How would I travel with a baby to some of the places I go?"

"I'm surprised Michael didn't suggest you give up your job." As soon as the words were out, I regretted them. I had promised myself I was not going to say nasty things about Michael.

Tess leaned back against the door. "He did suggest that once. When we were first married he wanted me to stay at home and be a good corporate wife."

"But you said no?"

"And lived to regret it. One evening I came home from a trip to the beautiful island of Jamaica and found my husband in bed with another woman."

"Oh, Tess, no!"

"You sound surprised. Did you think better of Michael?"

"Who was she?"

"Someone he'd picked up in a bar. A cute little coed, not much more than twenty-one. Perky breasts, a mane of flyaway blonde curls."

"Tess, I'm so sorry."

"I know you've never liked Michael."

"I have tried to like him, but he's never made it easy. You aren't seriously considering— What did you say when he suggested you get married again?"

"I told him I'd think about it."

"Tess—" I swallowed the words that I wanted to say. "Think carefully."

"I intend to." She pushed back her bangs and sighed. "All these years, he's claimed that seeing the look on my face—knowing how much he'd hurt me— He said it was because of the argument we'd had on the telephone the night before. He was angry, he went out and got drunk, and he met her in the last bar he hit. She was sweet and sympathetic."

"So he brought her home to your bed?"

"The question is, would he ever do it again? Can I trust him this time?"

"Yes. That's exactly what you need to think about."

"That and my baby." Tess opened the door. "See you in the morning, pal. Tomorrow, how about going into Penzance and then taking the bus to Land's End?"

"If you feel up to it."

"I'm on assignment, remember?"

Chapter Five

I slept as if I'd eaten pizza at midnight, and woke to the screeching of birds. Admitting defeat, I got up and went over to the balcony doors. The morning fog shimmered in the pale dawn light. I heard the door downstairs close. Dee came out, dressed in blue jeans and a white sweater, with her red backpack slung over one shoulder. She headed down the hill, toward the beach. I looked over my shoulder at the clock radio: 5:56 A.M. I was never going to be able to fall back asleep.

Before I could change my mind, I reached for the clothes I had tossed on the chair when I undressed the night before. If I was up at this hour, I might as well have an experience to remember. I crept down the stairs and let myself out the front door. I sucked in several lungfuls of the crisp air. I was almost functioning.

Dee was far enough ahead of me so I needn't worry about intruding on her morning ritual. By the time I got down to the beach, she would be up on the cliff path.

I headed down the hill, anticipating my solitary morning walk along the beach. But before I could set foot on the sand, I was brought up short by what I saw. There was a runner on the beach, coming in my direction, his long legs covering the distance in an easy lope. I swerved away, toward the paved path leading to the foot of the cliff walk. If the runner was who I thought he was, the last thing I wanted was an early morning encounter on the beach. I didn't want to see him again at all. It was always awkward encountering someone again after meeting in a muddled situation. What would we say to each other?

Hurrying past The Ship's Mast, the restaurant that Edith said served excellent seafood, I apologized to my body for the shock I was delivering to it, and climbed up the hill onto the cliff path.

Dee was too far ahead of me to be in sight. And anyway, it was a public path, so she couldn't expect to keep it all to herself.

I could see why she came up here every morning. The fog was melting away, revealing the sea. When I looked over my shoulder, I had a view all the way to the other side of St. Regis, of the buildings in town and the cliffs beyond. A white mist shimmered over everything. I started walking.

I saw Dee at the same time she saw me. She waved from her perch on a flat-topped boulder. "Hello," I said. "I saw you going out and got the idea of taking a walk myself."

She smiled. "Lovely, isn't it? I'll miss it when I leave here."

"You're going away?"

"There's not much to do here. We're all tourist trade, and the tourists have been going elsewhere. Besides, I'd like to live in London. I want to live in a city where there's always something happening and things to do."

"London's marvelous. But I live in a small town, too—Drucilla, Kentucky—and whenever I'm in a city like New York or London, I'm a little overwhelmed by the pace."

"I won't mind being overwhelmed. I'd like to lose myself for a bit."

"Then a big city's the place to go." I glanced at the plastic containers she had set out beside her. "I'll go now and let you get on with your breakfast."

"No need. I have enough, if you want to join me."

"I'm not really hungry, but if you wouldn't mind some company—" I sighed as I sat down. "I'm not used to all this early morning activity."

"Your friend Ms. Alvarez told us you were a slugabed."

"It's true that I am not a morning person."

"It's something you're born to. Sean—" She froze over his name as if she hadn't realized she was going to speak it. "He doesn't like to get up either." She opened a container, revealing a fruit salad with slices of peaches, strawberries, and grapes. She pointed to the other container. "Try those."

I reached for the container with the red plastic lid. "What are they?"

"Yummy balls."

"What?"

Dee laughed. "That's what Aunt Sarah calls them. She started making them for me when we found out I'm allergic to peanuts. I have such a yen for sweets, she wanted to make sure I wouldn't be tempted to eat something I shouldn't."

"What does she put in them?"

"She starts with oats and honey and chopped dates, and then she adds whatever she has on hand that's healthy but yummy—"

"And that's why they're called 'yummy balls.'" I plucked one of the dark, crunchy-coated balls from the container and took a bite. "Mmm, I think she used butterscotch flavoring. You're right, these are good."

"Have another."

"One more. Here, take this before I eat them all."

Laughing, Dee took the plastic container I was holding out to her. "Aunt Sarah made this batch fresh yesterday afternoon. I always keep a supply in my backpack to munch on. Much better for quick energy than chocolate bars."

I bit into my second yummy ball. "Except I'm a sworn chocolate addict."

"I would be too if it weren't for my allergies. But these make up for it." She popped one of the balls into her mouth, chewed, and swallowed. Her eyes went wide.

"Dee—"

Her face was red. She was wheezing.

"Oh, God, Dee . . . Dee, what is it?"

"Peanuts—" She pawed at her backpack, throwing things out. Her chest heaved.

"What should I do? Tell me what to do."

"My kit—" She gasped the words out. "I can't find it—"

"What does it look like?" I snatched up the backpack she had dropped.

"Sy-syringe kit—" She wheezed out the words through her swollen lips.

With the sound of her gasps in my ears, I dumped everything in the backpack onto the ground. Black and white polka-dot bikini bottom, crumpled tissues, lipstick, compact, sunscreen, keys, change purse, a tampon. A little purple dragon made of plastic. No syringe kit. "It's not here. Dee, it's not here!"

She had slumped to the ground on her back. Her eyelids twitched as I felt for the pulse in her throat.

Her tongue. She might choke on her swollen tongue. Head to the side. I was supposed to turn her head to the side. But what if she rolled back over while I was gone?

"Dee!" I grabbed the empty backpack and slid it under her head to elevate it. "Dee, I've got to go for help." But first I needed a stick.

He had ended his morning run at the restaurant and was sitting on the steps that led from the terrace down to beach. He shot to his feet as I stumbled toward him, his gray eyes sweeping over me, taking in my dishevelment. "What happened? Did someone—"

"I need to call— There's a medical emergency—" I said between pants. "She's—"

I sneezed. Sneezed again. *Sneeze in the morning, cry before evening*, Hester Rose said in my head.

"Dammit! Dee's up on the cliff path."

He looked blank. "Dee?"

I grabbed his arm and shook it. "The girl from Sunday evening—Dee and Sean—she's allergic to peanuts. She's having an allergic reaction. She's in shock."

"Use the telephone in there," he said, pushing me toward the restaurant. "They aren't open yet, but the kitchen crew's inside."

"Wait! Where are you going?"

"To see if I can help her."

"Are you a doctor?" I called after him, praying he would say yes.

"A cop."

He ran up the hill. I ran to the door of the restaurant and started pounding and yelling for them to let me in.

The grimness of his expression was enough. When our eyes met, he confirmed with a shake of his head what I suspected. We were too late.

The two paramedics who had hurried back with me along the path were trained not to accept the opinion of lay people. They bent over Dee and went to work, checking for her heartbeat, feeling for her pulse, doing all the things they were trained to do to try and reclaim someone from death.

The cop must have taken the stick out of her mouth. It would have been less than dignified for her to be seen like that by the small crowd which had gathered. I'd only put it there because I didn't want her to swallow her tongue. At least he had thought to take it out. Or maybe he had tried to give her mouth-to-mouth resuscitation.

The paramedics continued their efforts to revive her for several more minutes, but it was obvious she was dead. Finally, one of them mumbled, "No use, I'm afraid."

I walked away from Dee there on the ground in her white sweater and blue jeans with her long black hair shining with health. Out over the water, the fog was melting away. A bright summer day was being unveiled.

"The backpack. Is it yours or hers?" The cop had come to stand behind me.

"Hers."

"Were the things on the ground in the backpack?"

"Yes, we were searching for her adrenaline kit—"

"And it wasn't there?"

"If it had been there—" I caught my rising voice. "If it had been there, she would have been all right."

"But she thought the kit was there in her backpack?"

"Yes. Maybe she took it out for some reason and forgot to put it back."

"Would you forget something your life depended on?"

"She—" I looked toward the people who were watching the paramedics prepare Dee's body for transport. "Sunday night when she came back to the hotel . . . she'd had too much to drink. Maybe that was when—"

"So you think she misplaced her adrenaline kit during her evening on the town?"

"She was probably upset about the quarrel she'd had with Sean—"

"What about the peanuts?"

"The peanuts?"

"You said she had an allergic reaction to peanuts."

"That was what she said. She ate one of the yummy balls."

"One of the what?"

"In the plastic container with the red top. They're an oatmeal and fruit ball that her Aunt Sarah makes. Dee brought them along for her breakfast. She told me to try them. I did. I told her they were delicious. Then she ate one."

"And that was when she had the allergic reaction?"

"Yes, but her Aunt Sarah made the yummy balls. Her aunts know about Dee's allergy. They have a sign posted asking guests staying at the hotel not to bring in peanuts."

"Then how did the peanuts get into homemade yummy balls?"

"I don't know. It must have been an accident."

"An accident?" Cool gray eyes probed mine. "The peanuts got into the yummy balls by accident. And by some unlucky coincidence, she also happened to misplace the adrenaline kit that she usually kept in her backpack?"

"Dee. Her name was Dee." I lowered my voice. "And you can't think— No one would do what you're suggesting."

"Are you sure about that? What about her boyfriend?"

"He hit her. But this is different. If someone did this . . . you didn't see how she . . . someone would have to be incredibly cold-blooded to do this."

"And it's your impression her boyfriend wasn't that cold-blooded?"

"Didn't you see the look on his face when she told him to go away?"

"He looked angry."

"Yes, but he also looked hurt . . . wounded."

"I've got news for you, lady. Wounded people sometimes kill, and they do it in incredibly cold-blooded ways."

"We're ready to take her down now, mate," the older of the paramedics called to him.

"Hold on a moment." He flashed a glance in my direction, a measuring look, then he walked over to where the paramedics were standing with the stretcher. He spoke to them in a low voice. Their faces registered surprise. The younger of the paramedics pointed toward the path along which we had come.

A uniformed constable was striding toward us. The cop went to meet him.

The paramedics and the rest of us watched as they shook hands. Then for the next few minutes, the cop talked while the constable listened. When he was done, the constable reached for his police radio and began to speak into it. By the time he and the cop joined the paramedics, the onlookers who had gathered had begun to mumble among themselves.

The constable turned to them and said, "Ladies and gentlemen, if I could ask you to move along now. As you can see, there has been an accident here. We are about to transport the victim, so there is nothing more to see, and we would like to preserve this area for further examination. So if you would be so good as to go on about your business." Under duress, the spectators drifted away.

The cop walked back over to me. "The constable is going to stay here to guard the crime scene."

"The crime scene? You don't know that a crime has been committed."

"No, that's why the police need to gather any evidence that might be here so determination can be made about cause of death. The constable is going to secure the area until the evidence technicians arrive. Another unit is coming out to pick us up."

"To pick us up? Why?"

"Whatever this is—an accident or a homicide—we need to make statements. We're going to the station house to do that. Any objections?"

The paramedics walked past us carrying Dee's body strapped on the stretcher.

"No, no objections."

"Let's go then."

"Her aunts—someone will have to notify her aunts."

"Someone will."

I studied the backs of the paramedics as they trudged ahead of us. They didn't seem to be bothered by the load they were carrying, but then Dee hadn't weighed that much.

"I didn't get your name," the cop said. "I'm John Quinn."

"Lizzie. Lizabeth Stuart."

"Lizzie Stuart—from somewhere in the South. Where?"

How charming! We were going to make small talk. "Kentucky."

"Louisville? Lexington?"

"Drucilla."

"Drucilla?"

"I know. You've never heard of it."

"Afraid not."

The paramedics paused while the younger one reached down to adjust a strap, then they started to walk again.

"Philadelphia," John Quinn said.

"What?"

"I live in Philadelphia. That was going to be your next question."

"Was it? I'm glad you can read my mind. How long have you been a police officer?"

"Twelve years in Philadelphia."

"And somewhere else before that?"

"Military police."

I dug my hands into the pockets of the wrinkled shorts from yesterday that I had put back on this morning for my walk. I hadn't even showered yet, and I was going to be talking to the St. Regis police. "You're a detective? You've handled homicide investigations?"

"Yes, I am a detective, and, yes, I've worked homicide cases."

"And what about right now, Detective Quinn? Are you relying on your finely honed instincts? Your experience? Is that why you think this is foul play?"

"That's why I think it's murder."

I tripped over what must have been a stone on the path and almost fell. Quinn caught my arm.

"Thank you. You can let go now."

But he didn't. Obviously he thought I was on the brink of either fainting or fleeing.

I took a deep breath to calm whatever was fluttering in my chest. "So much for my nice, quiet vacation."

"Mine too."

"Your transport's here," the older paramedic called over his shoulder to Quinn and me as we reached the end of the path and started down the hill by the restaurant.

Another St. Regis police officer had arrived and was there among the people gathered on the terrace of the restaurant. He finished what he was saying to two children and strolled over to join us at the back of the ambulance. "A shame," he said, as he saw Dee's shrouded body.

"Nothing we could do for her," the younger paramedic said. He looked a bit pale. Maybe it was his first D.O.A.

The constable's glance swept over me and settled on Quinn. "I'm Constable Ingram. You must be the gentleman I'm to transport."

Quinn held out his hand. "John Quinn, Philadelphia PD."

The constable shook his hand. "I'll take you along to the DI."

"This is Ms. Stuart. She's a witness in this matter."

"Right, then. If you'll both come along to my vehicle."

We walked with him to where he had parked his police car on the access road above the beach. I sat in the backseat as he drove us the short distance to the St. Regis police station. In the front seat, he and Quinn engaged in casual discussion about policing in St. Regis during the summer tourist season.

The police station, a small building on one of the side streets, was a few steps up the hill from the cinema where, according to the posters in the window, several first-run American movies were being shown. In the station house vestibule, an interview room was on one side, the sergeant's desk on the other.

The constable excused himself to go find the DI. "Have a seat in the interview room if you'd like."

I didn't like. Quinn looked into the interview room with its table and three chairs, then back at me. I shook my head.

The DI was younger than I had expected, late thirties, recruiting-poster features, but with a look of quiet efficiency about him. "I'm Detective Inspector Thomas Cordner." He held out his hand to John Quinn, "I understand you're a police officer. Would you happen to be Ed Janowitz's former partner?"

"I gather he's mentioned me," Quinn said with a wry twist of his mouth.

"Indeed. He informed me of your arrival when he stopped in last week and promised to bring you by. It's a pleasure to meet you, Detective Quinn."

"And you, Detective Inspector. This is Ms. Stuart."

It occurred to me that by now my appearance probably resembled an unmade bed.

"Ms. Stuart," DI Cordner said with a nod. "If you'll excuse us, I'd like to have a word with Detective Quinn. Perhaps you could have a seat in the interview room. Shall I have one of the constables fetch you a cup of tea?"

"I'm sure Ms. Stuart would like a cup of tea," Quinn said.

He was sure about that, was he? I was tired and tense. The only nourishment I had consumed in over ten hours was one of Aunt Sarah's yummy balls that had quite possibly been used as a murder weapon. I was not in the mood to be agreeable. "No, I would not like a cup of tea. I am not Ms. Stuart. I am Doctor Stuart or Professor Stuart, a criminologist. I teach criminal justice and I do not care to be left sitting out here cooling my heels while the two of you confer."

"A criminologist," Quinn said. "You didn't mention that."

"You didn't ask what I do for a living."

"Well," DI Cordner said. "Isn't this fortunate? Two crime experts at the scene. But, Professor Stuart, I'm afraid I really must ask you to wait before I bring you in. You are a witness, as is Detective Quinn. I need to speak to you separately, or at least get Detective Quinn's statement before I ask you to join us. So if you would please try to make yourself comfortable, I promise we won't be long."

"All right. I'm sorry, I'm not usually—"

"I understand completely. It was rather an unpleasant way to begin the day, wasn't it?" He turned toward the listening sergeant. "Sergeant, could you arrange a cuppa for Professor Stuart."

"Yes, sir," the sergeant said.

DI Cordner turned back to me. "No more than fifteen minutes, then I'll call you in."

"Yes, thank you."

He escorted Quinn through the door leading into the inner sanctum of the police station. Having made a proper idiot of myself, I went into the interview room and took a seat.

A few minutes later, the sergeant brought me a steaming, milky cup of tea and two cookies (biscuits, he called them) on a saucer. I thanked him and took a sip of the tea. It was strong and sweet and sent an immediate jolt to my nervous system.

I reached for a couple of the pamphlets in the rack on the wall. The St. Regis police department was into community policing. Information about home burglary, rape, and domestic violence. A pamphlet on how to fill out a police report.

Nothing about murder. But murder was an atypical crime. Probably a once-every-five-or-six-years event in a town the size of St. Regis. Even less often if one counted only the permanent residents.

Just my luck to be there when a murder did happen—and even to be a witness. Just Dee's luck to be the victim. Just her poor Aunt Sarah's luck to have made the yummy balls that had somehow gotten spiked with peanuts. Just her boyfriend Sean's luck to have quarreled with her—struck her—with witnesses present, including a cop.

But maybe Detective John Quinn was wrong. Maybe his instincts had gone haywire. Maybe it had been an accident.

Yeah, and maybe wishing made it so. I had no instincts regarding homicide, but it felt wrong even to me. I leaned back in the wooden chair and took another sip of the sweet, bracing tea.

Detective Inspector Cordner was true to his word. No more than fifteen minutes had passed before a constable appeared in the doorway of the interview room to escort me into his office.

When I walked in, he and Quinn were sitting on opposite sides of his desk. Quinn was saying, "Another week or so. I have to get back—" He broke off as I came in.

To my surprise, both he and Cordner stood up. Obviously they had decided to smooth my ruffled dignity by displaying their best manners.

"Professor Stuart," Cordner said. "Please come in and join us. Sit here." He indicated the other chair in front of his desk.

"Thank you." I sat down and glanced around.

Sunlight filtered into the room through the vertical blinds on the two windows above a computer and printer on a wooden table. Folders were stacked on the table beside the computer and on top of each of the metal filing cabinets. Adjacent bookcases were stuffed with what looked like police manuals, legal tomes, and reports. A framed painting of a British bobby, circa 1880s, hung above a battered leather sofa.

But Cordner's desk might once have been in the office of a country doctor or lawyer, handed down from father to son. Dark maple, it glowed with the patina of age and care. An antique inkwell sat off to one side of the leather-edged blotter. On the other side was a picture frame, probably a photograph of his wife. He was wearing a wedding ring.

"Now, then, Professor Stuart," Cordner said, bringing my attention back to the matter at hand, "Thank you for waiting. Detective Quinn has filled me in on what he knows occurred. Now, if we could have your account. But first, would you like another cup of tea?"

"No, I'm fine, thank you."

"Then let's go on, shall we?" He drew a pad toward him. "Any objections to a recording?"

I shook my head, and he brought out a portable cassette player from one of the desk drawers. Hadn't he bothered to record the statement from his other witness, John Quinn? I bit my tongue before the question could pop out.

"And if you have no objections," Cordner said, "I'd like Detective Quinn to hear this."

"All right."

"Good. Then if you'll begin. Please describe what happened this morning."

I began with my impulsive decision to go for a walk when I'd seen Dee leaving, then my meeting with her on the cliff path. I didn't mention seeing Quinn and going in the other direction. Had he seen me?

Cordner asked what Dee and I had talked about.

I told him what Dee had said about her plans to move to London. Then I told him about the yummy balls, about eating one myself and passing the container to Dee, about her reaction when she ate one. I told him about running for help and finding Quinn there on the restaurant terrace.

'When my voice dwindled away, Cordner nodded. "Thank you, Professor Stuart. That was all I needed."

I reached up to adjust the collar of my sweater. My hand was shaking. I clasped my hands together in my lap. When I looked up, both men were watching me. "I'm sorry, I'm not— As you said, Inspector Cordner, it was an unpleasant way to begin the morning. And I got to bed late last night."

"Why?" The question came from Quinn.

"Because my friend was out and I was waiting for her to come in."

"Your friend? Someone else who's staying at the hotel?" Cordner asked.

"Tess Alvarez, the friend I came to spend the week with. She's a travel writer."

"Is she?" Cordner said. "So she's here to write about Cornwall, and you're here on holiday."

"Yes."

Quinn asked, "Where was she last night?"

Why had I brought Tess into the conversation? I considered not answering the question. But that would make them think there was something suspicious. "Her ex-husband is in St. Regis too. They went out to dinner together."

"Still friends, are they?" Cordner said.

"Yes. And by now Tess is probably wondering where I am."

"We've sent someone along to the Gull's Nest to tell them what's happened. However, under the circumstances, interviews will be required."

"Then you agree with Detective Quinn? You think that it's murder?"

"I think the matter needs looking into. But we'll know more when we have the report from the pathologist. And after we've talked to our young woman's relatives, friends, and associates."

Quinn asked Cordner, "Do you know the aunts?"

"By reputation only. They're said to be two rather kind old dears."

"They're not that old," I said. "But they are kind. You can't possibly think they would have anything to do with the death of their own niece."

"I don't think anything yet, Professor Stuart." Cordner pushed his chair away from his desk and stood up. "May I give you a lift back to your hotel? Would you care to come along, Detective Quinn?"

"If you wouldn't mind the company," Quinn said as he too got to his feet.

I looked up at Quinn, stalling for time until my trembling legs would support me. "I thought you were on vacation."

"I am."

Cordner smiled. "A busman's holiday, as we say. With any luck, we'll have this wrapped up in two or three days and then you'll both be able to enjoy the rest of your stay."

"Maybe Detective Quinn will be able to do that, Inspector. I won't."

Cordner's blue eyes met mine. "It would take rather a strong mind, wouldn't it? Even if we should wrap this up, I rather doubt either of you will be in the mood for beach lounging. But, as my mum always says, it never hurts to speak cheerfully." He paused. "Of course, one is tempted to stuff a sock in her gob when she says it."

Jolted into laughter, I accepted the hand he was offering to help me up from my chair. "Thank you."

"Have a hot shower when you get back to the hotel," Quinn offered.

"Excellent suggestion," Cordner said. "Nothing better for a bout of nerves."

"Except a stiff drink," Quinn said. "But we don't want to encourage you in bad habits."

Chapter Six

THE THREE OF US ARRIVED on the steps of the Gull's Nest Hotel at a little before 9 A.M., less than three hours, all told, since I had taken off on my great adventure—an early morning walk. I dug into my pants pocket for the key to the front door.

"I believe it's already open, Professor," Cordner said.

He was right. The door was not quite closed. I pushed it wide and we stepped into the hallway. The only sound was the ticking of the pedestal clock.

I glanced toward the board on the wall provided for guests to indicate their comings and goings, but that was no help. All the tabs were in the IN position from last night. I opened my mouth to call out—then shut it again and looked at the two men standing behind me.

"Why don't we try in there?" Cordner said, pointing to the closed lounge door.

I took a step toward the white paneled door and put my hand out toward the knob. The knob turned from the other side and the door was flung open.

"Aah, I thought I heard someone come in," Benjamin Stillman said, pushing at his glasses. "Forgive me, Lizzie, I didn't mean to startle you." He looked tired and a little rumpled with toast crumbs caught in his beard and a red stain on his white shirt. "Cranberry juice," he said when he saw where I was staring. "I was giving some to Benjy before they left. We spilled it."

"Benjamin, have you heard about . . . do you know about Dee?"

He nodded, "Her aunts had been worrying about where she could have gotten to when she knew there was breakfast to be served and morning chores to be done. Then the constable came to the door." His sad brown eyes looked into mine. "He said you were with her when it happened."

"Yes. I had gone for a walk, too. Benjamin, this is Detective Inspector Thomas Cordner of the St. Regis Police. Inspector, this is Mr. Stillman. He and his family are guests here at the hotel."

"Detective Inspector," Benjamin said, holding out his hand. But he was frowning. "You are considering Dee's death a matter for police investigation?"

"In cases of sudden death, an inquiry is routine procedure, Mr. Stillman," Cordner said. "Especially when the deceased is a young and apparently healthy person."

Benjamin was still frowning. "Except for her allergies. Isn't that what the constable said, that she had an allergic reaction?"

"That is what we believe happened, yes. But we're waiting for the pathologist's report. Meanwhile, we do need to initiate an investigation."

"Of course," Benjamin said, pushing at his glasses again. "Of course. If there is anything I can do to help—"

"Thank you, Mr. Stillman. I'd like you to meet a visiting colleague from the States, Detective John Quinn of the Philadelphia PD."

"Detective Quinn." Benjamin stepped to the side, reaching around me to shake Quinn's hand.

"Mr. Stillman."

I looked down at the two hands as they met, my eyes caught by the glint of the ring Quinn was wearing. A black and silver signet ring.

I hadn't noticed Benjamin's hands before. They were spatula-fingered and huge, hands that had done—could still do—hard work. And under his juice-stained shirt was a barrel chest. He stepped back and pushed at his glasses. "Philadelphia? I was in Philadelphia earlier this year in January. Snow and ice. Very nasty."

"You should try us in autumn," Quinn said.

"I have been there then too. I have many business acquaintances, all over the United States. My son and his wife lived for a while in Boston." With a half-smile and wave of his hand, he continued, "When my son was 'striking out on his own.' So I have had reason to come over quite often."

Quinn said, "So you've probably seen more of my country than I have."

"That is true, isn't it? We tend to neglect exploring what is at our doorstep." Benjamin tugged at his white cotton shirt, pulling the stained cloth away from his chest. "If you will excuse me, I will go change this as my wife ordered me to do before she left. I was sitting with Sarah . . . but now that you are all here—"

"Benjamin," I asked, "where is everyone else?"

"When the constable came with the news, Edith wanted to go immediately to her niece. Your friend, Tess, was good enough to drive her. Hildegard had already gone out to meet her group for a bird-watching expedition."

"And what about your family? Did you say they went out too?"

"Because of my grandson," Benjamin explained, speaking more to Cordner than to me. "Benjy, my grandson, heard what the constable was saying and became distressed. Dee had been playing with him yesterday . . . I came downstairs and found the two of them sitting on the floor in the lounge. She was telling him a tale about dragons and knights and beautiful ladies—"

"That's where I saw it," I said. "Benjy had a purple dragon—"

"Yes," Benjamin said. "He has such a dragon among his toys."

"No—what I mean is I think he must have given it to Dee. She had a purple dragon in her backpack."

"Perhaps yesterday when they were playing together." Benjamin shook his head. "When he heard that Dee was dead . . . it is difficult for a small child to comprehend such things. So we decided it would be best if his parents and his grandmother took him out for the day as we had planned."

"And what about Sarah?" I asked. "You said you were sitting with her?"

"When the constable told us how Dee died, Sarah—" Benjamin pushed at his glasses. "Sarah has never been strong, especially since the accident to her leg. She collapsed, and Edith and your friend Tess got her to bed. I said I would stay with her."

"Sarah collapsed when she heard? Does she know that the peanuts were in the yummy balls that she made?"

Benjamin frowned. "In the yummy balls? The constable told us only that Dee had died from what seemed to be an allergic reaction. The peanuts were in—?"

"We're waiting for the laboratory to confirm that," Cordner said. "But based on what Professor Stuart observed, the yummy balls do seem to have been the source."

"That is all this needs," Benjamin said. "Poor Sarah is having a difficult enough time already. Another blow—" He broke off in midsentence with a puzzled look on his face. "I'm sorry, Detective Inspector, I don't understand this."

"You don't understand what, Mr. Stillman?"

"I don't understand how Sarah could have made such a mistake. Sarah in the kitchen—when you watch her in the kitchen—you see how much attention she gives to her cooking. How could she have made such a mistake?"

"Perhaps something she bought was contaminated with peanuts," Cordner said. "The flour or the sugar."

Benjamin shook his head. "But she told me once that she always shops at the same market here in St. Regis. I'm sure she must have told them about Dee."

"And presumably they would then have warned her about possible contamination," Cordner said. "But we'll know more about that after we've had a chance to talk to Miss Crump."

"She is sleeping. I'm not sure it would be good to wake her."

"Has she been seen by a doctor?" I asked.

"Edith wanted to call their family physician, but Sarah refused."

"That's a good sign, isn't it?" Cordner said. "She's still enough in control to made her wishes known."

There was nothing in the expression on Cordner's pleasant face to suggest innuendo in the remark, but I wondered what he was thinking. Surely he couldn't think Sarah had done this. Even if for some reason she had wanted her niece dead, peanuts in the yummy balls she herself had made would have been an incredibly incriminating way to go about it.

"I will go up and change my shirt and then I will make us all some tea," Benjamin offered.

"Let me do that, Benjamin."

"Thank you, Professor," Cordner said. "Mr. Stillman, if you wouldn't mind, I do have a question or two I'd like to ask you after you've changed your shirt."

"Questions? Questions about what?"

"You seem to know the family well. I'd like to get a sense of the people here before I speak to the two Miss Crumps. I would like to avoid upsetting them any more than necessary."

"Yes. Let me put on another shirt and we will talk."

He went up the stairs. I turned to the two policemen. Cordner was watching Benjamin climb the stairs. Quinn was glancing around the foyer. Then they looked at each other, and I could have sworn a message passed between them.

Cordner smiled at me. "That tea really would be much appreciated, Professor."

"In other words, the two of you would like to confer. Of course, I'll be happy to go make the tea." A yawn caught me by surprise, almost splitting my jaw. "Excuse me."

"If you'd like to go upstairs and have a rest—" Cordner offered.

"No. Thank you, but I can't yet. I started this and I have to finish it."

"Started what?" John Quinn said.

"This. Dee's death. I was there when she— I can't just retreat to my bed and have a nap before we know what happened."

Cordner said, "Professor Stuart, I should tell you that if you intend to stay awake until this investigation is over—"

"You know what I mean. I can't just . . . I have to—"

Quinn broke into my stammering. "Then you'd better make that tea strong enough to keep yourself from falling asleep on your feet.

I don't suppose they have any coffee out there."

"I didn't sleep well last night," I said, responding to his tone. "And I'm not used to getting up at the crack of dawn. And, yes, they do have coffee. Do you want me to make some?"

"If it isn't too much trouble."

"Not at all. And you'll have tea, Inspector Cordner?"

"Yes, tea for me, please."

"Excuse me," I said. Then I turned back on a thought. "The yummy balls—Sarah would have made them in the kitchen. Do you need to look—"

Cordner shook his head. "I'm afraid we're not authorized at the moment."

"Oh . . . no . . . of course not. You don't have a search warrant. You do have to have those here?"

"Or permission," Cordner said. "When I speak to Sarah Crump, I'll ask about collecting her baking supplies for testing."

"Actually, the yummy balls weren't baked. I mean, they were a no-bake recipe. But you're right about the baking supplies anyway. Sarah might have used both flour and sugar in preparing them."

"We're glad you agree," Quinn said.

I ignored him, directing my words to Cordner. "I'll go make that tea now."

Quinn said, "Don't forget the coffee. Make it strong."

"And your coffee, Detective Quinn. Is saluting optional?"

A wave of color swept across his cheeks. Good grief, was he blushing? Before I could get over that, he hunched his shoulders and smiled, a real smile that started in his eyes and worked its way on down to his mouth. "Saluting is neither required nor expected. Sorry, Professor. Old habits. But I really would appreciate a cup of coffee. I didn't sleep that well last night either, and frankly, tea doesn't do a thing for me."

I swallowed. "Sure. Excuse me."

This, I instructed myself as I fled to the kitchen, was not the time to notice that John Quinn was an attractive man. Tess would have been astonished that I even had such passing thoughts. She swore I had checked my libido into a nunnery years ago.

God help us! Tess. Here she was pregnant and trying to decide what to do about it . . . about Michael . . . and now this. Dee dead. Tess gone with Edith Crump to wherever they had taken Dee's body.

Tess had gone to the morgue and so had the unborn child in her womb. Did visiting a morgue have a permanent impact on a baby's psyche? Hester Rose would have said it did. But Tess's baby was still only an amphibian with a tail.

Death touched you only if you knew what it was like to live.

Or if you had stood there watching while someone else struggled to hold on to life. Watched as she dangled over the precipice, eyes wide with terror, fingers clawing.

I had watched my grandmother, an old woman who should have been more at peace with death, struggle to hold on to life. And I had watched Dee this morning, much too young to even think of dying. She had struggled even harder.

Both had been terrified of dying, and I hadn't been able to help either one of them.

I turned on the cold water faucet and filled the tea kettle. Biting my lower lip to keep from giving way to the tears burning behind my eyelids, I reached for one of the two canisters on the counter. One was marked TEA; the other, COFFEE. I measured the rich-smelling black crystals into the coffeemaker.

My stomach growled, reminding me that life went on. I reached for a paper towel and scrubbed at my eyes.

Benjamin was right. Sarah's kitchen had a no-vermin-allowed, shelves-organized look about it. Appliances white with black trim. Walls painted white, with stenciled green vines climbing upward toward the ceiling. The aroma of cinnamon from that morning's breakfast or from Sarah's last baking lingered in the air. On a counter turnstile, corked bottles of spices, each labeled by hand, stood waiting to be added to roast or pudding. Not a kitchen in which unintended ingredients ended up in food being prepared.

The kitchen opened into a small garden room in which a bag of fertilizer and several clay pots of various sizes were stacked against the wall. Cushioned white wicker chairs and a round wicker coffee table provided a cozy nook at the other end of the room. A straw hat hung on the peg beside the outside door.

I came back inside and looked toward the door that must lead to the Crump sisters' suite. Edith had pointed out the foyer door behind the stairs that also led to their quarters.

Dee's room was on the third floor next to Tess's. Dee's room *had been* on the third floor.

Should I go and see if Sarah would like a cup of tea? But Benjamin had said she was sleeping. Best not to disturb her. What could I say to her?

The kettle began to whistle. I reached for it and poured the hot water into the pot.

Was Benjamin back downstairs yet? But it was unlikely that Cordner would invite me to stay for the interview.

While I was waiting for the coffee to perk, I put a sugar bowl and a small container of milk from the refrigerator on the tray I had found, adding cups, saucers, spoons, and the teapot. When the coffee was ready, I poured some into a carafe.

"Do not drop this tray," I instructed my shaky hands.

"Sorry," Dee had said, giggling. "I slipped." I looked away from the spot on the green and white tile floor where she had sprawled among broken pottery as we all stood there staring down at her.

I pushed open the kitchen door with my foot. Had anyone gone to tell Sean what had happened? Had Quinn told Cordner what he thought about Sean? Undoubtedly. But how did he think Sean had managed to tamper with the yummy balls?

I paused in mid-step. Dee had said she always carried a supply with her, in her backpack. Had she gone out last night? Gone out with a container of freshly made yummy balls? Seen Sean? Seen someone else who had sprinkled the yummy balls with peanuts and removed her adrenaline kit?

I had to tell Cordner what Dee had said about always having some of the yummy balls in her backpack. I had forgotten to tell him that part.

If nothing else, we knew Dee's killer had a perverted sense of humor. What a fine touch, a truly delightful touch, to do in your victim with something called a yummy ball.

And poor Sarah was never going to be able to get that out of her mind. The concoction she had created to preserve her niece's health had been used to kill her.

Benjamin's clean white shirt was tucked into his pressed gray trousers. He and Cordner sat on the sofa. Quinn, sitting across from them in one of the Crump sisters' wing chairs got up to take the tray I was carrying. "Where?" he mouthed as Benjamin went on talking.

I pointed to the sideboard. He carried the tray over and set it down. Then instead of returning to his seat, he leaned against the wall like a latecomer to a standing-room-only speaking event. Had he decided he could listen better standing up? He shook his head at my questioning look and nodded toward Benjamin to whom I was already listening with my other ear.

Benjamin was telling Cordner about having met Sarah and Edith's brother George over thirty years ago when he—Benjamin—was just starting up his own company. George had been the proprietor of a print shop, and Benjamin had been one of his customers. Over the years, they had become rather good friends. Then George and his wife, Joan, had been killed in a motor accident. Dee had been five years old when her parents were killed. And George—who was an excellent printer but not much of a business-

man—had left her little other than his debts. Once they were settled, poor Dee had been not only an orphan but almost penniless.
But she'd had her aunts. They had taken her in and used their own
nest egg to buy this house and convert it into a private hotel so that
they could care for their niece.

Not that they had seemed to mind becoming innkeepers. The
sisters were sociable types who enjoyed having guests in their
home, and people enjoyed coming here. Regulars like him came
every season. He had been coming since they opened their hotel.

"Still coming even though my family might prefer fancier accom-
modations," Benjamin said. "But loyalty . . . loyalty is important.
And where else can one feel so at home as here." He laughed. "Of
course, my wife tells me one does not go on holiday to feel at home."

Yes, Pamela would probably be of that opinion. And she was
actually quite right.

I handed Quinn his coffee. He shook his head at my silent offer
of milk and sugar. "Excuse me," I said, turning to Cordner and
Benjamin. "How would you gentlemen like your tea?"

"Two lumps for me," Cordner said, "with milk."

"Milk only for me," Benjamin said. "I am told by my doctor to
watch my weight, but I cheat with milk in my tea."

I poured their tea as Cordner posed his next question. "If you
wouldn't mind, Mr. Stillman, could you go over the past few days,
beginning with your arrival at the hotel?"

"We arrived on Friday. My family and I motored down from
London—Knightsbridge, to be exact."

Cordner made a note on the pad he was holding. "Is Knightsbridge— Thank you, Professor Stuart," he said in an aside, as I
put his cup and saucer on the table in front of him. "Is Knightsbridge your permanent residence, Mr. Stillman?"

"Yes, for the past six years. When my son and his wife returned
from the States, my wife and I decided to take a larger house and
invite them to live with us." Benjamin smiled. "Our new grandson,
you see. We are doting grandparents. We wanted to spend as much
time as possible with little Benjy, and it has worked out well for
his parents—they have live-in child minders."

"A handy arrangement," Cordner said. "Now, about your arrival
here—"

I passed Benjamin his cup. "Thank you, Lizzie. I'm sorry, you
were about to ask something, Inspector?"

"Before you go on," I said, "if there is nothing else anyone needs,
I'll take my own tea to drink upstairs and leave you all to talk—"

Benjamin said, "No, of course, you mustn't leave us. Sit down
here and have your tea. I have nothing to say that you cannot

hear." He grimaced. "And it will do you no good at all to go upstairs and brood on this."

I glanced at Cordner.

Benjamin said, "Unless you prefer to conduct this police matter in private, Inspector."

"Not at all, Mr. Stillman. If you don't mind having Professor Stuart present, I have no objections. In fact, the two of you might be able to jog each other's memories."

Benjamin gestured toward the sideboard. "Pour your tea and come and sit down, my dear."

"Thank you, Benjamin."

Quinn was still leaning against the wall with his cup in his hand. His amused look said he knew exactly how much I had wanted to stay.

"I offered to leave," I said under my breath as I picked up the teapot.

"I heard you offer," he whispered back. Then he pried himself away from the wall and said in a normal tone of voice, "Please have my chair, Professor."

I went back and sat down in the armchair opposite Cordner and Benjamin. Quinn brought over one of the straight-backed, velvet-cushioned chairs from the other side of the room, then he went to pour himself another cup of coffee.

Benjamin, meanwhile, was describing an accident he and his family had encountered on the motorway—a lorry accident that had kept them stuck in traffic for over an hour on their way down from London. "But forgive me, Inspector, you are not interested in traffic holdups. Everything was as usual when we arrived. The sisters were welcoming. Dee was here too. She presented Benjy with a cherry lollipop and a big red balloon."

"Benjamin, did you—"

All three men's heads swung toward me. Quinn paused in the act of raising his coffee cup to his lips.

"I'm sorry," I said. "Forgive me for interrupting."

Cordner smiled. "Not at all, Professor. Did you want to ask something?"

"I'm sorry. I was just wondering what Benjamin thought about Dee's drinking . . . about what happened Sunday evening. But I should let him tell his story—his account of what happened—in chronological order."

"No, I will answer your question now. I was shocked. Disturbed."

"Had you ever seen her like that before?"

"No. Never. She is . . . was . . . always such a responsible young woman. Drinking like that was unlike her."

"Do you think she might have been troubled by something?"

Benjamin hesitated. "I had noticed that she seemed preoccupied. She was quieter than usual. And then that episode on Sunday evening—as I have said, it was out of character, or at least what I know of her character. And I have known her since she was an infant."

"Benjamin—" I glanced at Cordner. "Did you know that Dee was planning to move to London?"

Benjamin frowned. "That I did not know."

"I just wondered if anyone had mentioned it. And that was my last question, Inspector Cordner."

"Your questions are relevant, Professor Stuart."

"But it is your interview."

"So it is. Returning for a moment to something you said earlier, Mr. Stillman. You said Dee seemed preoccupied."

"But that is in hindsight, Inspector. At times she seemed her usual self. Like yesterday afternoon, for example, when she was telling stories to Benjy. My observation about her preoccupation is only in hindsight."

Cordner nodded. "I understand. Could you give me some idea of the schedule you and your family have been following since you arrived in St. Regis?"

"When one is on holiday, one does not follow a schedule, Inspector. Or, at least, this is what I try to explain to my son. He is a great stickler for planning each day, checking in each morning with his secretary, ringing back the people who have left messages. Business, he says, must be taken care of. But I refuse to check with my secretary. I tell my son the company will be there when we return."

Quinn set his cup and saucer on the coffee table. "What kind of company do you have, Mr. Stillman?"

"Pharmaceuticals."

"Pharmaceuticals?" I said. "Tess's ex-husband, Michael, is in pharmaceuticals. I mean his family owns a pharmaceuticals company."

"Yes, I know. Michael and my son became acquainted when Jeremy lived in the States. Our two companies are now involved in a joint venture that we expect to be mutually profitable."

"You're involved in— Benjamin, do you—? Dee told me that Michael stayed here at the hotel last spring. She said it was he who recommended this hotel to Tess."

"And I recommended it to him. He was coming to Cornwall and wanted a comfortable place to stay."

"But you didn't mention—" I balanced my cup and saucer on my knee. "I haven't heard you mention knowing Michael. Does Tess know that you and Jeremy know him . . . that you're friends?"

"We are business associates," Benjamin said. "And, no, I have not had occasion to discuss that connection with Tess. From what Michael had said, Jeremy and I thought that Tess might not wish to discuss her ex-husband."

"I see. More tea, Inspector? Benjamin?"

They both held out their cups.

"Let me get the pot." I refilled their cups and brought Quinn more coffee, as I tried to digest what Benjamin had said.

Cordner was asking Benjamin to continue with his account of how the Stillman family had been spending its time in St. Regis. "Just to give us some sense of the comings and goings of guests in the house."

"We have had breakfast here each morning," Benjamin said. "Saturday and Sunday, we spent much of each day on the beach. My grandson loves building sandcastles and splashing in the water, so we have spent more time than his father would like on the beach. Me, I do not mind. I can help build sandcastles . . . or read my newspapers. But Jeremy is restless with such recreation. The ladies in our family are more indulgent, but they too have their limits. So yesterday and today, we planned outings, sightseeing—"

"You went to The Monkey Sanctuary yesterday," I said, remembering the conversation at breakfast.

"Yes," Benjamin said. "Then we drove to Penzance for lunch and to allow the ladies to shop, then back here."

"Returning at what time?" Cordner asked.

"We arrived back here at around four. To please Benjy, we walked down to the beach. And after that into town for dinner."

"And where was it that your family went this morning?"

"We had planned a trip to Tintagel Castle." Benjamin smiled at me. "Your friend Tess was telling Benjy about your own trip there. He wanted to go again—we went last year, you see." Benjamin pushed at his glasses. "But I am not sure where they went this morning. We were only concerned about getting Benjy away from here for a while. As I said, he was distressed."

"Yes," Cordner said. "Thank you, Mr. Stillman."

"I hope what I have told you is sufficient."

"Sufficient?" The question came from Quinn, not Cordner.

"To assure the Inspector that no one in my family has done anything that he or she should not have. None of us would have reason to do Deirdre harm."

"Deirdre?" I repeated.

"Her given name," Benjamin said. "A few years ago, she decided she preferred Dee. A young woman's growing pains."

"Do you know her boyfriend?" Quinn asked.

"Not a particularly prepossessing young man," Benjamin said. "Her aunts hoped she might do better."

"What did they object to about him?" Cordner asked.

"His general lack of prospects, Inspector. He dropped out of school and works part-time in a motorcycle shop."

Cordner nodded. "And now, I'm afraid I really do need to speak to Miss Crump. Perhaps you could try to wake her, Professor Stuart."

"Yes, of course." After all, I was the logical person. I was the only woman present. And, at any rate, I should speak to Sarah in private—to express my sympathy if nothing else.

Chapter Seven

I PUSHED OPEN THE KITCHEN DOOR and stood blinking as my eyes adjusted to the shadows in the back wing of the house. I found the light switch and flicked it. In the narrow hallway, there were three doors. The sisters would each have a bedroom. And a bathroom in between? Which room belonged to Sarah? I knocked on the first door. There was no answer. Feeling uncomfortable, but under orders from Cordner, I looked inside.

Against the far wall was a bed covered in a lightweight plain blue comforter. Matching blue curtains at the window. A blue throw rug on the hardwood floor beside the bed. A white dressing table with a mirror—a match for the one upstairs in my room. Fluffy pink bedroom slippers waiting beside an overstuffed armchair. On the side table, a pair of reading glasses and two books, one a hardcover, the other a glossy paperback. This must be Edith's room.

I started to close the door, then, with a glance behind me, I gave in to temptation. The books on the table were what I was interested in. I could never resist peeping to see what someone was reading. You could learn all kinds of things about someone from his or her choice of reading material. If nothing else, you might get a hint of a stranger's occupation or hobby. Or of what kind of mood a friend was in.

What I read myself was often a matter of mood. On some days I picked up a book for entertainment. If it was fluff I might even read it while watching television. On other days, I reached for a book that would sharpen my intellect and hone my soul. Literature—depending on what my definition of literature was on that particular day.

What Edith was reading was a memoir by a journalist who had come home to Cornwall after spending much of his adult life in Canada. His style was engaging and irreverent.

The other book, the paperback, was a historical romance by a best-selling author who specialized in Regency novels featuring spunky heroines and world-weary heroes. I had read it. It was one of the author's better efforts.

Too bad Edith and I wouldn't have a chance to sit down over a cup of tea and compare notes on our tastes in light reading material. I had the feeling they might be quite similar.

I tiptoed out of her room and closed the door. I had been sent to find Sarah.

Sarah was still asleep, the covers tucked up to her chin. With her dark curls ruffled and her cheeks tear-stained, she looked like a child grown old. I touched her shoulder and shook her. "Sarah? Sarah, it's Lizzie. Sarah, wake up—"

Her eyes opened—blue and damp. She shivered. "Hello," she said in a hoarse voice.

"I'm sorry to wake you, Sarah, but they need to talk to you— the police—"

"About Dee?"

"Yes."

The tears in her eyes overflowed. I looked away to give her time to compose herself.

Sarah's room was similar to Edith's, but her color scheme was peach. Her dressing table had been painted peach to match the curtains and the nubby peach and brown silk bedspread. Sarah had opted for a chaise lounge, covered in peach silk. At the window, the pale peach curtains collected the sunlight outside. On the dressing table, a peach and brown Chinese vase held a spray of dried flowers.

Sarah pushed back the covers and sat up in her bed. Her night-gown matched the room. It was of translucent peach silk, trimmed with ecru lace at wrists and neckline, and the neckline was not at all spinsterish.

"You were with Dee," she said as she rubbed at her eyes with a tissue. Her voice was the gentle, slightly hesitant voice of the past two days, the Sarah who wore flowered cotton dresses and limped as she carried her cane.

We all had two sides of ourselves, didn't we? There was the side we showed the world that might laugh and jeer. And that other private self we kept for ourselves and the few we allowed to intrude into our intimate space.

"Yes," I said when I realized she was waiting for me to say some-thing. "Yes, I was with Dee. I am so sorry." I touched her hand. Mine was toffee brown with nails that I kept short so that I could type on my computer and so that I did not feel obliged to wear pol-ish that I always managed to chip two minutes after I'd put it on. Sarah's hand was smaller, beige from exposure to the Cornish sun. She had beautiful, oval-shaped nails, and she was wearing peach nail polish.

Why hadn't I noticed that before? Probably because I had been distracted by the food she was carrying or by her limp.

"It had happened once before," Sarah said. "Dee went into shock in a restaurant during dinner. It was quite dreadful. But she had her adrenaline kit, and Edith and I knew what to do."

"We couldn't find it," I said. "It wasn't in her backpack."

"Where could it have been? She would never have been without it, not after that last time. It frightened her so. She said she thought she was going to die."

And this time she had. But this time perhaps by someone's intent.

"The peanuts," Sarah said. "Do you know how—? What was she eating?"

I hesitated, but her damp blue eyes demanded an answer.

"She was having her breakfast," I said.

"What was she eating?" Sarah asked again, frowning as she heard my reluctance to speak.

"She . . . the police are doing lab tests. But she . . . she had just eaten a yummy ball—"

"One of my yummy balls?"

"Yes."

Sarah wrapped her arms around herself. "I couldn't have . . . I'm always so careful. I don't know how I could have—" Her voice broke.

Oh, lord. Did Cordner want me to tell her what they suspected? "Maybe something was accidentally contaminated. The flour you used. Or the spices or the dates."

"No. I used the same ingredients—from new packages—last week when I did my baking."

"Sarah, I'm sure it wasn't your fault."

"Are you sure of that, Lizzie? I'm not." In a flurry of motion, she swung her bare legs over the bed and pushed her feet into her slippers. It was then that I saw the silver picture frame facedown on the floor beside the bed. I scooped it up before Sarah could step on it. She was wobbling slightly on her feet. With my other hand, I reached out to steady her.

"My cane," she said, pointing to where it leaned against the night table.

I brought it back to her.

"Thank you. I'm a cripple. I mustn't forget that."

I wasn't sure what to say. "You seem to get around quite well."

"Do I? Practice makes—" She broke off, staring at the picture frame in my hand. She held out her hand, and I gave it to her. As I did, I stole a glance at the photograph. It was of a young man with wavy dark hair and regular features, laughing, confident. An old photograph, taken when the cut of his suit had been the style for laughing, confident young men.

"It was such a stupid accident," Sarah said. "My own fault. I'd had a row with the man I was seeing. He'd told me he couldn't marry me, and I went dashing off and fell down a flight of stairs. I was young and silly then. I thought all I had to do was want a thing."

"Is he—" I indicated the silver frame in her hand. "Is that the man?"

Sarah glanced down at the photo. "You wonder why I would keep it? I keep it to remind myself of the high costs of silliness." Leaning forward, with a hand on the nightstand for support, she opened the single drawer and dropped the picture frame inside.

As she straightened, she smiled, a sad, distant smile. "He wouldn't have me. And after my fall, no other man would either. Or so I thought, and I made it true. I drew into my shell and shut out any other man who tried to show an interest. And now I realize quite clearly that he was a spoiled boy—charming and handsome—but the center of his own selfish little universe. I was one of his amusements for a while until I made the mistake of falling in love with him." Her eyes focused on me. "You look surprised, Lizzie? Because you had me pegged as a dried-up old prune? Or is it because you've always been too wise to fall in love with the wrong man?"

"No . . . I mean, I've never fallen in love at all."

"Never?" Sarah said. "Then your life has been much too sheltered. Find a man and lose your heart. Even if it doesn't work out, better that than going to your grave without knowing passion. Or so they say." Sarah shook her head. "She was so young. We had such hopes for her."

"I was wondering if . . . Dee's boyfriend . . . Sean—"

"Sean!" She said it almost the way my grandmother had said "that man." Almost, but without the same level of loathing. More with dismissal, annoyance.

"I think he was in love with her," I said, wondering if that was true. He had struck her. Hard to equate that with love. But I had seen the misery in his eyes.

"Oh, yes, he loved her," Sarah said. "But he was no more than a passing fancy for her, a stop on her way to growing up. And he had no idea at all how to deal with her." Sarah limped over to the wardrobe and opened its doors. When she turned, she was holding an unadorned blue cotton dress.

"Sarah, the yummy balls . . . Dee said they were freshly made. When did you make them?"

"Yesterday afternoon when I was doing my baking." Sarah

paused with the dress dangling from her hand. "Someone rang up. I was called out."

"Called out? You went out?"

"Yes. I don't know who he was. A man. He said he was ringing for Mrs. Evanston, one of our neighbors the next street over." The lines on Sarah's face had deepened. "He said that she was ill and that she had asked him to ring up and ask me to come right over."

"And you went?"

"Yes, but when I got there no one was home. I thought perhaps the man who rang had taken her to hospital. I told Edith when she came in, and she walked over later. The woman two doors down told her that Mrs. Evanston's daughter had taken her off to London for a stay."

"Did you think it was strange—the call?"

"Of course I thought it was strange. But we assumed it had been someone's practical joke. Send the cripple hurrying about."

Sarah and I stared at each other. Neither of us said what we were both thinking—that the call had been a ruse to get her out of the house.

"Did you . . . are you sure you didn't recognize the man's voice?"

Sarah hesitated, then she said, "It was no one I knew. He had a hoarse, rough voice with an odd accent."

"If someone were disguising his voice—"

"Then I was fooled," Sarah said. "They think someone killed her, don't they? That's what you're telling me."

"They—the police—are concerned because she didn't have her adrenaline kit . . . because the yummy balls shouldn't have had peanuts—"

Sarah nodded her head. She folded the dress from the wardrobe over her arm and limped toward the dresser. I watched as she opened one drawer, then another, finally pulling out a slip and a pair of white cotton panties.

"Sarah, was there anyone else here in the house when you left?"

"Everyone had gone out. I didn't hear anyone come back in."

"Do you usually bake on Monday?"

"Yes, I'm very predictable. Every Monday after our readers' group at the library, I come home to bake."

"So you always bake on the same day of the week at approximately the same time."

"'I know it's Monday afternoon because Sarah's baking,' Edith is fond of saying. Mondays at around three or thereabouts. That's when I do much of my baking for the week."

"Benjamin said he and his family got back from their day trip at around four."

"It was about that. I was just back from walking over to Mrs. Evanston's. I was in the kitchen washing my hands and about to get on with my baking."

I hesitated, then asked what I was thinking. "Are you sure they were just returning?"

"Yes, quite sure. Little Benjy was laughing with his grandfather. They both came out to the kitchen." Sarah swallowed visibly. "I gave Benjy a taste of the yummy balls I was blending."

"But it wouldn't have harmed him."

"No, only Dee."

Sarah limped over to the bed. She dropped the dress and the underwear down among the rumpled covers.

"The other Stillmans?" I asked. "Where were they?"

"They had gone upstairs." Sarah shook her head. "There is no reason why anyone in Benjamin Stillman's family would have wanted to harm my niece."

We both started at the rap on the door.

"Sarah?" It was Benjamin. "Lizzie? Is everything all right?"

"Yes," Sarah called back.

"The inspector asked me to remind you that he is waiting."

"Coming," Sarah said.

She pulled her peach silk gown over her head and dropped it on the bed. "Lizzie, please tell the inspector I will be right along."

"Yes," I said, as I spun toward the door. If she wasn't embarrassed, I was. Modesty kept me from stripping to my birthday suit in front of strangers.

But if I had a figure like Sarah's—the taut waist and full, high breasts more common for a woman in her twenties or thirties than in her late fifties—perhaps I wouldn't be modest either. No, I could suddenly find myself with a body like a runway model, and I still wouldn't be able to casually strip naked in front of someone I didn't know.

Of course, her mind was on more important things. But even so, Sarah was interesting. Not what I had thought.

And that made two for two. Neither Benjamin Stillman nor Sarah Crump was fitting neatly into the pigeonholes to which I had assigned them.

I did not sit in as DI Cordner interviewed Sarah. I went back to the lounge to tell him and Quinn—Benjamin was in the kitchen washing the cups and saucers—that Sarah would be right along. Then I excused myself and went upstairs to take the hot shower that Quinn had suggested for my nerves and that I was much in need of for other reasons. I felt sweaty and grimy, and I had the feeling I was beginning to smell.

I took my shower, adjusting my technique to the handheld European showerhead, then I scurried back to my room in my robe. I reached for shorts and then remembered this was a house in mourning. Slacks, then. I had packed only two pair. I had planned to spend most of my time in shorts or a swimsuit. A good thing I had also packed a dress and a skirt for London. Slacks would not do if we needed to go to church for a memorial service. I pulled on the navy T-shirt that matched the slacks and glanced at the clock radio on the bedside table. Only a little before eleven.

I rubbed a dab of texturizer-shine enhancer into my damp hair, then I ruffled it with my fingers the way Gino the stylist—whom I had stumbled upon in a mall beauty salon and who actually knew how to cut African-American hair—had shown me. If nothing else was going right, at least my haircut was standing up to the stress. Clean, dressed, and hair ruffled. Now what should I do?

I went over to look out through the balcony doors. Cordner's car was still parked on the street. Should I go back downstairs? The question was answered for me as I saw Tess drive up in her rented black coupe. She parked, and she and Edith got out of the car.

I took a deep breath and braced myself to face Edith. Why did I feel so guilty? I had done nothing to harm Dee. I had done everything I could to save her. So why did I feel so guilty? Because I had said to Dee, "These are good," and thus encouraged her to eat one of the yummy balls?

But she would have eaten one whether I had been there or not. If I hadn't been there, she would have died alone.

She *had* died alone. I had been running for help.

Edith gave me an unsteady smile as I came down the stairs. Like her sister's, her eyes were damp with tears. "I'm so sorry, my dear," she said to me.

I stared at her.

"It must have been so dreadful for you," she explained. "To see that . . . the way my niece died." Her voice broke and she pressed the back of her hand to her mouth.

"Edith, I don't know how to tell you how sorry I am."

Her hand—slightly tanned like her sister's but with blunt, unvarnished nails—came up to grip the hand I was holding out to her, then she nodded once and took a shuddering breath. "There must be an autopsy, they say. A sudden death—"

"The police are here now, Edith, in the lounge. They're talking to your sister."

"Sarah?" Edith whirled toward the closed door. "She's not fit to answer their questions."

"I spoke to her. She seems to be in control."

Edith drew herself up to her full height of five-eight or -nine. "Nevertheless, they have no right to harass her now." She opened the lounge door. The heads of the people in the room all turned. "Sarah, you needn't speak to these men now."

"It's best to get it done and over with," Sarah said.

Cordner and Quinn had gotten to their feet. Cordner came forward and introduced himself, and then John Quinn. Cordner said, "We do hate to trouble you at a time like this—"

"They think it's murder, Edith," Sarah said.

Edith's mouth opened, but no sound came out. She pressed her hand to her mouth. "Murder?"

"We're not prepared to say that yet," Cordner said. "However, the circumstances are somewhat suspect. The missing adrenaline kit—"

Sarah said to her sister, "If someone put the peanuts in the yummy balls I was making, then found an opportunity to take the adrenaline kit from Dee's backpack—"

Edith stared at Sarah. "Why? Why would someone—?"

"I don't know why," Sarah said. "But someone must have. How else could this have happened?"

"You don't think that—" I blundered on. "Could she possibly have misplaced her adrenaline kit? She was drinking on Sunday night—"

"No," Edith said. "Sarah's right. Even if Dee had been drinking, she would never have been so careless. She was terrified of those attacks."

Sarah nodded. "So you see, it must have been deliberate."

Edith gave her sister another anxious look. "Sarah—"

"We need to tell the police whatever we know, to answer their questions." Sarah took a sip from the cup she was holding. "They were asking me where you were yesterday afternoon. A routine question, the Inspector says."

"I'm sure you understand," Cordner said to Edith. "We need to develop a timetable of people's whereabouts."

"I was at the ladies' auxiliary. I volunteer to help with the charity sales during summer. I was there from noon until almost six. I stayed to have a late tea with two of the other workers."

"Thank you, Miss Crump," Cordner said.

Tess was there in the hallway behind us. She had followed Edith in, but I had been too involved in my conversation with Edith to acknowledge her presence. Now I edged back out into the hall. "The police are doing interviews," I said. "I think they'll want to talk to you."

"I need to go upstairs first."

"I'll come with you."

"Ms. Alvarez?" John Quinn called as we started up the stairs.

"Yes?" Tess said.

"Inspector Cordner asked me to tell you that he would like a word with you."

"Yes, I've heard, but first I need to use the toilet."

"You too, Professor Stuart?"

"Women always go in pairs. Don't you know that, Detective Quinn?"

"What I don't know about women would fill several books, Professor Stuart. Don't be too long." His gray glance held mine. "And try to remember that you're on your honor."

"On your honor?" Tess said as we continued up the stairs. "What does that mean?"

"Who knows? Military types talk like that."

"Military types? You said 'detective.' And he has an American accent."

She was requesting information. I didn't think being on my honor forbade providing her with some basic details. In fact, Cordner had said nothing at all about what I was or was not to discuss with other people. "He's the man I told you about . . . the one who showed up when Dee was arguing with her boyfriend. It turns out he's a cop from Philadelphia here visiting his ex-partner." I pushed my fingers through my hair. It was still damp.

We were on the second floor landing. The bathrooms were down the hall. Tess glanced toward them and then asked, "How did he get involved in this? Is he just observing or something?"

"Yes . . . well, no . . . I mean, he is actually involved. He was there this morning when Dee died. I saw him running on the beach before I started along the cliff walk and met Dee. Then when she collapsed, I ran back for help, and he was sitting on the terrace of that restaurant down by the beach. Anyway, he ran back to her to see if he could help while I called the paramedics."

"Obviously he couldn't help her."

"No one could have unless he or she happened to be carrying an adrenaline kit. Dee didn't have hers." I caught Tess's arm and turned her toward my room. "Come inside. I need to ask you something."

"Wait a minute, I need to pee—"

"This is important, Tess. We only have a few minutes." I unlocked my door and she followed me inside. "Hurry up. I only have a few minutes too." She leaned back against the sink. I sank down on my bed. Midday sunlight filled the room.

"What's so important?" Tess asked.

"Michael," I said. "Did you know that he and Jeremy and Benjamin Stillman are business associates?"

"Yes, he mentioned that last night."

"Last night? Don't you think it's odd that he didn't mention it before?"

"Why should he? When he recommended this hotel, he told me an acquaintance had recommended it to him and that he—Michael, I mean—had stayed here. There was no reason for him to mention Benjamin Stillman by name when I had never met him. The name would have meant nothing to me."

I thought about that for a moment. She was right. There had been no reason for Michael to mention Benjamin by name until after she had met him. "What about Jeremy? Did you ever meet him when he lived in the States?"

Tess shook her head. "Michael met him after our divorce . . . or at least after we were separated."

"Did Michael know that the Stillmans were staying here?"

Tess raised her chin. She was not pleased. "Michael knew that they always come here in August, yes. Are you trying to make some particular point?"

"No, just curious. I was surprised when Benjamin mentioned that he and Jeremy knew Michael, and I wondered if you knew."

"So we've covered that. Now—if there are no other urgent matters we need to discuss—I'm going to go to the bathroom."

I waved my hand. "Go."

"Thanks." She went out, closing the door behind her.

I'd put my foot in that one. I had the distinct impression that Tess was beginning to think of Michael as more than the father of her child, to feel protective toward him.

Because she was falling in love with him again? But how could you fall back in love with a man who had betrayed you? Or maybe she had never stopped loving him in the first place.

I went over to the sink and squeezed mint-flavored toothpaste on my brush. I had a sour taste in my mouth, probably bubbled up from my churning stomach.

John Quinn had said there were all kinds of things he didn't know about women. Somehow I doubted that. But it was true that there were things that I didn't understand about men and women and relationships. Although I tended to believe that I could learn almost anything I needed or wanted to know from books, sometimes that wasn't true. Relationships were a case in point. They had to be experienced. So maybe I should just stay out of this.

Except Tess was my friend, and I didn't trust Michael any farther than I could throw him.

As Benjamin had said they would, his family came back later that afternoon. I was grateful for their return. When they came in, I was having a nightmare. I was running through a dark forest, and branches were reaching out to grab me. Lightning flashed, and a pursuer's panting breaths were in my ears. I struggled out of the sheet that had wrapped itself around me and realized the panting breaths were my own.

Outside on the landing, Benjy was crying—screaming—at the top of his lungs. Jeremy was trying to make himself heard above his son's distress. "We'll meet you and Father downstairs in ten minutes."

I glanced at the clock radio on my nightstand. Almost five o'clock. I felt with my feet for my slippers, rubbing at my eyes, as I tried to orient myself. I was at the sink about to turn on the water when I realized Pamela and Benjamin were still out in the hallway. Without even thinking about it, I tiptoed over to my bedroom door.

Benjamin was protesting, "But I told the inspector I would call him when you returned."

"Then call. If he wants to talk to me, tell him to come down to the beach."

"Pamela, Dee is dead. We must show proper respect."

"Respect? My first concern, Benjamin, is for this family. Your grandson has spent the entire day driving us all to Bedlam with sulks, sobs, and screaming fits. We've tried everything else . . . now we are going to take him down to the beach and hope that splashing in the water will have an effect."

"Yes, my dear. Yes, you're right. Once he is out in the sunshine on the beach, Rosalind will be able to coax him out of—"

"Rosalind! Rosalind is useless."

"But she does try, my dear. You and Jeremy don't give her a chance to—" Their door closed. I drew my ear away from my own door.

I should have been ashamed of myself for listening. But they had conducted their conversation in a common hallway where, legally speaking, they had no right to expect privacy. And at the moment I felt at a decided disadvantage in this house and in need of all of the information I could get.

I splashed water on my face, then I paced back and forth in the narrow space between bedroom door and balcony doors. I was trying to wake up and think. On my sixth or seventh turn, I pulled open the balcony doors and stepped outside in my skimpy knee-length robe. I was not going to dress in order to get a breath of fresh air.

This had been one of the longest days of my life, but apparently the rest of the world was going on as usual. I could hear laughter and music from the beach, where seagulls soared in the sky out over the ocean. In the distance, a ship, perhaps a freighter, was visible. Across the street, someone had opened the windows of the house, and white curtains fluttered in the breeze. It was all very cheerful. Very sane. Glancing down to make sure I was not stepping in gull droppings, I edged closer to the railing. A blossom fell from the bedraggled potted geranium.

I peered upward toward Tess's room, immediately above mine. I couldn't see anything except that her window (she didn't have a balcony) was open. There were no sounds from her room. Maybe she was sleeping too. Or maybe she had gone out. She had knocked on my door after her interview with Cordner to say that she would be in her room. Nothing else. No invitation to come upstairs and dissect what had happened. But this was not the time for Tess and me to be engaged in our own cold war.

I turned back to close the balcony doors I had left open. Edith had warned me to keep them closed when I was out of the room. Not because of the risk of burglary, but because the gulls took open doors and windows as an invitation to come in. "And they make such a foul mess," Edith had said. The last thing she needed right now was a rug and bedding to clean.

But that did raise the rather interesting question of why she and Sarah had named their hotel after a bird Edith despised. A minor point, but the fact that it was only just occurring to me showed how oblivious I sometimes was to the obvious.

I pulled back on my slacks and top and opened my room door. The Stillmans had not left for the beach yet. When I stepped out into the hallway, I could hear Benjy crying upstairs.

Downstairs the telephone was ringing. I heard a man—was it Jeremy?—pick it up.

Benjamin Stillman opened the door of his room. "Aah, Lizzie. Are you feeling better?"

"Yes, thank you. I'm on my way up to see Tess."

"We are going to take Benjy down to the beach. I'm afraid he is still having rather a difficult time."

"I'm sorry. If there's anything I can do to help—"

"Thank you, but I think—"

I was not destined to hear what he thought. Jeremy was coming up the stairs. "The call's for you, Lizzie."

"For me? Who—? Did the caller say who it is?"

"No name. He said to tell you that he's the man you met when you were walking into town on Sunday evening."

Benjamin smiled with fatherly benevolence. "Aah, you have a suitor. Go and take your call, my dear."

"Excuse me."

John Quinn? Why hadn't he just given his name? The telephone was on the table outside the lounge door. "Hello?"

"Professor Stuart, this is John Quinn."

"As in the man I met on Sunday evening?"

"The same. I wasn't sure you'd want the other guests to think too much about any connection you might have to police officers, foreign or domestic. Was that Stillman, the younger, who answered?"

"Yes."

"The reason I called—I wanted to give you the telephone number where you can reach me if anything should come up."

"Such as?"

"Under the circumstances, any number of things. I thought you might feel better if you had someone other than the local police that you could contact. Not that Inspector Cordner's not a damn good cop. But we are US citizens in a foreign country—"

"On foreign turf?"

"And that can get dicey sometimes. So if anything should come up that you'd care to run past me—"

Somehow offering a sympathetic ear seemed a bit out of character for a man like John Quinn. Had Cordner suggested he cozy up to me in hopes that I would tell another American more about what I thought or suspected than I would a British police inspector?

Not that I had anything else. I had already told Cordner what I'd forgotten to mention—that Dee had said she always kept yummy balls in her backpack, that if she had gone out last night, she might well have had some of the new batch with her. I had nothing else, just vague suspicions. Did I dare share those with John Quinn? But I had no one else to talk to, and I did need someone who could be objective.

Quinn was saying, "The telephone number here is—"

I glanced toward the stairs and I could hear the murmur of voices. Benjamin and Jeremy were still out in the hallway. "Yes, I'd love to meet you for a drink," I said. "Where and what time?"

There was a distinct pause on the other end of the line. Then Quinn said, "I gather someone's listening."

"Possibly."

"There's a pub down by the harbor, near the fire station, called O'Hara's. I'll meet you there in an hour."

"Great. See you then." I hung up and turned toward the stairs. First, I would go up and speak to Tess.

My foot was on the bottom step when the front door opened. Hildegard Martin bustled in. "I've had a lovely day," she informed me. "I do hope you can say the same." I watched her set her backpack on the floor and shrug out of her hiker's vest.

"You haven't heard," I said.

"Heard what?" She dropped her battered hat on top of the backpack.

"About Dee. She—" I swallowed and tried again. "She died this morning."

"Good lord! What happened?"

"She went into shock after eating something with peanuts."

"But how could that have happened? She was always so careful."

"Somehow the peanuts . . . they seem to have been in or on the yummy balls that her Aunt Sarah made. But it isn't clear how they got there."

Hildegard said nothing for a long moment. "And what about the adrenaline kit she always carried?"

"Somehow it had been mislaid. It wasn't in her backpack."

"Where it always was. When did this happen?"

"Early this morning on the cliff walk. I was there when— I had gone for a walk too, and I ran into Dee. She invited me to join her for breakfast."

"So you ate what she ate?"

"Yes. But she said—Dee said—it was peanuts."

Hildegard nodded. "And without her adrenaline kit—"

"Yes. I ran for help, but she was dead before the paramedics could get to her."

Hildegard bent down and gathered up her backpack, vest, and the hat she had discarded. "I assume the police are conducting an inquiry."

"Yes. They've been here at the hotel. I think they want to talk to all the guests."

"Not that I can tell them anything useful." Hildegard tugged at her braid with her free hand. "And God help us if they have no more luck with this than they've been having with the one that's been all over the tabloids."

"What?" It was then that I realized I hadn't read a newspaper since Friday afternoon in the airport. "I'm sorry, Hildegard, I don't know what you're talking about. I'm behind in my newspaper reading."

"Some schoolboys found a young woman's body in a Sussex field. Nude. Strangled. Knife slashes on her breasts and legs. It happened last week, and the constabulary still don't have a suspect." Hildegard jerked at her braid again. "This one, we must hope, will be easier for them to unravel."

"Yes, let's hope so."

"I'll change and then go have a word with Edith and Sarah. See if I can be of any use."

I followed her up the stairs. She had dried mud on the heel of one of her hiking boots, and flecks of it fell in her wake.

"We'll carry on," Hildegard said as she bumped off down the hall toward her room with her backpack and vest.

I carried on up to the third floor. There was no sign of either Jeremy or his father. I knocked on Tess's door. Knocked again. "Who is it?" She sounded half-asleep.

"Lizzie."

"Hold on." Tess came to the door wrapped in her robe with her hair tousled and her eyes drowsy.

"Sorry," I said. "I woke up from my nap and thought you might have too."

"It's being pregnant," she said. "I'm sleeping more."

"Well, I'll let you get back to it. I just came up to tell you that I'm going to walk into town. Want anything?"

Tess stifled a yawn with the back of her hand. "No. Wait . . . a chocolate bar."

I smiled. "Which has nothing at all to do with your being pregnant."

Tess smiled back. "As one chocoholic to another."

"Tess . . . I'm sorry about earlier."

"Me too."

"Go back to sleep. I'll see you later."

She yawned again. "Okay." She started to close the door then pulled it open again. "Lizzie, don't stay out too late."

"I won't. I know you'll be waiting for your chocolate bar."

"You might bring me some real food too. A sandwich. Chicken or tuna."

"Chocolate bar and chicken or tuna sandwich. Got your order."

"See you later." She closed her door, and I turned away.

Not exactly our usual easy exchange, but a decided improvement over silence.

Chapter Eight

ONE OF THE THINGS THAT I HAD NOTICED about St. Regis was that not only were there fewer Americans than one might expect, there were almost no black people. So far in the three days I had been there, I had spotted one school girl among a group of horseplaying friends. And now, ahead of me in the throng meandering along the street by the harbor, was an older couple, arm-in-arm, laughing, as they spoke to each other in the musical accents of the West Indies. Not many black people about at all.

Not that I was unaccustomed to that. I had experienced it often enough in professional settings. But as I walked among them, I wondered if these holiday-makers with their pale (or tanned or dangerously reddened) skins wondered why I had come to Cornwall. A black American female, apparently alone. Or maybe they didn't bother to even give me a thought. Maybe I was invisible.

As Quinn had said, O'Hara's was a few doors up from the local firehouse, sandwiched between a sports equipment shop and a camera store. Like other drinking and dining establishments along the waterfront, the pub provided a few tables outside for customers who preferred the sea air.

But John Quinn was not outside. I stepped inside and stood there blinking as my eyes adapted to the change in light.

"Would you be Professor Stuart?" The question had come from a man who looked like a cross between a professional wrestler and a cherub. His head was bald, his full cheeks were pink. He wore a T-shirt with a Scottish terrier on the front, and he had a chest and biceps that suggested he spent a fair amount of time weight training. "Are you Professor Stuart?" he asked again. He was American, with an accent that sounded like the Bronx or maybe Chicago.

"I'm sorry . . . yes, I am. Who are you?"

He set his beer mug down on the windowsill and held out his hand. "Ed Janowitz."

I shook his hand, and then the name registered. "You're Detective Quinn's ex-partner."

"That's me."

I stepped out of the doorway to let two men in. "Is Detective Quinn here?"

"He had to go to the gents. He told me to keep an eye out for you." Janowitz retrieved his mug and gestured toward the back of the pub. "Come on. We've got a table back there."

"Thank you."

He led me back to a small table in a corner with an OCCUPIED sign on it. He folded the sign and stuck it in the pocket of the jacket that was over one of the three chairs. We sat down and I glanced around the noisy pub. Ed Janowitz looked at me.

"Is something wrong, Mr. Janowitz?"

He took a pull from his mug. "Why do you ask?"

"You were staring at me."

Janowitz's stare swept from my boyish haircut to what he could see of me above the table. "Yeah, I guess I was staring. The truth is I was trying to get a read on you."

"A read? Why?"

"A real good reason, Professor. Johnny's supposed to be on vacation . . . supposed to be getting some R and R, some downtime. Instead he's gone and landed himself in the middle of what looks like a murder investigation . . . not that that's altogether your fault. Cordner wants him in on this, and Johnny's just naturally drawn to dead bodies—"

"Is he? That's interesting."

He gave me a hard look, not pleased by my feeble attempt at levity. "Being a homicide cop comes natural to him. When he sees a dead body, he can't rest until he knows how it got that way." Ed Janowitz leaned forward, resting his bulging arms on the table. "But what he don't need right now, Professor Stuart, is a damn damsel in distress."

"I am not 'a damn damsel in distress,' Mr. Janowitz. In fact, I'm damn well able to take care of myself. I've been doing it for a long time now."

We locked eyes until he grinned. A grin that was somewhere between cherubic and I'm-about-to-smash-your-face-in. "Hell, maybe you are at that." He took another pull from his mug and wiped his mouth with his hand. "Anyway, I've gotta hope I'm reading you right."

"Reading me right about what?"

Janowitz sat back in his chair. "I gotta hope that I'm right and you aren't the type who would use what I'm going to say to play some damn female game."

"I don't play games. What are you going to say?"

"What I'm going to say is that Johnny is kind of bruised right now. He's had a bad year—one helluva of a bad year—getting zapped right, left, and sideways. So don't do anything to add to his grief. You understand me?"

Janowitz pushed back his chair and stood up. "About time you were getting back, Johnny. I kept the Professor company, now I'm going to get out of here and go have my dinner. I'll tell Fiona to put yours in the oven."

Quinn clapped his former partner on the shoulder. Although more slender in build, he towered over Janowitz by several inches. "Thanks, Ed. But I'll probably have something here."

"You're eating here when you could have Fiona's lamb stew?"

"Many more of Fiona's meals, and I'll have to buy new clothes."

Janowitz looked down at me. "What he means is that my wife is a world-class cook."

"One of the best," Quinn said. "And determined to fatten me up."

Janowitz nodded at me. "A pleasure to meet you, Professor Stuart."

Really? I nodded back. "And you, Mr. Janowitz."

His gaze held mine, he hesitated, then shrugged. "You might as well call me Ed."

I put pure saccharine in the smile I gave him. "Thank you, Ed. Please call me Lizzie."

Janowitz turned back to Quinn, who was watching our byplay. "You know Fiona. She's going to save you some stew regardless. You can have it for breakfast tomorrow."

"Yeah, give her a hug for me."

"Will do. See you at the house." Janowitz disappeared into the pub crowd. Quinn sat down in the third chair at the table.

And I sneezed. "Excuse me," I said. And sneezed again.

"Are you allergic to me?" he asked.

I looked at him over the hand I had pressed to my mouth. It was true that the only times that I'd sneezed during the past few days were when I was around him. "Maybe it's your aftershave."

"I'm not wearing any."

"Oh. But that wouldn't make sense anyway because I would go on sneezing." I thought about it. "It's probably just that you've happened to be there when I found myself in stressful situations."

"You sneeze when you find yourself in stressful situations?"

"When I was a child, I used to itch all over. So sneezing is a definite improvement. Although I never have—sneezed before, I mean. So it's probably only a coincidence, and I'm just catching a cold. Or maybe there's something in the air here in St. Regis. At least, we know it isn't bubonic plague."

"Bubonic plague?"

I sighed. I was babbling. "A documentary I saw. It was about the Middle Ages and the Black Death. Remember the children's nursery rhyme 'Ring Around the Rosie'?"

"What about it?"

"'Atchoo, atchoo, all fall down.' As did the plague victims. Except one of the experts in the documentary did point out that there are other versions of that particular nursery rhyme. And if it is about the plague, it seems odd that it would have gone underground and then reappeared in the eighteenth or nineteenth century as—" I broke off. "Sorry."

"Not at all. If I should ever find myself on 'Jeopardy.'"

"Well, you did ask, and it's worse when I don't explain." In fact, I had concluded long ago that it was better to explain to people what you had been thinking when you'd made an observation that seemed completely irrelevant to anything that was being discussed, rather than leave them to assume you had bats in your belfry. Did they have bats here in St. Regis? Probably. They had caves.

Quinn looked tired. He had looked tired the first time I saw him. *Bruised*, Janowitz had said. *One helluva a bad year.* What exactly did that mean?

"What did you think of Ed?"

The question caught me unprepared. "Ed—he seems very nice."

"Nice isn't how people usually describe Ed."

"Well, Ed is rather hard to describe."

"True, but he's a good friend. My former partner." The gray eyes probed mine. "And sometimes he thinks he's my mother."

"A mother with biceps like that?"

"What were the two of you talking about?"

"Nothing much. Chitchat."

"Ed doesn't make chitchat. What were you talking about?"

"If you're so concerned about what we might have talked about, why did you leave us alone in the first place?"

That brought a scowl. "I had to go to the john."

"Well, John, when you go to the john—"

"Did Ed happen to mention why I'm here?"

"Oh, that. He said you were here on vacation. To get some rest. Some 'downtime.'"

"That's all he said?"

"What else do you think Ed might have said?"

Irritation flashed in the gray eyes. But he looked wary too. "What would you like to drink, Professor?"

"What Janowitz said was . . . he said you'd had a bad year. That you're here to get some rest."

Quinn glanced away. "Like I said, sometimes Janowitz thinks he's my mother."

"But you still came here on your vacation?"

"Yeah, well—my mother always thinks she's my mother. Ed's a better choice."

"Good food and mother henning, but not too much?"

"Yeah. I guess that was it." He looked distinctly uncomfortable. "About that drink you asked if I wanted—"

"What would you like?"

"Something soft. No, make that a glass of white wine."

"Sure about that?"

"Yes. I'm in a pub, right?"

"That's where you are. I'll be back in a moment."

And when he returned I would relieve his discomfort by getting to the business at hand.

I looked around at the photos and paintings of famous pugilists that decorated the pub's walls. I got up and went over to have a better look at a lithograph of a bare-chested, bare-knuckled boxer in white trousers. Robert Fitzsimmons, born in Cornwall in 1863. "Ruby Robert." He was the one whose wife had created a major scandal during a bout in America by being at ringside in her husband's corner. Ministers had even preached sermons about it.

My grandfather had laughed when he told me the story. *"A woman with a whole lot of gumption."* My grandfather had been a boxing fan, especially of the black boxers, from the flamboyant Jack Johnson to the youthful Sugar Ray Leonard.

I went back and sat down at the table. At the bar, Quinn was placing our order with the barmaid. But I should probably call her a bartender. *Barmaid* was sexist. She poured my wine and filled a mug for him. He said something that made her laugh. She was still smiling as he turned away and started back to our table.

I went back to my contemplation of the lithograph of "Ruby Robert" Fitzsimmons. Whatever the source of Quinn's discomfort with me, it was not because of his self-declared ignorance about women. Maybe he really did think his friend Ed Janowitz had rambled on about his business. And what exactly had constituted Quinn's "helluva bad year"?

"One white wine," he said as he set the glass down on the table. "You didn't specify, so I asked for the house chardonnay."

"That's fine, thanks. I'm not a connoisseur."

"I wouldn't have guessed it."

"I'll overlook that remark, if you'll give me an objective opinion. Your professional opinion."

"About what?"

Did all police officers perfect an expression to make suspects feel ill at ease? Cordner, smiling. Janowitz, just plain staring. Quinn, cool and waiting. I took a small sip from my wine glass.

"You were saying, Professor Stuart?"

"I was saying that I need your opinion." I glanced at him, then back down at my glass in its damp circle. "Not that I'm actually sure that this is a police matter. It could be my overactive imagination. The fact that I've never liked the man might lead me to see things that are innocent as suspicious. And after what happened today with Dee, of course, I would be more prone to suspect chicanery—"

"Chicanery?"

I ignored his amusement at my choice of word. It was a perfectly good word, and it covered the situation. "What happened in London was too much of a coincidence. If there is some chance that he's— But if I'm wrong, and it isn't—"

"Professor Stuart?"

"Yes?"

"Not that I'm not finding your monologue fascinating. But if you want me to join in, you've got to tell me what we're talking about."

"Of course. I'm sorry. When I'm nervous, I sometimes ramble. I do that too when I'm trying to talk myself out of something."

"I'll keep that in mind."

"You have to promise me that this is in strict confidence."

"Is this something to do with Dee Crump's death? If it is, I can't promise you that I won't at some point—"

"I don't know who killed her. It isn't about her death. Or at least I don't think it is. I'm not sure what it's about . . . if it's about anything."

Quinn nodded. "That was clear. Now, tell me what it is that might or might not be about something."

"Do I have your promise that unless this does turn out to be related to Dee's death—"

"Or some other police matter."

"Oh." I sat back in my chair. "Then maybe I shouldn't—"

"You asked for this conversation, Professor Stuart."

"I know that. And stop trying to make me feel like a reluctant snitch on a cop show."

"Is this about snitching?"

"I don't know. It may be about nothing, but I need an objective opinion."

"Cops aren't always objective."

"When it comes to lawbreaking? Well, neither am I about my friends."

"This involves a friend? Tess Alvarez?"

I took a long sip of my wine. Quinn waited.

"It involves her ex-husband, Michael Donovan."

"What about him?"

"I think he may be mixed up in something. Up to something."

"Up to something criminal?"

"I don't know. I don't really have any evidence. Just because I was mugged after he had given me a package—"

"You were what?"

"Mugged. An attempted mugging. In London." I took another long sip of my wine. "It happened outside Madame Tussaud's." Before I could change my mind, I told Quinn what had happened. The gift-wrapped package that Michael had wanted me to bring to Tess and had shoved into my lap. The man with the slashed eye who had tried to grab it. My fall in front of the bus. "It sounds like a bad movie, doesn't it?"

"I don't suppose you looked in the package."

"Of course, I looked. I might have an overactive imagination, but I'm not a dimwit."

Quinn held up his hands. "Pardon me. Of course you would have looked in the package a mugger tried to steal from you. What was in it?"

I twisted the stem of my wine glass between my fingers. "Nothing anyone would want to steal. That's why this probably is my imagination. Or my dislike of Michael finding something to focus on."

"Why don't you like him? No, let's finish discussing the package first. What was in it?"

"A Winnie the Pooh figurine. And Michael had written a cute note: 'All my love, Christopher Robin.' So I wrapped the package back up again and brought it to Dee—"

"To Dee?"

"What?"

"You said you brought it to Dee."

I shook my head. "Did I? I meant I brought it to Tess."

"Did you tell her what happened?"

"No. Not about the mugging or about opening her gift."

"Has something else happened since London? Something else with Michael?"

"He's here in St. Regis. He didn't tell me he was coming. Why would he ask me to bring Tess a gift when he was coming here himself?"

"Maybe he wanted her to have the gift hoping it would soften her up before they saw each other again. As I recall, Benjamin Stillman implied the relationship between your friend and her ex-husband is somewhat strained."

"That's one way of putting it. Or, at least, it was. I'm not sure what's going on now." I took another sip of my wine. I was beginning to feel more relaxed. Depressed but relaxed. "Tess is pregnant."

"His baby?"

I nodded. "They ran into each other in Paris last month. Or, at least, Michael claims the meeting was accidental."

"You don't believe him?"

"That was where he and Tess spent their honeymoon. If he wanted to find a place where she would be vulnerable to his charm—"

"Vulnerable? You make it sound like he's preying on her instead of trying to win her back."

I met Quinn's glance. "I don't know what he's doing. All I know is that I got mugged in London and now Michael's here. And he didn't tell Tess until last night that he knew Jeremy and Benjamin Stillman."

"Had Tess ever met the Stillmans before?"

"That's exactly what she said when I brought it up. That there was no reason for Michael to mention Benjamin by name—to identify him as the person who had first recommended the Crumps' hotel—until after Tess had met him."

"She's right."

I set down my glass. "And you think this is all my imagination?"

"You want my professional opinion?"

"Yes, I want your opinion—your opinion as a trained police officer."

"Okay, as a cop, I find the mugging more than a little fishy."

"Fishy? Is that technical language."

"No." Quinn smiled. "But since we're on the subject, how about some?"

"What?"

"Fish. There's a restaurant around the corner that serves great seafood."

"You've been eating at restaurants when Fiona was cooking for you and Janowitz at home?"

"Sometimes one needs a solitary meal and an opportunity for contemplation."

"But tonight you're willing to share your restaurant with me?"

"I think I'd better. I need to sober you up before I see you back to your hotel."

"I'm not drunk."

"Not yet, but if you finish the rest of that glass of wine—" He reached out and took the glass from my hands. "You don't drink very often, do you?"

"About once or twice a year. Usually at a party or reception when I'm eating something." I straightened in my chair. "Do I seem drunk?"

"Not yet. Just a little too solemn."

"This is a solemn topic."

"So it is. Come on. We can finish discussing it over dinner and a cup of tea."

"You don't drink tea."

He pulled back my chair and handed me my shoulder bag. "Tea for you, coffee for me. And you can tell me why you don't like Michael."

"For all kinds of reasons. Don't let me forget that I have to buy Tess a chocolate bar and a sandwich."

"What was she doing when you left?"

"Sleeping. She says being pregnant has that effect."

"Yeah, it does."

"You've been pregnant, Detective Quinn?"

He took my arm, turning me toward the door. "My wife was once."

"Oh." I stopped walking and looked up at him. "I didn't realize you were married. You don't wear a ring. But, of course, some men don't—"

"I'm not married."

"You said your wife . . . you're divorced?"

"Widowed."

"I'm sorry—"

"Don't be. If she hadn't died, I would have divorced her."

The pub was jammed with people now. Quinn led the way to the door. I followed.

He would have divorced her if she hadn't died?

Chapter Nine

WE WALKED OUT OF THE PUB and around the corner to the restaurant. We did not continue with the subject of Quinn's wife. His tone of voice had not invited more questions, I didn't ask them. Why would he have divorced her? What had she done?

The restaurant we entered was comfortable, not fancy. Tables with white cloths and waiters in white aprons. A casual suggestion of a nautical theme in the form of pictures of ships on the whitewashed walls. And a lobster tank occupying place of pride by the kitchen door. We had only a short wait before we were installed at a corner table. Obviously, Quinn had been there often enough to be considered a regular.

"How long have you been in St. Regis?" I asked after the waiter had taken us through the specials for the evening and departed with our beverage orders.

"A couple of weeks. Long enough so that I'm beginning to think I ought to leave before I overstay my welcome."

"I doubt you could do that with Janowitz."

"Not with Fiona either. But it's time I thought about heading home."

"But you are going to stay until we know about Dee?"

"At least that long."

"Janowitz says you're a natural as a homicide cop, that you like to know how dead bodies got that way."

"It's more a matter of not liking loose ends. Getting back to Michael."

"Yes. Good old Michael."

The waiter set my teapot and cup in front of me. He poured Quinn's coffee and left a carafe.

"Why does the connection between Michael and the Stillmans bother you?" Quinn asked.

"I don't know. Maybe because nobody mentioned it right away. Maybe because both Michael and the Stillmans are in pharmaceuticals."

"Why is that significant?"

"Do I have to spell it out for you?"

"Sometimes I'm slow."

"Drugs, Detective Quinn. Pharmaceutical companies make drugs."

"You think Michael and the Stillmans are drug dealers? Illegal drugs?"

"I don't know what I think about the Stillmans. I wouldn't think anything about them if it wasn't for Michael." I straightened my fork and knife. Crooked silverware. Crooked people.

"Go on," Quinn said.

"I know that a man tried to mug me. I think it had something to do with Michael, with what the mugger thought was in the shopping bag he had passed to me. I'm scared to death Dee—I mean Tess—" *Why did I keep doing that?* "I'm afraid Tess will go back to him and that this time he'll do something even worse than before."

"What did he do before?"

I picked up my cup and took a sip. Reached for the sugar bowl.

"What did he do, Lizzie?"

"If you must know, John, he picked up another woman and brought her home to his wife's bed."

"When his wife was in it?"

"Cute."

"It happens."

"Tess was away on a business trip. She's a travel writer."

"You mentioned that earlier. And she mentioned it during her interview with Cordner."

"Well, she had been in Jamaica on assignment. She came home and found Michael in their bed with another woman. He said he was upset because he and Tess had quarreled on the phone and so he got drunk and picked up a woman."

"That happens too."

"Does it? So you did that kind of thing when you were married?"

Quinn said nothing. But a muscle in his cheek jerked. I had literally hit a nerve.

"I'm sorry." I shook my head. "That's none of my business. Forgive me. I'm upset."

He leaned back in his chair, his gray eyes shuttered now. "To answer your question, Professor, no, I did not do that kind of thing when I was married. But it happens. And it doesn't necessarily mean that the man doesn't love his wife."

"How can someone claim to love someone else and still betray that person?"

"Temporary insanity, or so I've been told. Getting back to Michael—"

"I have nothing else to say about Michael Donovan."

"Do you want me to ask Cordner to see what he can find out?"

"No, that's not what I want you do, I just wanted your opinion. You said the mugging sounded fishy."

"Which hasn't helped to answer any of your questions. Anyway, I think this is something Cordner should have to think about."

"You promised—"

"I said—"

"Ready to order?" The waiter asked.

"Give us a few more minutes," Quinn said.

"Certainly. Signal when you're ready."

"I know what you said, Detective Quinn. But if Tess finds out I've told you all this—even about Michael and the other woman—"

"I won't tell Cordner that part. Just about the package and the mugging. He needs to know that much, Lizzie."

I sighed. "All right. But would you, please, ask him to be more discreet than I've been?"

"British police inspectors are the souls of discretion."

At the table across from us, a man was cracking a lobster and digging for the meat. I loved lobster, but I didn't have it very often.

"Cordner's not exactly the inspector from *Midnight Lace*," I said.

"From what?"

"Nothing. A movie with Doris Day. She's an heiress, and her husband's plotting to drive her crazy and kill her."

"So you think that's Michael's plan? To kill his wife?"

"No, of course not. Why would Michael kill Tess? He's the one with the money. You said British police inspectors, and I thought silly movie. What I'm worried about is the fact that Tess is pregnant and in danger of actually marrying Michael again."

"John Gavin."

"What?"

"It just came back to me. A foggy memory of John Gavin as the British war veteran who rescues poor Doris."

"Actually, she manages to get herself out of her apartment, and then he climbs the scaffolding to help her down."

"Before homicidal husband Rex Harrison can get to her." Quinn gave me a thoughtful look. "Some nights when I'm too tired to sleep, I end up in front of the TV with the late, late show. That's how I happened to see that movie. What's your excuse, Professor Stuart?"

"I was up. It was on. I'm a night owl."

"Yeah, well, that's the other part of my problem. Which isn't good when you've spent your whole life getting up at 6 A.M. or earlier."

"Your whole life?"

"I was an Army brat. My father always expected his son to be up and ready for inspection before he departed for his office. Later

I went off to military school and then West Point."

"West Point. I'm impressed."

"It was expected. My father's alma mater."

"And after that?"

"Ten years in the military police. And all these years later, I'm still getting up at dawn. Philadelphia cops have to be on time for work."

"But you're on vacation, and this morning you were out running on the beach at sunrise."

"So you did see me."

"What—when?"

"Running on the beach this morning."

"Oh. Yes, I saw you. But then I decided to try the cliff walk."

He leaned back in his chair. "Why were you up and about so early? Dawn isn't exactly prime time for a night owl."

"But the other birds were noisy. I woke up. I thought I might as well go for a walk."

"On the beach?"

"Yes . . . no . . . I mean that was what I intended, but then I decided to try the cliff walk."

"Where you ran into Dee Crump."

"Yes."

I drew a breath, willing my suddenly tight muscles to relax. Did he think I had killed Dee? Were we playing a game of cat and mouse?

The man eating the lobster asked a passing waiter for more butter. He seemed oblivious to everything except his meal.

I smiled brightly at Detective Quinn. "Not that I've had that much more luck than you have with getting to sleep in. My grandparents were believers in the value of early rising."

"Your grandparents?" he said, allowing me to change the subject. "What about your parents?"

I took a sip of my tea. "My grandparents raised me."

Quinn smiled, a smile that didn't reach his eyes. "It sounds as if they would have liked my father."

"Well, they didn't make me stand for inspection, for which I'm grateful. What was your father's rank?"

"He made major general the year before he died."

"Your father was a general?"

"That was what he intended from the moment he put on his first uniform. And what my father set out to do, he accomplished, right up to the end."

Right up to the end? "There is something to be said for determination."

"All kinds of things to be said for it. Of course, he did make one early error in judgment. One of the few times in his life when, as he put it, he failed to fully evaluate the situation."

"A military error?"

"Personal. He married my mother. She didn't fit in well on an Army base."

"Oh."

"But the mistake was rectified. Actually, it was the best thing for both of them." Quinn turned his coffee cup in his saucer, then pushed it away. "When she was gone, he proceeded with his game plan. His record was good enough so that he was able to recover his lost ground."

"And your mother? What about her?"

"My mother went home to her people and went on with her life. She has the kind of life now that she would have had if she hadn't met my father. She's happy."

"But you stayed with him? With your father?"

"I was his only son. He had plans for me."

"He wanted you to follow in his footsteps as a soldier?"

"There are worse careers. If only the military didn't feel it absolutely necessary to be up and about at the crack of dawn. Decided what you want to eat?"

Change of subject again. All right. I picked up my menu and glanced again at the man across from us who was progressing through his lobster with obvious enjoyment. But lobster was so messy with melted butter, not to mention expensive. And how could I be starving at a time like this? My stomach had no sense of appropriateness. Of course, I had missed both breakfast and lunch. "I'll pay for dinner," I said. "To thank you for letting me bend your ear."

"Okay," John Quinn said. "In that case, I'll have the lobster too." This time his smile was real. A grin.

I put my menu down. "In that case, Detective Quinn, I'll be happy to let you pick up the check. As I seem to recall, you are the one who invited me to dinner."

"I'm glad you remembered that."

"Do you object to women paying their share?"

"Not at all. When you invite me, I'll be happy to let you pick up the tab."

"That sounds fair. What did you do about Sean? Did you tell Cordner about the argument Sean had with Dee?"

"I told him."

"And?"

"They're looking for the kid. He wasn't at his flat or at the motorcycle shop where he works."

"Do you think he ran away?"

"He's not where he should be. His girlfriend's dead, and he's missing."

"I still don't think he did it."

"So you've said. Why did you think of him all of a sudden?"

"I was thinking about mismatched couples. When I was talking to Sarah this morning, she said Sean was only a stage Dee was going through."

"He probably was."

"Probably." I picked up my tea cup. "But it's still sad. All of this is sad."

"I don't know how to break this to you, Professor, but sometimes life sucks."

"Thanks so much for telling me. Does this place run to chocolate mousse?"

"You'd better hope my credit card does."

"I'm sure Philadelphia cops are well paid. Why Philadelphia? You said you were an Army brat . . . you must have lived in a lot of places—"

"The Liberty Bell. I've always had a thing about that bell."

"Sure."

"And I had a friend or two in the area, guys I'd served with in the Army. Are you planning to stay there?"

"To stay where?'

"In Drucilla, Kentucky? Do you like it there?"

"Sometimes. There are other times when I hate it. But it's what I know."

"And where you intend to stay?"

"Probably. I don't know. Why do you ask?"

"When Tess was being interviewed, she mentioned that she had suggested you take a vacation because your grandmother, with whom you'd lived, had died recently."

"Tess mentioned that?" Why would she have told Cordner that? Although, given the fact I had just finished sharing her personal history with Cordner's colleague, I was hardly in a position to complain. "I don't know if I'll stay in Drucilla. I stayed before because my grandmother was there. But I still have the house, and I have tenure at the university where I teach. Job security. And it isn't as if I'm always unhappy there. I have friends."

"Job security and friends. Where have I heard that one before?"

"What?"

"Among the reasons I've been giving myself for staying in Philadelphia."

"You're thinking of leaving?"

"I have a job offer I'm considering." He pointed at my menu. "Last column on the right, under desserts. Chocolate mousse."

I opened my menu again. "When all else fails, there's chocolate."

"And lobster."

"At this rate, I'm going to have to start running again and—" Running. I was running through a forest with branches grabbing me and wrapping themselves around me. "I had a nightmare this afternoon. I was having a nap and I had a nightmare."

"And?"

"I've been trying to remember what it was I thought about as I was waking up. Benjy was crying in the hall, and I was tangled in the sheet. And I thought of something. Something about Benjy—"

"What about him?"

"I don't know. And I know you're sick of hearing me say that."

"Think about it. In the meantime, let's get our order in before our waiter gives up on us." Quinn signaled for the waiter. We both ordered lobster and I tried to recapture my former enthusiasm for my meal.

Something about the nightmare. Running. Then Benjy crying. Screaming. "A dragon. I thought a dragon had Benjy. It was probably the purple one in Dee's backpack. Nightmares never make sense."

"Yes, they do. Mine always do when I think about them."

"Well, this one didn't. I was the one who was running through the woods while tree branches grabbed at me and lightning flashed. Benjy wasn't even in my dream until I heard him crying outside in the hallway."

"What did the dragon symbolize?"

"You tell me, Sigmund."

"Dragons breathe fire. Knights slay them. Smearing on dragon's blood is supposed to make one invulnerable to stab wounds—"

"It is?"

Quinn nodded and continued, "A red dragon appears on the national flag of Wales. Dragons are also found in the mythology of almost every culture."

I joined in. "The Chinese use paper dragons in their festivals. In Chinese mythology, dragons are wise and powerful. Dragons come in various forms. Winged, tailed, horned."

"Puff was a magic dragon."

"And I think Benjy gave Dee that purple dragon. Benjamin told us that Dee was telling Benjy a story yesterday afternoon about ladies and knights and dragons. The purple dragon she had was probably Benjy's—" I snapped my fingers. "Why did he give her the dragon?"

"Because she was a beautiful young woman who played with him and told him stories, and he probably liked her a lot."

"No—I mean that was what I thought as I was waking up from my nightmare. I thought, *Why did Benjy give Dee the dragon?*"

"It would be the logical thing to give her after she had told him a story about—"

"Ladies and knights and dragons. All right. I told you my nightmare didn't make sense."

"It made sense. It just didn't tell us anything else we don't already know." Quinn paused with his coffee cup halfway to his lips. "On the other hand, if you get a chance you might ask Benjy why he gave Dee the dragon."

"Sure. If I can find an opportunity to do that without sending him into hysterics. He's still really upset."

"He was probably planning to marry her when he grew up."

"Someone else disappointed in love. As you said, Detective Quinn, sometimes life sucks."

"But the food here doesn't. So let's relax and enjoy it. Bread?"

"Thank you." I took a roll from the basket he was holding out.

I really did need to start running again. I used to before Hester Rose got sick. Was I going to stay in Drucilla?

I broke off a piece of my roll. "Could I have the butter, please? I'm starving." Stomachs have no sense of the proprieties. Or of pending decisions.

Chapter Ten

IT WAS AFTER EIGHT O'CLOCK when we left the restaurant. The chill of evening was settling in. I looked up the street—and grabbed John Quinn's arm. "There's Sean!"

"Where?"

"There!" I pointed up the hill, where the street curved. "Going around the corner. Sean!"

"Dammit, Lizzie, wait."

"He's getting away. Come on." I scrambled up the hill. As I turned the corner, I saw Sean shambling along in a kind of blind trot with his head down and his arms wrapped around himself. "Sean!"

He stopped and turned. His head was still down, his arms still wrapped around his body.

I approached him slowly. "Sean?"

He looked up. His eyes had a feverish glow. "Dee. They're saying she's dead."

"Yes."

"She's dead?"

"Yes, she's dead."

He sunk to his knees, there on the sidewalk. "Oh, God. Oh, God."

I stepped closer and put my hand on his shoulder.

"Lizzie," Quinn said. "Move away from him."

"Move away? Does he look like he's about to attack me?"

"Just get out of the way." He reached down and caught Sean by his arm. "Get up, kid. This isn't the place for it."

Sean looked up at him with tears running down his face. "I loved her."

"And love's a bitch. Get up."

Sean stumbled as he got to his feet. Quinn steadied him.

Sean straightened and wiped at his face with the sleeve of his leather jacket. "What do you two want? I heard it was the coppers that were looking for me."

"They are," Quinn said.

"Where have you been, Sean?"

"I was . . . I went up to London to visit a mate."

"Without letting your boss at the motorcycle shop or your land-lady know?" Quinn said.

"I don't have to account for my every move to them. That job at the shop is only when I'm available."

"And you weren't available today or the day before," Quinn said.

"No. I needed to go up to London."

"Because of your argument with Dee?" I asked.

"I needed to get away for a day or two and cool off. I didn't mean . . . what you saw . . . I had never hit her before." His Adam's apple worked as he swallowed. "I loved her."

Quinn appeared unmoved by this declaration. "Come on. You need to go talk to the police."

"And supposing I don't want to."

"I'm a cop too, kid. Let's do this the easy way."

"I should have known. I should have known from your bleeding smell."

Quinn said nothing. Sean shook his head twice like a punch-drunk fighter. "Okay. Let's go and get this done. I've got things to do."

"So do we all," Quinn said. "Lizzie, I'll drop you off at your hotel."

"Oh . . . but I thought you said I might not want the other guests to know that I've been hobnobbing with the police."

"All right. I'll drop you off at the top of your street."

"But it's out of your way if you're driving Sean to the police station. I can walk."

"You can. Or if you'd rather come along, and be dropped off later—"

"That would work."

"I thought it might."

I ignored what he was implying about my curiosity. I was as involved in this case as he was. Even more involved. I had been there when Dee was dying.

Sean sniffed again like a small boy with a hurt and swiped at his nose with his sleeve. I was half out of my chair when I realized that unlike the offices of doctors and funeral directors, police stations probably did not keep boxes of tissues conveniently at hand. I sank back down into my chair and reached for my shoulder bag. Neither Cordner nor John Quinn raised any objection as I slid the small purse pack of tissues across the table to Sean. He took one and blew his nose, then grabbed for more as the first one turned soggy in his hand.

Cordner leaned back in his chair at the table looking as if he had all the time in the world. His patient pose was at odds with the way he'd hurried back to the police station. He'd walked through the door less than fifteen minutes after the constable at the front desk called him to say we were there.

Quinn, looking equally unruffled, was leaning against the wall with his arms folded. Part of the strategy for intimidating the suspect? One detective across from him at the table, the other leaning against the wall, listening, was classic American cop show.

Not that the two of them had been particularly intimidating thus far. Cordner hadn't even disagreed when Sean looked up with a sullen glare and mumbled that there was "no reason for the American cop and the woman to go, is there? They already know all about Dee and me." He didn't want "no sodding mouthpiece"—lawyer—but he didn't mind having Quinn and me stay. He had almost asked that we stay. Maybe because John Quinn and I had been there when he had his argument with Dee and we had been there when he fell to the ground weeping for her. Compared to a cool and official Detective Inspector, we might even seem a comforting presence.

"I'm not sure I understand, Mr. Etling," Cordner said. "You say that you and Miss Crump had been having some problems—"

"I told you, we had different ways of seeing things."

Cordner said, "And that was what the two of you were rowing about on the beach path on Sunday evening—your different ways of seeing things?"

"Yeah, that was it."

"What things exactly?"

Sean glanced from me to Quinn, and I had the feeling that he regretted saying that we could stay. Hard to lie in front of witnesses. Sean glanced around the room. "You ain't going to leave it alone, are you?"

"We can't leave it alone," Cordner said. "The circumstances of Miss Crump's death—"

"Are suspicious. You said that. I told you, I ain't got nothing to say. We had a row that's all. She was doing something—I thought she was doing something—that I didn't like."

"You thought she had gone to see someone," I said, remembering his challenge to Dee.

"I want them to leave," Sean said. "Get them out of here. I've changed my mind."

I stood up.

Cordner said, "Mr. Etling, we will find out. For your own sake and for Dee's, it would be better if you told us now."

Sean let his breath out in a hiss. His shoulders sagged again. "There was talk. But it wasn't that way. She said she didn't."

"She said she didn't what?" Cordner asked.

"Sleep with that dyke."

The proverbial pin might have dropped and been heard. I doubt either Cordner or John Quinn was shocked. But it wasn't what any of us had expected Sean to say.

"What dyke?" Cordner asked.

"That dyke artist—Felicity Hollingsworth." Sean turned the name into a sneer. "She paints pictures of people—portraits. She's supposed to be famous. In magazines and stuff."

Cordner nodded. "I've heard of her."

"Dee met her at a pub. She said she wanted Dee to sit for her, told her she had 'magnificent bone structure.'"

"And did Dee sit for her?"

"She did. But then I heard about her—about Hollingsworth being a dyke—and I told Dee. Told her to stay away from her. But she said she liked her. She said she could talk to her about all kinds of things. Things I couldn't understand."

"You were jealous?" Cordner asked.

"Why would I be jealous of a dyke? I just thought Dee ought to stay away from her so that people wouldn't get the wrong idea. I didn't want no talk about Dee."

"I see. Was that what you had your row about on Sunday evening?"

"That was it. Are you going to charge me?"

"No, Mr. Etling. We have no grounds on which to hold you. We will, however, verify your statement that you were in London until this afternoon."

Sean got to his feet. "My mate will tell you."

"Stay in town," Cordner said. "We might need to speak to you again."

"I'll be around. I have to be here for Dee's funeral."

He went out the door, his head down, walking fast.

In the interview room, there was silence until Quinn said, "This gets more and more interesting."

"Yes," Cordner said. He looked at me. "I don't suppose Dee happened to mention Felicity Hollingsworth during your conversation with her."

"I would have told you if she had. What do you think it means?"

"It might mean nothing. But then again—" Cordner stood. "It's been a long day. Shall we try again tomorrow?"

At the beginning of the interview, when Cordner had asked Sean if he knew of anyone who would want to harm Dee, Sean had looked as if he were stunned by the question. Then he had blurted,

"Harm her? No one would want to harm Dee. She was a good person. No one would want to hurt her." He shook his head. "Why would someone kill her?" Cordner had gone over again the reasons why the police found Dee's death suspicious—the peanut-spiked yummy balls, the missing adrenaline kit—but Sean had shaken his head, still unable to believe that someone had killed Dee. It was only Cordner's next question about his quarrel with Dee on Sunday evening that had snapped Sean out of his bewilderment. If someone had hurt her, it was not he. Sean was emphatic about that.

"So who did it?" I asked, verbalizing my thoughts. "If Sean didn't kill her—and I never thought he did—who did? What was the motive?"

"You tell me, Professor," Quinn said. We were stopped at a traffic light. Across the street, a couple entered a dance club and the live performance of a rock band poured out into the street. Then the doors closed. St. Regis after dark, in full swing.

"I think," I said, "that whoever killed Dee must have hated her. To kill someone like that—to know that she'd die fighting for breath—requires hatred."

"Does it?" Quinn said. "Maybe the killer was simply looking for a way to do the deed and be somewhere else when it happened."

"All right. That's possible. But who? It would have to be someone who knew Dee well enough to know about her allergy, to know that she kept the adrenaline kit in her backpack, to know that Sarah made yummy balls for her—"

"And to have a good reason for wanting her dead."

We had left the holiday merrymakers in the center of town. Upper High Street was as quiet as it had been on Sunday night when Tess and I encountered each other there. Light and shadow. The sea in the distance.

"All right," I said. "Someone with a reason for wanting her dead. What are some of the reasons that someone would want another person dead? Greed, hate, revenge, fear—"

"Jealousy, lust—"

"Lust?"

"As in 'If I can't have you no one else will.' Usually accompanied by jealousy or obsession or both."

"If Sean's story holds up, that might leave Felicity Hollingsworth."

"Or someone else that Sean didn't know about." As he spoke, Quinn turned onto my street and stopped the car.

I gathered up my shoulder bag and the paper bag containing Tess's sandwich and chocolate bar and reached for the door handle. "Thank you for the ride, Detective Quinn."

"Not at all, Professor."

"Good night."

"Lizzie?"

I paused in the act of closing the door and leaned down to look back into the car. "Yes?"

"Don't ask the people at the hotel a lot of questions."

"But you told me to try to speak to Benjy."

"I know what I said about Benjy. Just don't go playing detective with the adults."

"Meaning you think one of them did it?"

"A guest at the hotel would know about Dee's allergy and have ample opportunity to get to both Sarah Crump's baking supplies and Dee's backpack."

"What about motive? Do you think Hildegard Martin or one of the Stillmans would have a motive for killing the nineteen-year-old niece of the owners of the hotel where they're guests? They've been coming to the hotel for years."

"Time enough to develop a motive or two."

"Are you going to speak to Cordner about Michael?"

"Tomorrow. I thought you'd rather not be there when I did."

"No, I'd rather not."

"Let me ask this one more time. Do you have any reason to believe Michael might have killed Dee Crump?"

"No . . . I just think he should be checked on. But Michael was at the hotel last spring, wasn't he? And Dee knew him well enough to say he was 'a lovely gentleman.' Maybe they knew each other quite well."

"You're suggesting an affair?"

"Well, that would give him a motive, wouldn't it? If he'd had an affair with Dee and was afraid she'd say something to Tess—"

"Then why suggest the Crump sisters' hotel to Tess in the first place?"

I sighed. "It sounded good. For a moment, it sounded good."

"Did it? Are you so anxious for Tess and her ex-husband not to get back together again that you want him to be a murderer?"

The question caught me like an unexpected jab to the mid-section. Did I really dislike Michael that much? Did I really think Tess would be better off if the father of her child was arrested for murder? "I— No, of course not. I didn't mean— But if he did do it, I don't want him to get away with it, that's all. Good night." I turned away and started down the street.

"Lizzie?" Quinn was leaning out his window. "Remember what I said."

I flapped a hand at him in response and kept walking.

The car's engine gave a muffled roar as he reversed out of the street. A dog in the backyard of the house opposite barked twice in response, then fell silent. No one else was about. Street lights gleamed on polished car hoods. From a house a few doors up from the Gull's Nest, music drifted through an open window, something light and melodious and thirties. Cole Porter?

I stopped to listen. A strange place to hear Cole Porter, here in a seaside town in England. No, not really. He'd had British connections. And music was universal.

So was murder, even in Cole Porter melodies. What was that strange little song of his? Ella Fitzgerald had sung it straight. But a male friend of Porter's had sung it as high camp at dinner parties. A woman who regretted she couldn't keep her luncheon engagement because she was about to be lynched for shooting her lover. Murder among the upper crust, among the ladies who lunched. No stranger than murder on a cliff walk in Cornwall. Neither the stuff of Raymond Chandler's "mean streets."

But it had been mean and nasty. Dee's murderer was someone who didn't mind causing pain if it was expedient, if it suited his or her purpose. Quinn had said I was not to ask questions that might irritate a killer. And, of course, I should also pray that the killer wasn't Michael, pray that Tess wouldn't have to deal with that. But if I could suspect Michael of not only having an affair with Dee but of killing her, it would seem I liked him even less than I thought I did.

Why was that? What had Michael ever done to me other than find me amusing? Was all this righteous indignation on Tess's behalf? Was I outraged that he had cheated on her with another woman? Was I so outraged that I could believe a man who could commit adultery should quite naturally be the prime suspect when a murder was committed?

I climbed the two steps to the door of the Gull's Nest Hotel. As I fumbled my key into the lock, I admitted to myself that I might be biased.

But I also knew when someone bore watching, and Michael Donovan did.

Chapter Eleven

EDITH CRUMP STEPPED INTO THE HALLWAY as I opened the front door. Her short salt and pepper hair stuck out here and there as if she had been raking her fingers through it. "Lizzie, I'm so glad you're back."

"What's wrong?"

"It's Tess, my dear. She's been taken to hospital."

"She's been— Why? What happened? Is it the baby?"

"The baby? Tess is pregnant?" That quivering question came not from Edith, but from Rosalind Stillman as she stepped out of the lounge. The expression in her green eyes made me uneasy. I felt as if I should snatch back my words before she could grab them up.

Then Jeremy was there in the doorway behind her. His hands came to rest on her shoulders. She twisted her neck to look up at him. The open collar of her white blouse slid downward, revealing the bruise on her delicate skin. A hickey? I had a sudden, too vivid, and completely unwanted image of Jeremy's mouth on his wife's neck as the two of them made love.

"Michael's, I assume," Jeremy was saying. And he was actually smiling. He looked younger and more relaxed than I had seen him.

"What?" I said.

"The baby that Tess is carrying. You did say she's pregnant?"

"She—" I turned back to Edith. "Tess—you said she's been taken to the hospital. When? What happened?"

"Michael took her," Rosalind said.

"Michael? He was here? What was he doing here?"

"Visiting Tess," Jeremy said, looking puzzled. "They were upstairs in her room. Then Michael came downstairs carrying her—"

"Carrying her?"

"He said she had passed out," Edith said. "We thought it might be no more than a faint, but he was insistent about taking her to hospital."

"So he carried her out of here and took her away?"

"Looking more than a little anxious," Rosalind said. "Fathers-to-be do tend to overreact." Her smile fluttered and disappeared. "Of course, in my case, poor Jeremy was always right to react as he did. With me, there was always something wrong."

"Roz," Jeremy said.

She smiled up at him and touched his cheek. "I know. I mustn't dwell on the past. We have a beautiful, healthy son now." Her glance came back to me. "You see, Lizzie, I had three miscarriages before Benjy, and then I almost lost him too. It was touch and go toward the end."

"I'm sorry you had such a difficult time," I said. "But Benjy is a wonderful little boy."

"Yes. His mother's pride and joy. Jeremy says I spoil him, but I am so grateful to have him. I don't know what I'd do without him. He's out with his grandparents right now. It's been such a dreadful day, they wanted to take him out for ice cream to try to cheer him up a bit."

Jeremy gave Edith an apologetic look over his wife's head. "We all need cheering up a bit under the circumstances. But we're getting off the subject, aren't we? Lizzie's concerned about Tess."

Rosalind said, "But I'm sure she's all right, Lizzie."

"I think I'd like to go to her," I said. "Edith, do you know which hospital?"

"There's only one here in St. Regis," Edith said.

"I'll run you over," Jeremy offered.

"Oh, yes, do, darling," Rosalind patted his hand. "We women will all be fine until you get back. Sarah's tucked in bed, Hildegard is sitting behind the screen meditating, and Edith and I will go back into the lounge and have another cup of tea."

The look Jeremy gave her as she looked up at him was hard to interpret. It was both tender and uncertain. It was definitely not detached. If she had been fluttery on Sunday evening, tonight she was ranging from blithely cheerful to downright brittle. I rather suspected Rosalind might be on the patient list of some London therapist who billed her for weekly sessions during which she poured out her neuroses.

"Right," Jeremy said. "Shall we go, Lizzie?"

"If you're sure it wouldn't be too much trouble," I said.

"Not at all. Ready?"

"Yes." I looked down at the paper sack in my hand. "Tess asked me to bring her a sandwich."

Edith held out her hand. "We'll put it in the fridge for her."

"I doubt she'll want it tonight."

"Hard to know," Rosalind said. "I used to get such cravings at the most ridiculous moments."

"Off we go," Jeremy said, gesturing me back toward the door. "I won't be long, darling."

"We'll be fine until you return," Rosalind said. "We'll lock all the doors."

Edith's face flushed pink. "Yes, we'll be perfectly safe here," she said. "That isn't a concern."

Rosalind shook her head, looking abashed. "No, of course not, Edith. I didn't mean that security is a concern. The police aren't even definite about Dee. And even if they were, we certainly wouldn't have to worry about anyone attempting anything else."

"Certainly not," Jeremy said. "There's nothing at all to worry about."

Edith nodded, accepting his attempt to make up for his wife's lack of tact. "And we do keep the doors locked at night as a matter of course."

"And common sense," Rosalind said. "You and Sarah are such sensible women."

I heard Jeremy sigh. "Back shortly," he said as he held the door for me to precede him.

Did Rosalind have a streak of malice in her makeup? Or was she simply unsettled by what had happened today, tactless in her uneasiness? At any rate, making love to her seemed to have repaired Jeremy's ragged edges. Or, at least, I assumed that was what had done it.

Still, it was an odd time for lovemaking—when someone had just died, probably been murdered. But I had always read that in moments of crisis, people found lovemaking a life-affirming act, a way of shaking their fists at death. I, on the other hand, had dealt with the situation by stuffing myself with lobster and chocolate mousse while I exchanged murder theories with a cop. A cop who in all likelihood did not consider me above suspicion. Arguably, Jeremy and Rosalind had made better use of their time.

"This is my car right here," Jeremy said, unlocking the door. "Here, let me have that." He took the shawl I had picked up from the passenger seat and tossed it in back.

"It's really nice of you to drive me to the hospital," I said when he had gotten in on the driver's side of the dark blue sedan.

"Not at all," he said as he twisted the key in the ignition. Then he turned his head to look at me in the dim light of the car's interior. "The truth is, Lizzie, I do have an ulterior motive. There's something I want to speak with you about."

Really? And did that explain his unexpected shift to niceness and concern? "What?"

"It's about my wife. My wife and Michael, actually."

"Michael and Rosalind?" I said.

"And Tess."

Chapter Twelve

"AND TESS? THE THREE OF THEM? I mean, what about them?"

"Let me get us under way, and then I'll try to explain."

I watched as he maneuvered us out of the tight parking space and into the street. Michael, Rosalind, and Tess? Could Michael have been involved with Rosalind? But that didn't make sense. Jeremy and his father wouldn't be doing business with Michael's company if he had been.

A few minutes later, we were on High Street, headed away from downtown. "Right, then. I was about to explain about my wife."

"And Michael."

"It's more about Rosalind's awkwardness around Michael, which has carried over to Tess, I'm afraid."

"Rosalind is awkward around Michael? I've never seen the two of them together."

"No, you were out when he arrived tonight. But I'm sure Tess noticed. I want to explain to you, so that you can explain to her."

"Can't Michael explain whatever it is?"

"I'm not sure Michael understands what it is, or even if he has noticed."

"I see."

"You don't, of course. Let me try to do a better job of this. I don't want you to get the wrong idea about Rosalind. She—" He hesitated, then, with a wave of his hand, continued, "She's a bit nervy. More so, since the miscarriages. But she really is a wonderful person—bright and talented. We met when she came to work for our company. Hildegard referred her, as a matter of fact."

"Hildegard? Why would Hildegard refer—?

"Sorry—I thought someone had mentioned it. Hildegard owns one of the top office temp firms in London. Any type of office assistance one happens to need on a temporary basis, from secretaries to accountants and technical consultants."

"And Hildegard referred Rosalind to your company," I repeated, to make sure I had gotten it straight. Hildegard, the bird-watcher, owned a high-profile office temp firm, and she had brought Jeremy and Rosalind together. And now, she and the Stillman family were vacationing here in St. Regis during the same week. Were they here at the same time every year?

"My father had mentioned to Hildegard that we were looking for a computer consultant."

"Rosalind is a computer consultant?" I hadn't meant for it to come out with quite that note of incredulity.

But Jeremy smiled. "I know. You wouldn't guess it to look at her, but she is really quite adept with computers. A whiz, actually." He paused. "She's a lot of other things too."

Including good in bed? Shame, Lizzie. Slap yourself on the wrist for that one and pay attention to what the man's saying.

"But," Jeremy said, "what I want to explain is why she's uncomfortable around Michael. You see, we first met Michael about seven years ago in the States. I was out on my own—or rather working for a company other than my father's. That company had business dealings with Donovan Pharmaceuticals. Michael and I did some work together on a couple of projects, and we began to socialize. That was how he and Roz came to meet."

Jeremy stopped at a traffic light. I waited for him to go on with what he was saying.

"You see, both Michael and Roz were going through a bad patch at the time. Roz had miscarried again for the third time a few months earlier. The doctor she was seeing had cautioned her about getting pregnant again. The truth is we were battling a bit about that. I didn't want her to risk her health. She insisted she was going to give me my heir."

"And Michael? What was the bad patch he was going through?"

"Shortly after we began to see Michael socially, he and Tess had their breakup. We never even met Tess. We were going to have dinner with the two of them when we could coordinate our schedules, but then Tess was gone—had left Michael. And the poor chap was in a bad way. I suppose that was the reason."

"The reason for what?"

"That he and Roz struck up a friendship. Fellow feeling, you see. Both suffering through a loss."

"But you were there, and you had also had a loss."

"Yes, but Roz was upset with me because I had vetoed the idea of trying for another baby."

"What was it that happened between Michael and Rosalind?"

"Not an affair, if that's what you're thinking. Not that. But Roz did share a bit more of her feelings with Michael than she likes to think about now. As she told me later, she felt worse than if she had slept with him, because she had told him her intimate thoughts."

"But if your wife feels that way, isn't it awkward having Michael as a business associate?"

"You see, that's the thing of it. Michael doesn't seem to realize what Roz shared with him. How much of herself. Michael's the gregarious type—" Jeremy glanced at me and smiled. "Part of the American character, isn't it?"

"Not all of us. And for a reserved English type, you're being rather forthcoming."

"The aftereffect of my sojourn in the States. But, as I was saying, being the gregarious type, Michael doesn't realize that for someone as reserved as Roz, self-revelation can be embarrassing."

"You've talked to him about it?"

"Indirectly. I wanted to feel him out a bit. The truth is, I think when Roz was rattling on, his mind was on his own problems. And, in fact, they only shared a few lunches and attended the theater a time or two together. All open and aboveboard. Michael even asked my permission to escort her. I was tied up with a rather time-consuming project at work, and Roz was on her own."

"Didn't Michael have work to do?"

"Michael is one of those people who manages to get a prodigious amount of work done while taking two-hour lunch breaks and playing racquetball three times a week."

Good for Michael. "So from what you've gathered, Michael found nothing out of the ordinary about his conversations with Rosalind. Nothing out of the ordinary between two people who were becoming friends."

"And in Roz's mind, those conversations are still enough to make her cringe. She had a rather difficult childhood, you see. Her father was not the best of parents. And there was an unpleasant incident when she was at university. All of which she more or less poured out in the course of her conversations with Michael."

"Rather like talking to a therapist?"

"Exactly," Jeremy said. He turned onto a side street. "Almost there. Would you mind explaining what I've told you to Tess? I don't want her to misinterpret Roz's reaction to seeing Michael."

"Hadn't Rosalind seen Michael at all in the past six years?"

"On occasion. But she always had time to prepare herself before hand."

"To put on her social face?"

"But this evening, she didn't have time to do that. She'd had such a wretched day with Benjy and his upset over Dee that she was practically in tears. My parents had taken Benjy upstairs. Then there was Michael coming through the door, and Tess coming down the stairs. Poor Roz looked from Michael to Tess and bolted upstairs past Tess without saying a word. I tried to smooth it over, but I could tell Tess wondered what was going on."

Jeremy turned onto another street, and I saw the sign for the hospital.

"Lizzie, I don't want my wife caught up as an innocent third party in someone else's marital difficulties. I know what I'm asking is an imposition—"

"No, it isn't. I'll be happy to tell Tess what you've told me. Her life is complicated enough already without any unnecessary misunderstandings."

"Yes, I rather thought it might be when I heard about the baby. Is she likely to take him back, do you think?"

"Do you know why she left him?"

"More or less. Michael and I also had several conversations, sharing our marital woes."

"Everyone's friend and confidant is our Michael."

"And you don't like him very much at all, do you?"

"Michael and I don't have a great deal in common." Jeremy turned into the parking lot of the hospital, a modern, multi-floored building with glowing signs over its entrances. If Tess was having trouble with the baby, this hospital looked capable of coping. "Michael's not a complete rotter, you know," Jeremy said as he drew up in front of the hospital main entrance. "He once did me a rather enormous favor."

"In the name of good business relations?"

"This particular favor wouldn't be found in any of the business manuals. Lizzie, I think he honestly does regret having hurt Tess."

"And from now on, he'll be faithful and loyal?"

"Quite possibly."

I reached for my door handle. "Thanks for the ride, Jeremy."

"Not at all. Thank you for agreeing to speak to Tess for me. Are you going to be all right getting back?"

"Sure. I'll get a taxi or get Michael to give me a lift. Maybe he and Tess are ready to leave by now."

"Let's hope. Give them Roz's and my best."

"Will do. See you later." I watched his car pull away, and then I took a deep breath and turned toward the hospital.

Chapter Thirteen

MICHAEL WAS THERE IN THE WAITING ROOM the nurse had pointed out to me. I stood in the doorway for a moment watching him stare out the window. Then he turned and saw me. "Lizzie—I'm glad you're here."

"Are you? How is she? What happened?"

He shook his head and came over, dropping down into one of the armchairs. I sat down in the chair across from him. "What happened to Tess, Michael?"

He closed his eyes and rubbed his hand over his face. "It was my fault. We were having an argument. I was pressuring her to marry me. She was sitting there on the bed, and then she stood up to tell me to go, that she needed to be alone for a while—" He shook his head again. "And she just passed out. I tried to catch her, but she was on the floor before I could get to her."

"What do the doctors say?"

"They say, sit down in the waiting room and wait."

"Do they know what happened? Is she conscious yet?"

"She wasn't when they put me out of the room about an hour ago." Michael stood up. "Do you want a cup of coffee?"

"Thanks, but I never touch the stuff."

"Oh, yeah, that's right." He looked around the room as if he were searching for something. Then he wandered back toward the window. If he was acting, it was a magnificent performance.

"Why didn't you call the paramedics?"

"The paramedics? That never even occurred to me. I saw her pass out and all I could think about was getting her to the hospital."

I nodded. "You probably did the best thing just putting her in the car and bringing her here." But having conceded that much, I couldn't resist probing a bit. "Of course, it is lucky that you knew where to find the hospital. But you've vacationed here before, haven't you?"

"Last spring. I had some business in the area and I decided to take a few days off. I knew there was a hospital. Edith told me the street." He turned from the window and took a few steps toward the door. "What's taking them so long?"

"They're probably doing tests. Jeremy Stillman gave me a ride over. He said to give you his and Roz's best."

Michael paced back to the window. "If anything happens to Tess or the baby— I shouldn't have pressured her."

"You shouldn't have gotten her pregnant."

"You think I did it deliberately."

"Didn't you?"

"Tess was there too."

"And obviously not in her right mind."

Michael shook his head. He came back over and sat down. "Lizzie, you're really one of a kind."

"So are you, Michael. Did I mention I was the victim of an attempted mugging while I was in London?"

"An attempted mugging? Are you joking?"

"Completely serious. It happened as I was leaving Madame Tussaud's. A short, ugly man with a scar tried to steal your shopping bag."

"The shopping bag? That was what he tried to snatch? Not your purse?"

"Not my purse. He wanted the shopping bag. I held on, and he shoved me. I fell into the street in front of a bus. The driver was able to stop in time. Otherwise I wouldn't be here."

"My God!" Michael surged to his feet. He frowned down at me. "This man—" He cleared his throat. "Describe the man again."

"About five-nine and stocky build. Short, sandy blond hair. Blue eyes. One of his eyes . . . it looked like someone had slashed a knife down that side of his face and almost put his eye out. He had a kind of zigzagging scar through his brow, down his cheek."

"That's a pretty complete description," Michael said. He was trying to smile but not quite managing to pull it off. "Bet you even noticed what he was wearing."

"No," I said. "I was too busy noticing how mean his eyes were."

Michael rubbed his hand over his chin. "I'm sorry, Lizzie."

"That I was mugged? But that had nothing to do with you, did it?"

"No, of course not." He jammed his hands into the pockets of his khakis. "I can't take this waiting. I'm going to go find someone who can tell us what's going on."

He went to do that. I leaned my head back against the chair and closed my eyes.

Michael had recognized my description of my mugger. It had not been a random incident on a busy London street. That man had wanted the bag Michael had given me.

* * *

The doctor came before Michael returned. In her fifties, a tan shirtwaist dress under her white coat, she exuded calm. "I'm Dr. Nielson. I was told Mr. Donovan was waiting in here."

"He stepped out for a moment. He said he was going to go look for someone to tell us something. I'm Lizzie Stuart, a friend of Ms. Alvarez. Is she going to be all right?"

"She should be. She's conscious now. From what we can tell, the fainting spell was caused by a drop in her blood pressure. And she seems to have hit her head when she fell."

"Is that why she was unconscious for so long?"

"That's what we believe. But I want to do some additional tests. I'm going to keep her here overnight."

"May I see her, please? I'll only stay a moment."

The doctor tapped her pen on the edge of the clipboard in her hand and considered my request. "Only for a moment. I want her to get some rest."

Tess opened her eyes and smiled up at me. "Hi."

"Hi, yourself. How do you feel?"

"A slight headache, but nothing spectacular. I felt woozy when I tried to sit up."

"Then don't try to sit up."

Tess peered past me. "Where's Michael?"

"The men's room, I think. He should be along in a moment."

Tess looked too washed out to suit me. I hesitated, then I asked the question I had to ask. "About Michael—he said you passed out while the two of you were arguing—"

"Discussing. I'd had enough for one day, so I stood up to put him out and suddenly the floor was coming up to meet me."

"I've never fainted before. It must be a weird experience."

"Not anything you want to try." Tess's fingers gripped the sheet. "They think everything's all right with the baby."

"That's good, isn't it?"

"Yes." The word came out as a sob. "I think I want this baby, Lizzie."

"Then I guess you should have it."

"I still need to decide what to do about Michael."

I leaned over to kiss her on the cheek. "Think about it tomorrow, Scarlett. I'm going back to the Gull's Nest and eat your chocolate bar."

"I don't think I could handle it tonight anyway," she said as I left.

Michael and I met in the hallway as I was coming out of Tess's room.

"Tess? The doctor said she's awake."

I nodded.

He rushed past me.

I heard him said, "Tess—sweetheart, you scared me to death. Darling, I'm so sorry—"

I stepped away from the door. I needed to find a telephone and call a taxi. I didn't feel up to parrying with Michael anymore tonight. All I wanted to do was to crawl into bed. Preferably my own bed in my own room back in Drucilla, Kentucky.

Michael knew something about the thug who had tried to mug me.

Sneeze on Sunday and spend the whole week trying to keep one step ahead of the Devil. Hester Rose had been right about that.

Chapter Fourteen

I lifted my head from my pillow, told the birds to shut up, then flopped back down again. When I woke up the second time, so much sunlight flooded the room that I knew I had overslept. But it took me another ten minutes to convince myself that I needed and wanted to get out of bed.

My eyes felt as if I had been walking through a sandstorm. I had a crick in my neck, and my right arm was numb because I had been lying on it. I staggered over to the sink and splashed cold water in my face.

I'd fallen asleep at some point after my last glance at the clock radio at 2:49 A.M. Before that I had tossed and turned as I enjoyed a technicolor, looping replay of yesterday's events.

It was now 8:26 A.M. Breakfast ended at nine, assuming that after yesterday Sarah and Edith were even up to providing breakfast. Not that I was that concerned about food, but missing breakfast also meant I would miss an opportunity to talk to and observe the Stillmans and Hildegard Martin.

During the taxi ride from the hospital, I had admitted to myself that even if Michael knew something about the man who had mugged me, the mugging was one thing and Dee's murder could be another matter entirely. As far as I knew, no scarred thug had been hanging around the Gull's Nest.

I tucked the sheet in and pulled the comforter up. It wasn't much, but it would be one less thing for Sarah and Edith to do. They should not have to think of making people's beds at a time like this.

That telephone call. Could the thug have made the telephone call that Sarah said she'd received on Monday afternoon? A telephone call from a man who had given her a bogus message from her neighbor, a message that had made her leave the house in the middle of her baking.

But, no, that didn't work. There was no way that a thug from London could have known Sarah baked on Monday. Or known the name of Sarah's neighbor. Unless he was a thug from St. Regis who had made a special trip up to London. Or unless Michael had remembered Sarah's baking schedule and told the thug about it. But why on earth would Michael have done that? Why would Michael want Dee dead?

Quinn had been right when he questioned the idea of an affair between Michael and Dee. Why would Michael suggest Tess stay here if he was concerned about what Dee might tell her? Unless he had hoped to make Tess jealous. But then that would give him even less of a motive for killing Dee.

A shower. I needed a shower, and then I would try to make my foggy brain work.

As I was trying to manipulate the dangling showerhead and rub soap over myself at the same time, I realized I needed to go up to Tess's room and have another look at the Winnie the Pooh Michael had sent her.

Tess would be back from the hospital any time now, and I must do it before she arrived. Of course, I could wait until she came and go up to her room with her, and while carrying on a casual conversation, I could pick up the figurine and play with it. That was assuming it was sitting out on her dressing table. But I had no idea what she had done with it after she left my room. She might even have given it back to Michael.

No. It would be better to go look for it now. Then I would be able to shake and prod Winnie without having to worry about being too obvious. Of course, I had looked at the damn thing when I unwrapped the package, but maybe I had missed something.

But why would Michael have given it to Tess, if it was something someone wanted? For safekeeping? But then he had come straight to St. Regis himself. Anyone who was following him would connect him with Tess and know that she might have it.

All right. Enough thinking. Just go upstairs and have another look. Unless Michael had locked Tess's door when they were leaving. No, not likely. He had been carrying her. But maybe Edith had gone up and locked the door later.

I finished toweling off and reached for my robe. Only one way to find out.

As I pulled on teal blue shorts and a matching top, opting for sneakers rather than sandals, I rehearsed what I would say if someone saw me. Nothing suspicious here, folks. I want to pick up a gift for Tess—something to cheer her up. I was thinking perhaps a scarf, and I wanted to have another look at the new blouse she showed me. I wanted to make sure I remembered the colors.

As I started up the stairs to the third floor, I could hear voices in the downstairs hallway. I stopped to listen. Sarah and Benjamin. Rosalind. And Benjy, who was still unhappy, judging from the loud

"No!" he had just uttered. That left Edith, Hildegard, Pamela, and Jeremy.

On the third floor landing, I paused to eye the door of the room that Jeremy and Rosalind shared with their son. It was closed, no sound came from behind it.

Down the hall, at the back of the third floor, was Dee's room. That door was closed too. Had the police searched Dee's room yet? Would they? Of course they would if they decided it was murder.

In the meantime, maybe I could just peep inside and— No, don't be stupid. Getting caught in Tess's room was one thing. Being found in Dee's would be harder to explain.

Besides, I didn't even know what I was looking for. And the detectives on the case, Cordner and Quinn, were capable of conducting their own investigation. So concentrate on what I did know something about.

The knob of Tess's door turned under my hand, and I stepped inside, leaving the door ajar. I went over to the closet and took out the blouse, a scarlet and hot pink concoction that suited Tess's dramatic coloring.

I held it up to verify the possibilities in terms of accessorizing with scarf or earrings. I really did intend to buy her a welcome home gift. Having established my veracity, I got down to the business at hand.

The Winnie the Pooh figurine was there on the dressing table. I picked it up and turned it over. Nothing on the bottom except the manufacturer's name. I shook it. Nothing sloshed or rattled. It looked solid. I prodded Pooh's chubby body and his honey jar. Rubbed at the paint. Nothing. I was beginning to feel like an idiot. It was a figurine. Plain and simple. It was not whatever the mugger had thought it might be.

I put Pooh back in his place beside Tess's makeup bag and the framed photograph of her family. The Alvarez family consisted of mother, father, Tess, and her four sisters. In the studio photograph, the sisters—all five of them—stood behind the parents. Tess stood to the right of her two older sisters, the middle child of the five. A handsome group. Beautiful in the case of the women.

Tess's sisters were all married. Together they had provided their parents with eleven, soon to be twelve, grandchildren. A houseful and then some when the daughters, their husbands and children, and the assorted aunts, uncles, and cousins gathered for a family occasion.

According to Tess, Michael had managed to fit right in from the first time she had taken him home to meet her family. He had praised her mother's cooking and charmed her sisters. He had played gin rummy with her Aunt Sophia and accompanied one of Tess's nieces on the piano when the teenager was persuaded to sing the song she was doing in the school play. Then Michael had retired with the men to the den to drink beer and watch basketball on TV. Tess's family had all loved him.

They had been shocked and horrified when Tess decided to divorce him. She hadn't told them why she was doing it. She hadn't told me either. Now I knew.

I walked back over to the closet and hung up her blouse.

What now? Downstairs to see who was still around. Then call Quinn and see if he had spoken to Cordner yet about Michael. I couldn't ask him that on the telephone. Maybe I could meet him again. Go with him to the police station. I had changed my mind about not wanting to be there when he told Cordner about my suspicions concerning Michael. Michael had changed my mind last night when he reacted to my description of the mugger.

I eased open Tess's door and slipped back out into the hallway. Then I remembered that I was supposed to have a legitimate reason for being in her room. I pulled the door shut, making no attempt to be quiet about it.

But I almost jumped out of my skin when the door to Dee's room opened and Edith came out. She was carrying a navy blue dress over her arm.

"Good morning, Lizzie." The lines in her face had deepened overnight, but she tried to smile. "Would you like your breakfast now?"

"No—thank you for offering, but I'm not terribly hungry."

"Are you sure? Some neighbors were by first thing this morning with more food than we have room to store."

I shook my head. "My stomach isn't quite up to it."

"Neither is mine. A strange custom, isn't it? But food is always supposed to make one feel better."

"Yes." I nodded toward the dress over her arm. "Is that for Dee? For her—"

Edith took mercy on my stammering and held up the dress. "One of Dee's favorites. I thought she'd like to wear it." She shook her head, shaking away the huskiness in her voice. Then she went on briskly. "When they release her body, that is. They said perhaps later today."

"Is there anything I can do to help, Edith?"

She hesitated.

"Please, if there is anything."

"I wonder if you would . . . there's something I need to return. Dee seems to have borrowed something. I need to send it back to the person to whom it belongs."

"Of course, just tell me who to take it to."

Edith turned back to Dee's door. I darted after her, following her into the room. Dee's color scheme was white. White curtains at the windows, white comforter on her bed. White cushion on her white wicker armchair. A small white desk by the window with a white fountain pen in a white porcelain holder. White bottles on her white dressing table. The room would have been virginal in its whiteness, if not for the posters on the walls.

On each side of the dressing table and on the wall that the bed was pushed against, there were movie posters of Madonna. Madonna as the sexy chanteuse in *Dick Tracy*. Madonna as Argentina's first lady Eva Peron in *Evita*. Madonna as lawyer Willem DaFoe's lethal client in *Body of Evidence*, her flirtation with film noir.

Aside from the Madonna posters, on the table beside Dee's bed there was a portable CD player and several CDs. Madonna, blonde and sultry, pouted up from the CD that was on the top of the small pile. Obviously Dee had been a Madonna fan. What had she liked so much about her?

But there was something else—a small painting on the wall facing Dee's bed. It was a black and white abstract in a black lacquer frame. I stepped closer to peer at it. It looked rather like two ducks dancing. Or tulips bowing to each other. Or two people holding hands—or maybe holding something else.

The painting was cleverly done. Humorous, as if the artist were saying, "Here's my version of the Rorschach test. Read into it what you will."

"Pardon me," Edith said, moving around me to get to the painting. She reached up and removed it from the wall. Her mouth was tight when she turned back to me. "Would you return this to its owner, please?"

"Who is the owner?"

"The artist," Edith said. "Her name is there." She indicated the signature as I took the painting. The signature in the bottom right corner was a slashing *Felicity*, followed by an *H* that disappeared into the scrawl of a last name.

"I . . . uh . . . I can't make out the last name," I said.

"Hollingsworth. Felicity Hollingsworth. I'll give you the address of her studio." Edith hesitated again. "If you're sure you wouldn't mind taking it around to her."

"No, not at all," I said. Then conscience got the better of me. "But, Edith, I'm not sure we should remove anything from Dee's room until the police . . . in case the police should want to have a look—"

"They've looked in this room. They looked yesterday before they left. They took Sarah's baking supplies from the kitchen, then they came up here." Edith raked her fingers through her hair, leaving it standing in little tufts. "That Inspector said it was 'a matter of routine,' if we had no objections, of course." Edith nodded her head toward the wall. "The painting was right there for him and that American policeman to see if they'd had any interest in it. What they were interested in was pawing through Dee's closet and the drawers of her desk and dressing table. Looking for what, they didn't say."

Well, they hadn't been looking for artwork. They hadn't known about Felicity Hollingsworth at the time. "Did they find anything that they thought was interesting?"

"Nothing. And they seemed disappointed about that."

"Edith, I'm sure they didn't mean to upset you. It is routine when someone dies under sus—" I started again, "Under unexplained circumstances."

Edith nodded. "I know. I've seen it often enough on the telly, haven't I? I just don't like it when it's my Dee." Her blue eyes met mine. "On those shows, they always find something, don't they? Something in the victim's life—"

"I'm sure there's nothing in Dee's life. Even if she were . . . even if someone did this . . . I'm sure it wasn't because of anything she had done."

"That would make it worse," Edith said. "If someone decided to kill her when she hadn't done anything, that would be worse." She gestured at the painting. "Please, if you would return that to its owner, it would be a great help."

"Yes, I will."

"Thank you, Lizzie. I do appreciate it." Edith frowned. "I didn't even think to ask if you'd mind walking into town—"

"No, I was going anyway. I want to pick up a back-from-the-hospital gift for Tess. That was what I was doing in her room. I wanted to have another look at her new blouse so that I could find her a scarf to go with it."

"That's a lovely thought. I'm sure it will make her feel better."

"I hope so. You haven't heard anything this morning, have you? Last night, the doctor said she wanted to keep Tess overnight for tests."

"No, no one's called this morning," Edith said. "And, please, do forgive us for not waiting up last night to hear how she was. When Jeremy came back at about the same time as his parents and little Benjy, we realized we were all of us done in."

"So was I. So I was glad to be able to go right upstairs to bed."

"But I should have thought to ask right away how Tess was—"

"Edith, there are times when we can't be expected to remember all the niceties. I'm going to go down and call the hospital, and then I'll be off."

"You're sure about breakfast?"

"Positive. I'm not at all hungry." Hungry, no. Guilty, yes. Because I couldn't take the painting back to Felicity Hollingsworth without first showing it to Cordner and Quinn. And I didn't think that was what Edith had in mind.

I stopped by my room and got my backpack and sunglasses. Sunscreen too. It looked sunny enough outside to need it.

No one was in the downstairs foyer by the time I came down. The Stillmans and Hildegard had probably gone out. Sarah might be in back, in the kitchen or her bedroom.

I dialed Ed Janowitz's number. It rang. No one answered. And, unlike many homes in the United States, there seemed to be no answering machine.

Glancing toward the stairs, I hung up and reached for the telephone book. Then I saw the list of local phone numbers on a card stuck in a corner of the bulletin board. The number for the hospital was there.

When Edith came downstairs a few minutes later, I was replacing the receiver. "I called the hospital."

"Is Tess going to be released today?"

"She was out of her room. But she hasn't signed out yet. So I suppose we'll have to wait and see. In the meantime, I'll go take this back." I picked up the painting from the side table. "Do you have a bag of some sort that I could put it in?"

"Of course. I'm sorry, I should have thought of that." Edith bustled away through the lounge door, and I wondered if I had been wise to request another shopping bag for a package I had been asked to deliver.

But this was Cornwall, not London. And my mugger was probably still plying his trade in the metropolis. Unless he was as hot on Michael's trail as he had been in London.

Edith came back with a department store shopping bag and some white tissue paper. We wrapped the painting and tucked it into the bag. She came outside to wave me off. I left her standing there on her doorstep as I started down the hill toward the path above the beach.

I would go around to the police station and ask for Cordner. With luck he would be there, even if Quinn was out who-knows-where. But it wasn't as if I could expect John Quinn to sit twiddling his thumbs until I called him with something else on my mind. Except I would have felt better if I could have spoken to him about this before I went to Cordner.

My next thought brought me to a dead stop. What if Cordner confiscated the painting? What if he wouldn't let me deliver it to Felicity Hollingsworth because it might be evidence of some sort? How would I explain that to Edith? Would I say that I happened to run into the Detective Inspector, and with his X-ray eyes he had seen what was in my shopping bag and demanded that I surrender the painting? Demanded that I surrender the painting that she said he hadn't even noticed?

I had reached the steps leading down to the pedestrian walk. I sat down on the top one. The rough cement, heated by the sun, would not have been my seat of choice. But I needed to collect my thoughts.

I swatted at an insect as it buzzed past my face. "Think, Lizzie."

When the sergeant on duty informed him that I was there, Cordner came out into the vestibule to greet me.

"I hope I haven't caught you in the middle of something."

"Not at all, Professor Stuart. Please come along to my office."

When I was seated in one of the chairs opposite his desk, I opened the shopping bag and took out Felicity Hollingsworth's abstract. "I thought you might want to see this," I said as I passed it across the desk to him.

"I've seen this before. It was hanging on Dee Crump's bedroom wall."

"Look at the signature."

Cordner did. When he looked up, there was a question in his eyes. Before he could ask, I said, "Dee's aunt—her Aunt Edith—asked me to return it to Ms. Hollingsworth. She said Dee must have borrowed it, and she wants to return it to its owner."

"Does she?"

I waited while he examined the painting and its frame. "I need it back again. I just thought I should show it to you before I delivered it as I promised Edith I would."

"I think perhaps I should keep this until the lab—"

"Oh—but I've already called Felicity Hollingsworth—"

"You've what?"

"From the telephone booth on the corner. I wanted to make sure she would be at her studio. And then it occurred to me that I should show it to you before I took it back."

Cordner smiled. "Professor, has anyone ever told you that you're less than convincing as an actress?"

So much for that. "All right . . . I did call Felicity first in case you wanted to keep the painting. But I promised Edith—"

Cordner held up his hand. "How soon is Felicity Hollingsworth expecting you?"

"Within the next hour."

"You might have given me a bit more time."

"I did intend to. But she said she was meeting someone for lunch, and she wasn't sure about her plans for the rest of the afternoon. She asked me to please bring whatever I had for her straight over."

"So you didn't tell her what it is you're bringing?"

"I said I had a package someone had asked me to bring round to her. I thought if she wasn't expecting the painting she had given Dee that perhaps her reaction—"

"Yes," Cordner said. "However, it seems I'll have to rely on you to relay an account of that reaction."

"I'm afraid you will. She might wonder, if I brought along police officers."

"I would imagine she has heard about Dee Crump's death by now."

"In a town the size of St. Regis, I would think so. So you haven't spoken to her?"

"Not yet." Cordner frowned down at the painting again. "Damn," he said.

"I'm sorry. I know I shouldn't have— But I did promise Edith and—"

Cordner's smile was a bit thin this time. "And you found yourself with two competing obligations."

I nodded. "I'm so glad you understand. By the way, have you heard from John Quinn this morning?"

"Briefly." Cordner stood up. "May I get you a cup of tea, Professor?"

I stood too. "No, I'd better be going. About Quinn—"

"I spoke to him around eight this morning. He said he was going with Ed Janowitz and his wife into Penzance."

"Oh," I said. "I just assumed he was interested in the case."

"He *is* on holiday," Cordner said.

"Yes. Of course. Well, I'd better be off."

Cordner walked with me back to the vestibule. "Please check in with me later, Professor Stuart."

"Of course, Inspector. A full report."

Cordner looked from my face to the bag I was carrying. "When you arrive, be sure to remind her that you were asked to do this."

"As in 'I'm only the delivery person and my whereabouts are

known'?"

Cordner did not appreciate the joke. "This is— I wonder if I should even allow you to— "

"I'm going to be late," I said, scooting toward the door. "I'll check back with you later."

In spite of Cordner's second thoughts about my mission, I was not too concerned. Not knees-knocking concerned anyway. As far as Felicity Hollingsworth would know, I was only doing a favor for Dee's aunt. She might not like what the return of the painting implied, but the woman was hardly likely to kill me over the insult. Especially not in her own studio.

And I had promised Edith, who certainly wouldn't have asked me to do it if she had any reason to think Felicity Hollingsworth might be responsible for her niece's death.

Chapter Fifteen

FELICITY HOLLINGSWORTH CAME TO THE DOOR with her short blonde hair still wet from the shower and a towel knotted around herself. She was no more than 5'4" with a pleasant, freckled face and a wide smiling mouth. Still she managed to pull off "coolly sophisticated" with nothing more than the expression in her blue eyes. A good trick, that. Wish I could learn it.

"Hello," I said. "I'm Lizzie Stuart. We spoke on the telephone."

Felicity Hollingsworth eyed my shopping bag. "Now this is intriguing," she said. Her voice was throaty and as amused as her glance. "Who has sent me what? And why are you playing delivery person?"

"May I come in?" I asked. "This might take a few minutes to explain."

"Hmm," she said. "Well, you don't look as if you'll do me bodily harm. Come in. Pour yourself a drink. The bar's over there. I'll be back as soon as I get some clothes on." She disappeared down the hallway and into the back of the house that Edith had described as her studio. But she apparently lived here as well. In fact, there was nothing to indicate that she did anything but live here. There were a few paintings scattered about on the white walls, seascapes—washes of blues and purples and lavender—that picked up the colors of the cushions on the upscale wicker and knotty wood furniture. But nothing to indicate that this was the studio of a working artist.

She must be able to confine her work to one room. Maybe it was easier when you were working on canvas. With papers and books it was more of a challenge. Now that I had a whole house to myself, I was starting to overflow from the den I had claimed as my office into the other rooms. Books were finding their way onto the kitchen table. Manuscript pages and index cards were establishing residence on the living room sofa.

Neatness when you were in the midst of creating anything took effort. Maybe—probably—Felicity Hollingsworth had a housekeeper.

I selected a bottle of orange juice from the varied choices available in the mini refrigerator under the bar and filled a glass with ice from the bucket.

About five minutes later, just as I finished glancing around the room and sat down on the sofa, Felicity came back. She was buttoning up the sleeveless white blouse that she was wearing with a white knee-length skirt and bare feet.

I thought of Dee's room. White on white. Except for the Madonna posters and Felicity's painting.

"Let me pour myself a gin and tonic, and then I'll sit down and you can tell me all about it."

She brought her drink over and sat down on the sofa beside me. Or rather she folded herself onto the sofa, legs tucked under her. I was always impressed by women who could sit like that and actually stand afterwards. "You have something for me," she said.

"I was asked to bring you this," I said as I drew the painting out of the shopping bag and held it out to her.

She tilted her head to one side. "Dee Crump asked you to bring this to me?"

"Then you . . . you haven't heard about Dee?"

"Heard what about her?"

"About what happened yesterday."

"Yesterday I was incommunicado. I needed to get some work done, so I didn't answer the phone or the door. I was tempted to do the same today, but I broke down and picked up the phone on my way to get another cup of coffee. That was your call."

"And you haven't spoken to anyone else?"

"No one. The phone has rung twice since you called. I've ignored it." Felicity Hollingsworth reached over and took a cigarette from the porcelain box on the coffee table. "What happened yesterday?"

I watched her light the cigarette with the matching white porcelain lighter. "Dee died yesterday."

Felicity Hollingsworth choked. She coughed twice and then stabbed out the cigarette in the ashtray on the table. "Bloody hell! Died? How?"

"It seems to have been an allergic reaction. To peanuts. She ate a yummy ball and—"

"Her aunt makes those things."

"Yes. But somehow peanuts—"

"And so she died gasping for breath." Felicity Hollingsworth unfolded her legs and got to her feet. "Do you want a drink? Something stronger than that damn orange juice."

"No, thank you. It's too early for me."

"Not for me. Another gin is most definitely in order." She unscrewed the bottle and sloshed more of it into her glass. "So what do you have to do with all this?"

I got up and went over to the bar. "I'm a guest at The Gull's Nest.

I asked Edith, Dee's aunt, if I could do anything to help. She asked me to bring back the painting. She thought Dee must have borrowed it."

"Borrowed it." Felicity stirred her drink. "I just bet she thought that."

"That was what she said."

"And you do know why she said it, don't you?"

So much for subtle probing. I started to say "no" to her question. But Felicity Hollingsworth was giving me a straight-on look. "You mean because she probably doesn't approve of your sexual orientation?"

"Right you are." Felicity tossed back half her drink. "From what Dee said, I gathered that if her aunts knew of me—and obviously they did—they would not have approved. At least, Aunt Edith wouldn't have. I gathered Aunt Sarah might be something of a closet rebel."

I smiled. "Yes, I've gotten that impression."

Felicity finished her drink and refilled her glass from a bottle of Perrier. I took another sip of my orange juice as I looked around the room again.

"Nice place," I said.

"Thanks so much," she replied. "Shall we skip the bull dung?"

"The bull—"

"You're just panting to know, aren't you? That's why you brought the painting back for dear Aunt Edith."

"What is it that you think I want to know?"

"Whether I seduced sweet little Dee." Felicity's glance was still direct. "That cloddish boyfriend of hers was convinced I would contaminate her by looking at her."

"I heard she did some posing for you."

"You heard that?" Felicity came around the bar. She flicked another cigarette from the box and lit it. "Well, that, my friend, is all you're going to hear."

"Then why did you bring it up?"

Felicity turned. She stared at me for a long moment. Then she laughed. "Because, obviously, I sometimes still feel as if I need to defend my lifestyle."

"We all feel that way sometimes."

"All empathy, aren't you?"

"I try. I'm going to leave now."

"Just as well. I probably won't be decent company for a while." Felicity stubbed out the cigarette and followed me to the door.

"Did you know Dee planned to move to London?" I asked.

"I knew. I suggested it."

"Why?"

"Because there was nothing for her here. What? Marriage to her cloddish suitor?"

"She told me she wanted to lose herself for a while."

"Sometimes, the great philosopher said, that's the only way to find yourself."

"Do you live in London during the rest of the year?" I asked as I opened the door.

"I have a flat there. But I didn't invite Dee to share it. I like my privacy."

I nodded. "You should probably expect to hear from the police. They think there's something suspicious about Dee's death."

"What did you say?"

I looked from her colorless face to the fingers digging into my forearm. "I said—"

She let go of my arm and turned away, her back to me. "Bloody hell!" She whirled back around. "Are you telling me that they think that someone deliberately did this?"

"Dee's death was unexpected. They're investigating."

"Because they think she was murdered?"

The word hung there between us.

"Because they think it might not have been—" I nodded. "Yes, because they think it might be murder."

"So, of course, they'll want to talk to me."

"They've been talking to everyone that Dee— To her friends and acquaintances." Or, at least, I assumed they had. I had no idea whom they had talked to other than Sean and the guests at the hotel. Cordner had not mentioned his interview schedule. Was he still waiting for the lab reports on Dee? I hadn't thought to ask.

Felicity was staring at the painting on the coffee table. Or maybe she was staring at her cigarette box, wanting another one.

"Good-bye," I said.

"Having dropped your bombshell," she said. "Cheers, Lizzie Stuart."

I closed the door behind me and stepped from the shade of the archway back out into the sunlight. Felicity's neighbor was sitting at a pottery wheel in her yard. She was singing to herself as she worked.

Bearer of bad news. That was me. And I still didn't know a whole lot more than I had before about Dee's relationship with Felicity. Lovers or not?

And did it even matter? Let Cordner find out if he wanted to know.

Chapter Sixteen

I FOUND A SCARF FOR TESS in the first shop I tried. Probably because my heart wasn't into shopping. I was happy finding something that Tess would like rather than driving myself crazy looking for exactly the right scarf.

I paid my money, accepted my purchase, and edged my way back out onto the crowded sidewalk. All around me, people were laughing, talking. Death on the cliff path had not cast gloom over St. Regis. Or did many of these people even know about what had happened?

There was a supermarket a few doors down. I went inside and picked up a hand basket. I found grapes, bottled water, and a newspaper, then added a bottle of orange juice and scooped up a cheese scone from the bakery case.

Efficiency in action. I was through the checkout line and back out on the sidewalk in less than ten minutes. It took me a bit longer to find a place to sit down. Finally I climbed up the hill, taking one of the streets that led away from the waterfront, and went into a small, shady park.

I sat down on an empty bench and took out my grapes and considered whether eating them without washing them first would result in E. coli or something else I didn't want to deal with. Sighing, I opened my bottled water and poured half of it over the bunch of grapes. Digging in my backpack, I found tissues. Grapes patted dry, orange juice and scone at the ready, I settled down for my impromptu breakfast picnic.

When the grapes and half of the scone—all I could choke down—were gone, I took out the newspaper, the St. Regis Record. I wanted to see if there was anything about Dee's death.

But the death that was garnering front page coverage was the one Hildegard Martin had mentioned. The nude woman who had been found in the Sussex field by schoolboys. POLICE MAKING LITTLE PROGRESS, the headline announced.

The story went on to explain that the police investigation had turned up no information about the identity of the victim or leads as to who might have strangled her and left her there in the field. A police artist's sketch showed a pretty young woman with wide-set eyes and a rounded chin. Her hair fell to her shoulders in cascading curls. High cheek bones set off a soft, curvy mouth.

According to the report her hair was blonde and her eyes blue. Age between twenty-five and thirty. A small rose tattoo on the wrist of her right arm. Not much help that. Nowadays everyone from corporate execs and lawyers to Hell's Angels and punk rockers had tattoos.

Hildegard had mentioned knife slashes on her breasts and legs. Had her killer left her face unmarked? But the sketch artist would have omitted any damage done to her face. That was not the kind of thing one would want to show in a family newspaper. And the point of the exercise was to have a relative, friend, or passing acquaintance see the photo, recognize her, and come forward to identify her. They wouldn't recognize a face swollen and distorted with cuts, bruises, and the aftermath of exposure to the elements. But the likelihood that anyone would come forward was getting slimmer. She had been found a week and a half ago.

I turned the page, looking for anything about Dee. On page two, edged from page one by murder and politics, I found a brief report of the "death of a local woman, Deirdre Crump, on the Coastal Path" yesterday morning. Apparently a fatal allergic reaction, although the authorities had yet to announce the cause of death. The report noted that Dee had worked as a housekeeper for her aunts, Edith and Sarah Crump, who had come to the area to open their hotel almost fourteen years ago. Dee was nineteen, a few months short of her twentieth birthday, and she had recently completed training as a computer programmer.

That was something I hadn't heard before. Dee had gotten training. Were there no jobs for computer programmers in St. Regis, or had she gone on working for her aunts out of a sense of loyalty?

But she was planning to leave them and go to London. Had she intended to support herself there as a computer programmer? Had she spoken to Hildegard, who owned a temp agency, or Rosalind, the computer consultant, about finding work? I would have to remember to ask them.

There was no mention of Sean Etling in the story, and only the statement that funeral arrangements were pending. I closed the newspaper and leaned back against the bench.

What now? Damn Quinn. How could he have just taken off to Penzance for the day. I needed to find out if he had spoken to Cordner about Michael. But if he had, wouldn't Cordner have said something when I stopped by his office?

Well, I needed to go back by to tell him about my meeting with Felicity Hollingsworth. I could tell him myself about my suspicions concerning Michael. I didn't need John Quinn to speak for me.

It was just that I had been counting on Quinn to present it to Cordner as one police officer to another. Something you might want to check into. Probably nothing to do with Dee Crump's death, but something might be up with the guy.

If I went in and told Cordner that I wanted him to investigate Michael, my best friend's ex-husband and a corporate vice president, he would probably think I was feebleminded. Dotty. A good British word that. Dotty Lizzie.

Well, what if he did? I wasn't. And I would have to make sure he understood that. Someone had tried to mug me, and I had reason to suspect Michael might know who that man was.

What reason? Cordner would say.

Michael's reaction when I told him about it, I would answer.

And why on earth wouldn't Detective Inspector Cordner be convinced by that? Had I even convinced Quinn? Maybe that was why he had gone to Penzance—to avoid the whole mess. But Janowitz had said Quinn was tenacious when it came to homicides. Apparently not when he had to deal with other sticky messes in the process.

Stuffing what was left of my breakfast into the plastic grocery bag, I stomped over to the trash receptacle and dropped it inside. I was about to toss in the newspaper too when it occurred to me I should save the article about Dee. I tore it out and dropped the rest of the paper into the trash.

"Oh come on, Ash! I do not believe that!" The protesting voice was teenage, female, and region-undefined American.

Her friend Ash responded in a voice that was as Southern as okra. "It's true. My great-aunt Geneva swore it was true. She saw it."

"That is so bizarre. You're telling me that this dead woman's body exploded?"

"Because back in those days some mountain people didn't believe in embalming. So her family wouldn't let the undertaker do it. And it was summertime, and all the gases that build up in a dead body when you don't embalm it built up—"

"And she exploded?"

"She sure did."

"Explain to me again why you want to be a doctor. I mean that is gross, Ash."

I had stopped on that street corner to get my bearings in St. Regis's maze-like streets. I wanted the most direct route back to the police station for my check-in with Cordner. While I was standing there, I had become aware of the two girls' conversation. Now I was shamelessly eavesdropping as I pretended to read the brochure about scenic day cruises that someone down the street had been handing out.

Sneaking another look at them, I almost burst out laughing. They looked like an ad in a teen magazine as they leaned there against the wall of the snack shop eating ice cream bars. One was blonde, one was redheaded, both were slender and fresh-faced. And they were chatting about exploding bodies.

Or had been. Now the redhead, who was "Ash," said, "Your daddy's going to be put out with us because we didn't go to that play."

"Who wants to sit on a pile of rocks and watch *Macbeth* when we could be sitting on the beach checking out guys?"

"Yeah, but we did tell him that we were going to go see the play. And I did kinda want to see it."

"You would. Ash, you have the absolutely weirdest taste in entertainment of anyone I know."

"I can't help it," Ash said. "*Macbeth* is one of my favorite plays." Her head had come up and her green eyes were staring straight into mine.

"Mine, too," I said without thinking.

She flashed me a grin, nodded her head, and turned her attention back to her ice cream bar.

I turned and stepped off the curb—right into the path of a car. The driver tooted on his horn, and I waved to him as I scurried out of his way.

I walked for almost half a block before I took a deep breath and glanced at my watch. Eleven thirty-eight. Did I have time to make it to the tour bus station on Upper High Street? Did I even want to have to explain to anyone what I was about to do?

I was not superstitious in the way that my grandmother was. No salt tossed over my shoulder when I spilled it. No fish on New Year's Day so I would swim in money. I had even walked under ladders and opened umbrellas in the house. I didn't believe in signs and portents and good luck charms.

But I did believe in synchronicity—in the flow of events in the universe and the possibility that what seems to be a coincidence might not be purely a matter of chance. I did believe that the universe sends us information. Information to which, as Carl Jung argued, we'd be wise to attend. Synchronicity. Not superstition. Not the same thing at all.

On Sunday evening, as I had been walking along the path into town, I looked at the bright sunshine and wondered how the

Merrimont Theatre handled the staging of matinee performances of *Macbeth*. On Monday, when Tess and I were in the tour bus office picking up our tickets for the day trip to Tintagel, I had noticed the flyers for the theater. I had reminded Tess that the Merrimont Theatre was one of the places I wanted to go to while we were in Cornwall. She had suggested we go to the matinee on Wednesday. That was today. But, of course, I hadn't thought of it again with everything that had happened yesterday.

I hadn't thought of it again until Ash, with her cat green eyes and her Southern drawl, looked straight at me and said, "*Macbeth* is one of my favorite plays." And just before that she had been telling her friend one of those gory tales my grandmother might have told.

I had stopped there on that street corner because I was trying to decide in which direction to go. And now I knew. I was going not to Cordner's office but instead to the Wednesday matinee performance of *Macbeth* at the Merrimont Theatre. I was going to go and sit there in that amphitheater overlooking the sea and wait for what came to mind.

Tess would laugh her head off. John Quinn—who had taken himself off to Penzance—would undoubtedly share her opinion. But if I had learned nothing else in my thirty-eight years, I had learned not to ignore what my instincts were telling me simply because it was taking my rational mind a bit longer to catch up.

And that was not superstition. It was good common sense.

"Yes, you're in time," the ticket clerk assured me. She was trying not to laugh because I was leaning against her counter for support. I had sprinted up that last hill. "Only one ticket?" she asked.

"Yes," I said, wondering if she saw someone else with me.

"I noticed you were with a friend when you came in on Monday for the Tintagel tour."

"Oh. She's not coming along," I said. And I needed to let Tess know where I was going to be.

Clutching my ticket, I looked outside to make sure the bus wasn't there yet. Then I dug into my backpack to find coins for the pay phone in the corner. "There's no telephone book here," I called to the clerk. "Do you have one I can use? I need to look up the number for the hospital."

"No need," she said. "I used to work there."

She rattled off the number for the main switchboard.

No one answered when the hospital operator connected me to Tess's room. The bus was pulling up as a nurse on Tess's floor came on the line. Tess was still not back in her room, she told me.

"But Mr. Donovan—Ms. Alvarez's husband—is here, if you would like to speak to him."

Ex-husband, I thought, but I didn't correct her. From the tone of her voice Michael had charmed her. "No," I said. "I haven't time to talk to him. But could I please leave a message for Ms. Alvarez?"

"Of course."

"Please tell her that Lizzie—"

"Lizzie?"

"Yes, she'll know who I am. Tell her that I'm going to the Merrimont Theatre because . . . because there's something I need to do. But I should be back by six o'clock, and I'll call then to check on her." The nurse repeated my message. I thanked her and hung up the phone.

"Enjoy the show," the ticket clerk called to me as I bolted out the door for the bus.

"My last passenger," the driver greeted me. "I thought we'd have to leave without you, dear heart."

"Sorry," I said. "I had to make a phone call."

The bus was not even half full. As Dee had said, in spite of the illusion one had of crowds jamming the streets of St. Regis, in some quarters tourism was not booming.

But this was the matinee performance. Maybe on a beautiful sunny day, most tourists would rather be at the beach than sitting on a pile of rocks watching a play about a man destroyed by ambition—his own and his wife's.

It would be interesting to see how this production company would deal with the matter of atmosphere. Hard to create visual gloom and foreboding on a splendid summer day. Hard to believe in the weird sisters stirring their cauldron. It was too fair a day for such foulness. "So foul and fair a day." Yesterday had been too.

I leaned my head back against the cushioned seat and closed my eyes. I was tired. As I had discovered when Hester Rose was dying, coping with death is exhausting.

Dammit, what was going on with Tess? Had the doctor changed her mind about everything being all right with the baby? I should have gone to the hospital to make sure she was all right. Of course, she was all right. She had to be.

And Michael was there playing the devoted spouse, and the one thing I didn't need was another encounter with Michael. If she wasn't at the hotel by the time I got back, I would go to the hospital. I couldn't be in two places at the same time, and I needed to do this now.

The driver had announced that the trip to the theater would take a little over an hour. Time enough for a nap, which was absolutely necessary if I was going to stay awake during the play. Maybe I needed vitamins.

Against a bleak stage backdrop, with fog swirling around them, the weird sisters spoke to Macbeth and Banquo, delivering their prophecy. By the time Macbeth and his lady huddled on the stone steps of their castle conferring about the sleeping grooms whom she urged him to go back upstairs and smear with Duncan's blood, I had forgotten that the sky was blue and it was early afternoon.

The talented cast and the imaginative staging that made full use of the bare rock amphitheater succeeded in luring me and the rest of the audience into the world of the play. Even as we munched on snacks purchased in the overpriced gift shop, we were drawn into the drama of ambition and murder unfolding in front of us.

At intermission, I made my way to the ladies' room. As always, there was a line.

"A lovely theater, isn't it?" the woman in front of me asked. She had the look of someone who would chat with anyone who was breathing.

"Yes, it is lovely."

"It took years and years to build. From scratch they did it, bringing the rocks and placing them by hand. They were from London, you know. A writer and his wife who moved into that house down the lane and thought how marvelous it would be to build an amphitheater overlooking the sea."

"I'm glad they had the idea," I said, as the line edged forward.

"So am I. I come here every chance I get. The production of *Great Expectations* earlier this summer was lovely. But I do enjoy Dickens, don't you?"

"Yes, I do."

"He's like Shakespeare in that, isn't he? Catching all the oddities of people and the things that they do to end up destroying themselves and all the people around them. But it does make you think, doesn't it?"

"Think? About what?"

"About the price to be paid for getting what you want." The woman shook her head. "Still, I can't help but feel sorry for her, can you? For Lady Macbeth, that is. Some women are like that, aren't they? Strong women who try to live their lives through their husbands."

"Yes, I suppose some do."

"Certain politicians' wives, for example." She gave me a sly look and smiled. "You do have a bit of that in the States, don't you, dear?"

I smiled back. "Yes. But so far, none of our political wives has actually encouraged her husband to murder his way to the top."

The woman laughed. Then she shook her head again. "But it does make you think."

"Yes, it does." About ambition gone awry. About lethal couples, locked in duets of love and murder. But what did any of that have to do with Dee's death or Michael's chicanery?

What had I gained by coming here? I had been watching and waiting for that revelation I had thought would come if I hopped on a bus and came to a matinee of *Macbeth.*

Maybe I had just needed an excuse to escape for a while. A time-out, so the world would go on without me for a few hours. That was all right, too.

The second half of the play was as riveting as the first. I leaned forward as the actor playing Macduff—with a deadly smile on his face—informed Macbeth that he was not "of woman born" . . . had been "untimely ripped" from his mother's womb.

"Lay on, Macduff!" cried Macbeth.

Then it was over. Macbeth's head displayed on a pike as the son of Duncan assumed his rightful place as king. The audience applauded, rising for a standing ovation, then picking up the hired cushions they had been sitting on, shaking off the fantasy as they reconnected with a world in which the sun was shining.

I glanced around, looking for the other people who had been on the bus. The driver had said we would have twenty minutes after the performance ended. I had enough time to pop back into the gift shop and buy the picture book of the theater that I had looked at earlier and put back when I saw the price.

When I came out of the gift shop and started up the hill toward the parking lot, I spotted a man and woman from my bus. I recognized them because they were so much a pair. Both in their sixties, both the same height, no more than 5'5", both wearing khaki hats and vests. They walked arm-in-arm, in stride. They were rather an adorable little couple.

I followed them and the rest of the stream of theatergoers across the main parking lot. Cars were leaving and had to be dodged.

I caught my breath as I ran full tilt into a man who was crossing my path. "Excuse me," I said and tried to step back.

He grabbed me, pulling me against him. "Janey Shore! Give us a hug!" His hand moved between us.

"Like that?" he whispered in my ear. "Yeah, you like it." His hand brushed upward, over my breast. "Another dead bitch."

He stepped back, freeing me from his embrace. "See you soon, old girl." And then he was gone, walking away off across the parking lot.

I stood there. People streamed past me. No one was looking at me. No one had noticed. No one had seen. I turned and started walking toward the bus. In another moment, I was running.

The bus driver looked up from his clipboard. "Slow down, dear heart, slow down. You've plenty of time." I could feel the other passengers staring as I staggered blindly down the aisle.

I had sworn I would never let that happen to me again. I had sworn I would fight back if I were ever touched like that again.

Chapter Seventeen

BY THE TIME THE BUS REACHED THE OUTSKIRTS OF ST. REGIS, I had gotten past the shame and paralysis of being touched in a way that had taken me right back to the schoolyard and a fifth-grade molester named Gary Vincent. I had begun to deal with the more important point. The mean-eyed, ugly thug who had tried to mug me in London was here in Cornwall, and he had said I was "another dead bitch." He had said he would see me soon. He had known where to find me to tell me those things. The only person who could have told him where to find me was Michael.

I had left a message for Tess, and Michael had gotten it. Michael had sent him after me. Unless he had been following me. Maybe he had been following me since I left London. No, he was interested in Michael. Michael's package. But he had said I was dead. Another dead bitch. Another? Dee? Had he meant Dee?

I staggered out of the bus as blindly as I had staggered on. The driver caught my arm and steadied me. "All right, love?"

"Yes, thank you." I licked my dry lips. "I was— I'm fine." He didn't look convinced but decided not to pursue it. I glanced around me and took a deep breath. There were lots of people on the street. All I had to do was get back to the hotel. Get back to the hotel and call Cordner.

The police station. I half-turned as I thought it. No, what if Cordner wasn't there? It was almost six o'clock. He might be gone for the day. Get back to the hotel. Call from there.

Everyone staying at the Gull's Nest Hotel seemed to be congregated in the hallway outside the closed lounge door. All four adult Stillmans and Hildegard Martin were there. As I eased the front door shut behind me, Hildegard put her finger to her lips and nodded her head toward the parlor.

"What's going on?" I whispered.

"The DI and his American colleague arrived a few minutes ago," Hildegard whispered back. "I heard them tell Edith that they have the results of the autopsy and the crime lab reports, then they went in and closed the door. We're waiting to hear."

"Should we be waiting out here in the hallway?"

"Of course we should," Pamela Stillman said, looking down her nose at me. "This matter concerns all of us."

"You see, Lizzie," Benjamin said, his eyes sad. "We care about Edith and Sarah. They are old friends."

I wondered if that was what Pamela cared about. I had a feeling she was more concerned about anything that might inconvenience her family.

Rosalind made a half-movement toward the stairs, "I suppose I really should go back up to check on Benjy. I left him playing with his toys."

"I'll look in on him," I said. "I have to go up to my room."

Pamela's glance swept over me. "Thank you, but Rosalind will do it."

But Rosalind was feeling rebellious. "Actually, Pamela, if Lizzie doesn't mind looking in on him, I would rather stay down here."

Pamela's eyes flared. Between almost closed lips, she said, "Then I'll do it—"

"Pamela—" Benjamin shook his head at her. "Lizzie has offered to check on Benjy. I'm sure she can handle it."

Pamela bit her lip. "Thank you, Lizzie. If you wouldn't mind—"

"Thanks, Lizzie," Jeremy said as I passed him.

The better I got to know his family, the more I liked Jeremy. Or at least sympathized with him. It must be less than joyful to be caught in the middle between his wife and his mother, and he was clearly cast in the role of son to a benevolent patriarch. Maybe he should have stayed out there on his own.

But I had my own troubles. With one foot on the stairs, I turned and caught Hildegard's eye. "Hildegard, when they open the door, would you please tell Inspector Cordner that I need to speak to him before he leaves?"

She nodded and started to say something. But then, on the other side of the closed door, one of the sisters, Sarah or Edith, gave a loud wail of anguish. I ran up the stairs, away from that cry of pain. What had Cordner or Quinn said to provoke it? What could be worse than the fact of Dee's death?

On the second-floor landing, I glanced toward my room. I'd better go up to Benjy before I did anything else. Pamela's suspicions of my incompetence would be confirmed if something happened before I got around to looking in on him.

The dragon. This was my opportunity to ask Benjy why he had given Dee the dragon. I hurried up the stairs to the third floor. I had to talk to him before Pamela got away from Benjamin and came to check on her grandson herself. The only problem was I knew nothing at all about talking to small children.

When I turned the doorknob and walked into the bedroom which he was sharing with his parents, Benjy was sitting on the floor banging together two brawny male action figures as he supplied the dialogue for their fight. He froze in mid-motion when he saw me.

"Hi," I said. "I didn't mean to interrupt your battle. Your mom's downstairs and she asked me to check in on you to make sure you have everything you need."

Benjy said nothing. He was not the same lively little boy he had been when he greeted Tess and me at the door on Sunday evening. There was a wariness about him now. Had Dee's death done this to him? I dropped down to the floor beside him. "What are you playing?"

"Fighting."

I gestured toward the action figures. "Who are they, anyway? I think I've seen them on television, but I don't remember their names."

"Santo the Magnificent and Zorta the Strange," Benjy said, holding up each figure in turn.

"Which one's the bad guy?"

He held up Zorta—who was indeed strange with horns sprouting from his head and feathered wings on his back. But I would have backed him as a winner against the clean-cut and muscular Santo. I would have bet Zorta knew all kinds of dirty tricks, and sometimes the bad guys did win.

But in the end, good would triumph and evil would be undone. Or so Mrs. Ingram, my Sunday school teacher, had always claimed.

Benjy had gone back to banging his two combatants together. But he was doing it silently, with a quiet intensity.

"I think I remember seeing you with a dragon," I said, as I picked up a miniature shield and examined it. "A purple dragon. Do you still have him?" Benjy shook his head. His corn silk blond curls glistened in the late afternoon sunlight coming through the window. He was really a handsome little boy. "Your dragon . . . did you give him away?"

"Yes."

"To Dee?"

To my horror, tears welled up in his eyes.

"Benjy, sweetheart, don't cry."

"He was supposed to protect her until she found her way home," he sobbed.

"To protect her?"

"Like in the story. The princess was lost and she didn't know who she was or where she 'longed . . . until she met the dragon and he protected her . . . and then he helped her remember and then she found her way home to her castle . . . Dee said sometimes she didn't know who she was or where she 'longed . . . so I gave her the dragon so he could protect her—" It all came out in one long run-together sentence, punctuated with sobbing breaths.

"Oh, Benjy," I put my arms around him and drew him into my lap. "Oh, Benjy, it's all right."

"I want to kill him. I want to kill whoever hurt Dee." I smoothed his baby soft hair and hugged him tighter, while he cried some more. He smelled of bubble gum and well-scrubbed child, and I ached with him.

When Pamela marched in we were still sitting there on the floor. Benjy had sobbed himself into a gentle case of the hiccups and I was wondering what to do next.

"I'll take him now," his grandmother said as she bent down to remove him from my arms. "What did you—? Why has he been crying?"

He was half asleep, and she kissed his damp cheek. She did love him. Whatever her faults—and perhaps I gave her more than she deserved because I had decided she was a snob—Pamela Stillman did love her grandson.

"I'm sorry," I said. "I mentioned Dee."

Pamela's head came up. "What did you say to him?"

I rose awkwardly from my position on the floor.

"I asked what you said to him." Pamela's tone was annoyed, tense.

I decided to tell the truth. Benjy would probably tell her anyway. "I had seen a dragon that he had. One like it was in Dee's backpack the other morning. I asked him if he gave it to her, and he said he did. I'm sorry, I didn't mean to upset him again."

Pamela turned toward the child's bed, opposite the larger double bed. "I would appreciate it, Lizzie, if henceforth you would not speak to my grandson about Dee."

"Yes, of course. Excuse me." As I closed the door behind me, Pamela was tucking Benjy into bed as she told him that grandmother was there now, and everything was all right. If only that were true.

I unlocked the door to my room and dropped my backpack on the floor. I pulled at my blouse, which was damp from Benjy's tears. I felt hot and sticky. Did I have time for a shower before Cordner was done with Edith and Sarah? I should go downstairs in case Hildegard forgot to tell him that I needed to speak to him. But he would probably be looking for me anyway to ask me about my meeting with Felicity Hollingsworth. So I could just wait to be called.

I sank down on the bed. A seagull was sitting on the balcony rail.

He looked like the seagull who came each morning. But then it was hardly stereotyping to say that all seagulls do look alike. Maybe not to each other. He arched back his neck and flapped his wings and, having had a good stretch, settled back down to staring into the room. What was he thinking? What was I thinking?

I made it to the sink just before I threw up. When there was nothing left in my stomach, I washed out the sink and reached for my toothbrush. Then I went to take a shower.

Hildegard pounded on the bathroom door as I was soaping myself again. "Lizzie? Lizzie, are you in there? The inspector's waiting."

"Thank you," I called back. "Please tell him I'll be right down."

Hildegard was back upstairs and waiting on the landing when I came out of my room. "They're sure now that it was murder," she said in a stage whisper. "The autopsy confirmed that Dee died of heart and respiratory failure brought on by anaphylactic shock. But there was nothing in Sarah's baking supplies. No peanuts."

"No peanuts? Then how—? I saw Dee eat— She said—"

"The peanuts were in the yummy balls," Hildegard said. "But the yummy balls weren't Sarah's. Someone substituted ringers."

"Ringers?"

Hildegard nodded. "They looked like Sarah's. That wasn't hard. Dark, crunchy cereal balls. But according to the lab, these balls contained both peanut butter and ground nuts. They also contained preservatives . . . were commercially made—"

"So someone bought them and substituted—"

"And that's why the good inspector and his colleague are now convinced that Dee was murdered. The substitution couldn't have happened by accident."

"No," I said. "It couldn't have. Excuse me, Hildegard, I'd better go down."

"Wait! Why do you need to see the inspector?" On the shadowed landing, she was suddenly too close. I could smell the peppermint on her breath. "Do you know something about this, Lizzie?"

"Hildegard . . . I need to go downstairs."

She stared at me, her chest rising and falling under her camouflage vest. Then she laughed and stepped back. "Do forgive me, Lizzie, murder isn't conducive to calm nerves."

"No. No, it isn't. Excuse me." It was as I reached the bottom stair that it occurred to me that the peppermint might be a coverup for the liquor she had been consuming. I looked back up toward the landing. She was still standing there.

"Professor Stuart." Cordner had come to the lounge doorway. "Please join us."

I stepped inside, and he closed the door to the hallway. The one to the dining room was already closed. On the other side of the room, John Quinn was standing to one side of the window, looking out into the street. He didn't turn around when I came in. "Please sit down, Professor," Cordner said. I took a seat on the sofa. Cordner sat down on the chair across from me.

"Is he looking at anything in particular?" I asked, nodding toward Quinn.

"Our friend Sean," Quinn said. "He's up the street a bit, leaning against a car while he smokes a cigarette."

"Watching this house?" Cordner asked.

"He seems to be."

"Why?" I said. "Why would he be standing there watching the house?"

"Good question," Quinn said. And then, as if he had lost interest, he strolled across the room and dropped down into the other chair.

Cordner exchanged a glance with him, then cleared his throat. "We've had the reports from the pathologist and the crime lab."

I nodded. "Hildegard told me. No peanuts in Sarah's baking supplies. Instead someone substituted fake yummy balls containing peanut butter and ground nuts. So now you're sure that it was murder . . . that Dee was murdered."

My hands were shaking. I clasped them together in my lap. When I looked up, Quinn's cool gray eyes were on my hands. Did I look guilty? Like Dee's murderer? Certainly, if I were going to kill someone, how better to deflect suspicion from myself than to be there when she died. To have run for help, tried to save her. "So we are all now officially suspects," I said.

Cordner smiled. "Actually, Professor, we are inclined to put you at the bottom of our suspect list. But, yes, everyone residing in this hotel is on that list. It also includes Sean Etling and Felicity Hollingsworth and anyone else who might have had a grievance against Dee Crump."

I looked at Quinn. He was watching me. "Did you tell Inspector Cordner that someone tried to mug me when I was in London?"

"I told him."

Cordner said, "He also told me that you have concerns about Michael Donovan."

"Some concerns," I agreed. "Even more after what happened this afternoon."

"What happened?" Quinn said. "Where were you this afternoon?"

"I played tourist. The same thing I assume you were doing in Penzance."

"I'll tell you about Penzance later. Right now, we'd like to hear how you spent your afternoon."

"Yes, we would like to hear about that, Professor Stuart. I gather something unsettling happened."

I nodded. "I went to the matinee of *Macbeth* at the Merrimont Theatre—"

"You did what?" Quinn said.

"I went to . . . you heard me . . . I had a perfectly good reason for going. I needed some time to think." I licked my dry lips. "When the play was over, I was walking back across the parking lot to the bus when I encountered my London mugger—"

"Your London mugger?" Cordner repeated. He leaned toward me. "Encountered how?"

I looked away from his probing glance. "I . . . he bumped into me."

"Is that all?" Quinn said.

"No, of course, it isn't all. Isn't it enough? A man who shoved me in front of a bus . . . he could have killed me in London."

"Lizzie, calm down."

"I am calm." I stood up. "Shouldn't you go outside and see why Sean's standing out there?"

"He'll wait," Quinn said. "Sit down and tell us what happened."

"I am trying to tell you. The two of you keep interrupting."

"You're quite right," Cordner said. "Please sit down and tell us about your encounter with your mugger."

"He isn't *my* anything. I shouldn't have called him that."

"With the mugger," Cordner corrected. "Please sit down, Professor Stuart."

I sat down. I didn't want to do this. I felt the way I had felt that day when my grandmother marched me into the principal's office to demand that he do something about what Gary Vincent had done to me in the schoolyard in full view of a group of laughing, jostling boys. Some of the girls had seen too. One of them had told her mother, and her mother had called my grandmother.

I swallowed down the sweet sick taste in my mouth. I was not going to throw up here in front of these two men, I was simply going to tell them what had happened. I was thirty-eight, not ten. "He bumped into me," I said. "I didn't realize who he was at first. I apologized and started to back away, but he grabbed me up against him. He said, as if we knew each other, 'Janey Shore! Give us a hug!' And then he—" I pressed my hand to my mouth, swallowing hard.

John Quinn, the soul of patience, said, "And then he what?"

"And then, Detective Quinn, he shoved his hand hard between

my legs. He whispered in my ear, 'Like that? Yeah, you like that.' He brushed his hand over my breast and said, 'Another dead bitch.' And then, satisfied that he had gotten my attention, he said, 'See you soon, old girl,' and walked away."

By the time I'd gotten to the end, my glance had fallen back to my hands twisted together in my lap. "He called me Janey Shore," I said into the silence. "Maybe he has me confused with someone else."

Cordner cleared his throat. "In Cockney rhyming slang, Jane Shore means . . . Jane Shore would be a prostitute."

"He was calling me a whore?"

Cordner said, "Don't let it upset you, Professor Stuart. This man is obviously—"

"Michael knew where I was going."

"Donovan?" Quinn said. "What does he have to do with this?"

"I am telling you what he had to do with it. I called the hospital to speak to Tess, but she was out of her room. I left a message with the nurse saying that I was going to the matinee at the Merrimont. Michael was there at the hospital. The nurse said he was there and she asked if I wanted to speak to him."

Cordner said, "Then it's quite possible he either saw the message or was told about it by the nurse or Ms. Alvarez."

Quinn stood up. "So it seems we need to have a conversation with Michael Donovan."

"Yes," Cordner said. "I'm inclined to agree."

"You'd better come along," Quinn said, directing the comment to me.

When I looked at Cordner, he said, "I know it has been another trying day, Professor. But if you wouldn't mind coming with us, perhaps we might have a better chance of eliciting information from Mr. Donovan."

I got up, shoving my shaking hands into my pockets. "I'll be happy to punch him in the mouth if that will help."

"If all else should fail," Cordner said.

"Let's go," Quinn said. Out in the hall, he stopped and turned to look down at me. "Go get a sweater or a jacket."

"I'm not cold, I'll be in the car."

"Lizzie, go get a sweater. You're already shivering."

"Did I happen to mention I don't like being given orders? Did I mention that?"

"Sorry to interrupt," Cordner said.

I glanced at him, considered punching him in his smile, then realized the fact that I felt like punching people probably meant I was not completely calm, cool, and collected. "Excuse me," I said.

"I'll only be a moment."

Quinn said nothing, which was probably just as well.

Had I said that Rosalind was high strung? Right now I could give her lessons. Take a deep breath and calm down. I counted backward from one hundred as I unlocked the door to my room and walked over to the closet to look for my sweater.

It was after seven, but still full-light outside. Summer evenings on the Cornish coast. I edged closer to the balcony doors and peered out to see if I could spot Sean.

There he was in his leather jacket and white T-shirt. He had even added a leather-brimmed cap. And he had the attitude down. Cigarette drooping from his mouth, legs crossed at the ankles, as he leaned against a red sports car.

Was he working at getting himself arrested?

I had my answer when we stepped out of the door of the hotel. Sean called out, "Hey, coppers, I want to talk to you." Cordner and Quinn observed his approach, apparently deciding he wasn't armed and dangerous.

"What is it, Mr. Etling?" Cordner said. "What can we do for you?"

Sean tossed aside his cigarette. "Look, I know you're going to catch me on it . . . on that story I told you about being in London—"

"Are you saying you weren't in London, Mr. Etling?"

"I was here in St. Regis Monday afternoon—the day before Dee died. I know someone must have seen me on my bike or talking to her."

"Then you would be well advised to tell us what really happened, Mr. Etling."

Sean shoved at the cap on his head, then he took it off and let it dangle from his fingers. "She— I came back and I wanted to talk to her and try to work it out."

"Where did you see her?" I asked. "Did you come here to the hotel?"

Sean glared at me. "So she did catch on that it was me that rung up."

"Who did you ring up, Mr. Etling?" Cordner asked.

"Dee's Aunt Sarah. Did the old bag know it was me? Why didn't she say nothing?"

"Why don't you tell us about the call?" Cordner said.

Sean shoved his cap back onto his head. He dug his hands into his jacket pockets. "I rung up. I knew she'd be here doing her baking and I needed to get her away—out of the house—so I could come over and see Dee without having her aunt about looking disapproving."

"It was you who pretended you were calling for Sarah's neighbor," I said.

"I knew she'd go rushing over, or rushing as fast as she could with that gammy leg. I thought that would give me time to get to Dee. I was at a call box around the corner."

"Did you come here to the hotel to see Miss Crump?" Cordner asked.

"No, I never made it this far. I saw her coming up the street before I got here. She'd been to market. We got into a row right on the pavement. That's how I know someone must have seen us."

"What was your row about?" Quinn asked.

Sean ducked his head. "I was trying to apologize to her. She told me it was over between us, to bugger off. She said she was going up to London at the end of summer."

"And what did you do, Mr. Etling?"

"I sodding well didn't kill her! I jumped on my bike and went tearing off out of town again."

"Back to London?" Quinn asked.

"No . . . well . . . I never went to London, see. I went to Truro, then I came back on Monday afternoon. After Dee and me had the row, I went back to Truro. I spent another night at my mate's flat. We got pissed and it took me most of the next day to get my head on straight. I didn't know Dee was dead until I got back here that evening."

"Your mate's name, Mr. Etling?"

"Kevin Parrish."

"And his address?" Cordner asked as he scribbled into his notebook. Sean gave him the address. "We'll check out this new version of your story, Mr. Etling. In the meantime, please stay available here in St. Regis."

"I ain't got no place else to go," Sean said. He turned on his booted heel and took off up the street.

"I think he was telling the truth," I said.

"We'll see," Cordner said. He tapped his pen on his notebook. "But we were on our way to speak to Mr. Donovan."

"Are you sure he's still at the hospital?" I asked. "Is that where we're going?"

"There first," Cordner said. He gestured me forward and opened the back door of his dark brown sedan. "If he's not there, we'll see if Ms. Alvarez can tell us where to find him."

"No," I said. "We can't upset Tess."

"We'll talk about it on the way," Quinn said. "Get in the car."

"I'm not going to allow you to upset Tess. She's pregnant."

"We know that, Professor Stuart. But under the circumstances, with a man on the prowl who might well be dangerous, we do need to find Mr. Donovan and see what he can tell us."

"We'll let you go into her room and ask her where he is," Quinn said.

"Can't we check his hotel first to make sure he isn't there?"

"We did that on our way over," Cordner said. "Mr. Donovan was not in his room."

I rested my hand on the warm metal top of the car. "Why were you looking for him on your way over? You didn't know yet what had happened at the Merrimont."

"We were looking for him," Quinn said, "because you insisted he was up to something that should be investigated."

"We also needed to ask him about his acquaintance with Dee Crump," Cordner said. "And quite frankly, neither one of us was anxious for that session with Dee's aunts."

"Get in the car, Lizzie," Quinn said.

I had my mouth open to respond when I saw the weary twist of his mouth. I got in the car.

Know when to fight your battles, my grandfather had often advised me.

"But we are not going to upset Tess," I said from the backseat. "I don't even know what's going on with her and the baby." Neither man responded. Babies and pregnant mothers were not a topic they cared to discuss.

I contemplated the passing scenery. The conversation between Quinn and Cordner moved from a discussion of the staffing of the Truro police department—prompted by the need to have someone there check on Sean's alibi—to a story Cordner related to Quinn about the havoc a Truro constable had been called upon to deal with when two goats escaped from their enclosure.

Chapter Eighteen

WE WERE A COUPLE OF BLOCKS FROM THE HOSPITAL, when Cordner glanced over his shoulder and said, "Do forgive the shop talk, Professor Stuart."

"No problem," I said. "Would you like to hear about my visit with Felicity Hollingsworth now or later?"

"Now, please. In fact, I was about to ask you about that."

Quinn half turned in his seat. "So? Were she and Dee Crump lovers?"

"She refused to comment on that. She said she didn't intend to satisfy my curiosity. But she did offer me a drink and a seat. And when I asked if she knew Dee planned to move to London, she said she was the one who had suggested it."

"And why was that?" Cordner asked. "Or did that fall under not satisfying your curiosity?"

"Felicity said that she thought Dee would be better off in London."

"Living with her," Quinn said.

"No. Felicity says she did not ask Dee to move into her flat in London. She likes her privacy."

"Then why did she encourage Dee to leave St. Regis?" Cordner asked.

"Because, according to Felicity, there was nothing for Dee here. Only marriage to Sean, her cloddish boyfriend."

"I wonder if Dee thought that was her only option," Quinn said.

"She took a computer programming course," I said. "They mentioned that in the article in the newspaper. So I would think that even if she had stayed in Cornwall, she would have been able to have a career if she had wanted one."

"A career?" Quinn said. "Don't you consider being a housekeeper a career, Professor Stuart?"

"Only if chosen freely, Detective Quinn. Some people actually enjoy whizzing through rooms with a vacuum cleaner and polishing furniture to a high gloss. But my grandmother was a domestic for most of her life, and her advice to me was to stay in school. So I never had to clean up after anybody but myself and my family. And, as I recall, her last statement on the matter was that the Good

Lord—knowing me—would undoubtedly understand if I played
'Miss Lady' and hired someone to pick up my mess before I tripped
over it and broke my neck."

Cordner laughed. Quinn said, "So you have a housekeeper?"

I studied the lighted windows of the hospital as Cordner guided
the car into a space opposite the main entrance. "No. I'm still having problems with the idea."

"For the sake of your neck, hadn't you'd better resolve your
problems?"

"For the sake of my neck, I hope the two of you can get something out of Michael Donovan."

Cordner said, "We will do our best, Professor Stuart. Assuming,
of course, he has something of interest to tell us."

"He does. You just have to get it out of him."

Quinn opened his car door. "Third degree still allowed over here,
Thomas?"

"I'm glad you're amused," I said as I climbed out of the backseat.

"Donovan will be too. I'm always fun when I'm enjoying myself."

"I'm sure you are, John," Cordner said, "but I'm afraid we will
have to abide by the rules."

"Now, that's a damn shame, Thomas." Quinn gestured for me
to walk ahead of him. "Maybe we could bend a rule or two for
Professor Stuart."

Maybe he did bend a rule or two back home in Philadelphia.
Maybe he thought the right to engage in verbal and physical abuse
was one of the perks of his profession, especially when dealing with
a designated "scumbag."

I glanced at Cordner as I passed him. He looked unconcerned.
Obviously he wasn't worried about having to pull his American
colleague off the man they were about to interview. Good. I might
not like Michael, but I didn't want to have to explain to Tess how he
came to have his face rearranged.

And the truth was, I would just as soon Quinn didn't turn out
to be a goon with a badge. That would certainly disillusion me
about the value of a West Point education. Although, even at West
Point, honor and integrity must be struggling against high tide
these days.

And undoubtedly the Ivy League university Michael had
attended was proud to claim both him and his generous contribu-
tions to the annual fund.

Tess was sitting up in bed watching a game show on television.
She looked a whole lot better than she had the last time I saw her,
but I could tell at a glance that she was not enjoying her leisure.

"Hi," I said as I kissed her on the cheek. "When are they going to let you out of here?"

"Tomorrow, if I'm good. How was the Merrimont Theatre?"

"Great. A fantastic production of *Macbeth.* I think I really needed some downtime."

"And I need some work time." Tess plucked at the sheet over her lap. "I'm supposed to be out researching an article, not here in bed contemplating my belly button"

I sat down in the armchair beside the bed. "You can finish researching the article when you get out of here. You can't have that much more left to do."

"I was actually hoping we'd get to spend some time together," Tess said. "If you'll recall, this was supposed to be the week when we'd have a chance to see more of each other."

"Well, you could always come to Drucilla for a couple of weeks. Think what a great article you could write about a historic small town on the Kentucky River."

On the bedside table, in a crystal vase, a single long-stemmed red rose basked in its own perfection. No need to ask where it had come from.

"So where's Michael?"

"He went to get coffee." Tess brushed back a lock of dark hair. Then she smiled, a reluctant, self-conscious smile. "Believe it or not, that's been the one good thing about the last two days."

"What has?"

"That Michael and I have had a chance to talk. To really talk."

"And have you reached any conclusions?"

"Not yet. But I think I owe it to the baby to consider all the possibilities."

"So you have definitely decided to go ahead with the pregnancy?"

"Yes. That I've decided. It's the what-happens-when-baby-arrives that I haven't figured out yet."

I gestured toward the crystal vase on the table. "So Michael is helping you figure it out by wooing you with flowers?"

Tess wrinkled her nose. "Michael is doing his best to get what he wants by wooing me with flowers. One flower, in this case. And you must admit that's a lot less extravagant than the dozen red roses he used to send every Saturday when we were dating?"

Every Saturday because that was the day they had met. Michael was a master of the romantic gesture.

The door swung opened and he came in carrying a coffee mug and a glass of milk. "Hi, Lizzie. I hear you spent the afternoon at the theater."

"Yes, I did. How did you spend your afternoon, Michael?"

"Right here with my favorite pregnant lady." He said this with a wink at Tess as he handed her the milk. She smiled up at him.

I dug my fingernails into my palms. "Michael, that reminds me—there's something I need to ask you. Could we step outside for a moment?"

"Hey, what's going on?" Tess protested. "What do the two of you have to talk about that you can't discuss in front of me."

"The stock market. I know how totally uninterested you are in the Dow-Jones average, and I could use some advice from a pro." I took Michael's arm. "If you wouldn't mind, Michael . . . I heard about a new growth stock from this man I was talking to at the theater, but I'm not sure about it and he said I should act quickly."

Michael gave me a quizzical look, but he set his coffee mug down and let me guide him toward the door. "This won't take long, sweetheart," he said to Tess.

I waved my hand at Tess and smiled. "See you later, pal."

"Fine for you. You come to see me and stay all of five minutes. Some friend you are."

"An awful friend . . . but you know how much I hate hospitals. I'll see you at the hotel in the morning. I even have a welcome-home gift."

Tess made a face at me as I drew Michael out into the hall. I knew she was hurt. From her point of view, I was not earning any stars as best pal and buddy.

When we were several feet from her room, Michael stopped walking and I let go of his arm. "Advice from a pro?" he said.

"I had to make some excuse. The truth is, Michael, that there are two police officers in the waiting room who would like to chat with you."

"About what?"

"They'll tell you. Shall we join them?"

I thought he was going to refuse, then he shrugged. "Why not?"

When the introductions had been made, we all sat down in chairs in a corner of the waiting room.

"Mr. Donovan," Cordner said, "I believe you know that Professor Stuart was the victim of an attempted mugging in London."

"Yes, I was shocked when she told me about it."

"Then the mugging came as a complete surprise to you?" Quinn said.

"Of course, it did. Why would I anticipate that she might be mugged in broad daylight on a busy London street?"

"As to that, Mr. Donovan," Cordner said, "Professor Stuart believes you may know something about the man who mugged her."

Michael turned to me with a frown on his face. "Lizzie, come on, you can't really believe that." He gave a comic grimace. "Do you really think I hang out with thieves and muggers?"

"I'm sure you don't count them among your friends. But, yes, I do think you know who the man was . . . is. I think you know why he's after me." I held Michael's glance. "I saw him again today when I was at the Merrimont Theatre. Did you tell him where to find me?"

"Of course I didn't. How in the devil could I tell him where to find you when I don't even know who he is? Lizzie, have you gone paranoid?"

"I'm not paranoid, Michael. When I saw him at the Merrimont Theatre today, he threatened me. He said I was 'another dead bitch.'"

"Another—?" Michael rubbed his hand over his chin. "Are you saying that this man implied that he had killed someone?"

"That's what I'm saying."

"That's incredible."

"Any idea who his other victim might have been?" Quinn asked.

"At the risk of repeating myself, Detective Quinn, how could I know anything at all about this man when I don't even know who he is?" Michael shook his head at me. "Lizzie, this guy sounds like some kind of psycho. You'd better give him a wide berth."

A wide berth? A seafaring expression from his Martha's Vineyard summers? Michael, the skipper, speaking. And Michael, the liar, looking me right in the eye as he did it.

"Thank you for that helpful suggestion, Michael."

"Lizzie—" Michael held out his hands in a gesture of defeat. "I know you don't like me. I know you don't trust me. But I swear to you, I don't know anything about this."

Quinn said, "Did you tell anyone that Professor Stuart would be at the Merrimont Theatre this afternoon?"

Michael turned to Quinn with a thoughtful frown on his face. "You mean after Tess showed me the message from Lizzie? As a matter of fact, I did. A few minutes after that Edith Crump called to check on Tess. Tess had gone into the bathroom, so I answered the phone. Edith mentioned speaking to Lizzie about Tess this morning. And I mentioned that Lizzie had called to say that she was going to the matinee at the Merrimont, so she hadn't been to the hospital yet." Michael braced his hands on the knees of tailored beige slacks. "Gentlemen, if there is nothing else, will you excuse me? I would like to get back to Tess."

I said, "Did you tell the staff here that Tess is your wife?"

"I told them she's my ex-wife. But you might as well know,

Lizzie, I have asked Tess to marry me again."

"You've asked before, Michael. She always says no."

"Yes, but this time is different, isn't it? This time we're going to be parents." Michael turned to Cordner. "If that's all, Inspector—"

"As a matter of fact, Mr. Donovan, we would like to know about your acquaintance with Dee Crump."

"Dee? I couldn't believe it when I heard she was dead."

"She was murdered," Quinn said.

"Murdered?" Michael seemed to be genuinely shocked. "Murdered? Who would want to kill Dee?"

"How well did you know her?" Cordner asked.

Michael rubbed at his jaw again. "Not that well. I stayed at the hotel last spring. She was the housekeeper there. My impression was that she was a very sweet girl—not someone anyone would have a grudge against." He shook his head. "Why would someone murder her?"

Quinn said, "So you haven't any thoughts about that? About possible suspects?"

"None."

Cordner said, "Thank you, Mr. Donovan. That's all for now."

As Michael was about to walk out the door, Quinn called after him. "One thought, Mr. Donovan."

"Yes, Detective Quinn?"

"The thug who's after Professor Stuart . . . he seems to have targeted one woman he saw you with. It is possible that he might go after another, your ex-wife, for example."

Michael went as still as a spooked rabbit, then he smiled. "I really don't think I need to worry about that, Detective Quinn. This fellow has nothing to do with me. It was only a coincidence that Lizzie and I happened to be in the wax museum together before she was mugged."

"I was carrying your package, Michael."

"My package—as you must know by now—was a figurine of very little value."

"But he might have thought it was something else—something you—"

"Lizzie, dammit, I don't know this creep. He has nothing to do with me."

"But how can you be certain of that, Mr. Donovan?" Cordner asked.

"What?"

Quinn said, "If you don't know who he is, then how can you be sure he isn't someone who has a grudge against you? How can you be sure he hasn't targeted the women around you?"

"That's ridiculous," Michael said. He turned and walked out of the door.

I watched him go. "At the risk of repeating myself, gentlemen, he's lying."

"You might be right, Professor Stuart," Cordner said. "But short of roughing Mr. Donovan up, there really is nothing more we can do to persuade him to cooperate." He glanced at Quinn. "Unless, of course, something should turn up in the bit of checking we're doing."

"Then you are investigating him?" I asked.

"Informally," Cordner said.

"As far as we know, Donovan hasn't committed any crime," Quinn said.

I twisted in my chair to face him. "I don't care what you know. Michael—"

"Was lucky he wasn't hooked up to a polygraph. But knowing he was lying through his teeth and proving it are two different things."

"At least you know now why I don't trust him."

"Because you're paranoid?" Quinn said.

"Aah, but that doesn't mean no one's out to get me."

He reached down and picked up my white knit sweater from the floor where it had fallen. "Come on, Professor Stuart, it's time all good little paranoids were tucked in for the night."

Cordner gave me a reassuring smile. "Never fear, Professor. With or without Mr. Donovan's help, we will get to the bottom of this."

"Hopefully before I've had another encounter with my least favorite thug."

"Before would definitely be better than after," Quinn said.

"What a comfort you are, Detective Quinn."

He draped the sweater around my shoulders. "Thanks, I learned it in cop school."

I picked up the miniature purse, into which I had shoved my keys and the essentials, from the end table. As I looped the strap over my hand, I asked the question that had been nagging at me. "Do you think he—the thug, not Michael—could have anything to do with Dee's death?"

Cordner said, "I rather doubt it. From what you've told us, this man hardly seems the type for subtlety."

"No, he's more the type who would like to have his hands around his victim's throat as she gasps for—" I stared at the two of them. "The girl in the field."

"What?" Quinn said.

"That story in the newspapers. Hildegard mentioned it. The girl—the young woman—that the schoolboys found in a Sussex field. She had been strangled and—"

Cordner was shaking his head. "That's rather a leap, Professor."

"Why? Have you had any other murders? Any other women killed?" It was an incredibly stupid question. I should have hung my head in acute embarrassment when it popped out of my mouth. Of course the British police had more than one open case in which a woman had been murdered. Spouse murders. Rape-murders. Serial killers. The United States had no monopoly on male violence against females.

Cordner was saying, "We do have homicides here in England. Not nearly as many as you do in the States, but enough to keep us busy. And since we don't know how long ago this other woman— assuming this man did kill someone—"

I nodded. "Yes. You're right. It could have been months ago or even years. But I didn't get that impression."

"You were frightened," Quinn said.

"That doesn't mean I was rendered witless. He said 'another dead bitch.' I think he meant what he said. I think he was referring to a crime that he had personally committed sometime in the recent past."

Cordner said, "We will check into the possibilities, Professor Stuart but I really don't think we should suspect a link between your thug and the Sussex murder."

"All right. It was just a wild idea. I'm ready to go back to the hotel now."

Cordner looked at Quinn.

"Inspector Cordner and I had a talk about that," Quinn said. "You aren't going back to the hotel."

"I'm not? Where am I going?"

"You're coming with me to Ed and Fiona's."

"Why?"

"Because Inspector Cordner doesn't have an officer he can assign to keep the hotel under surveillance, and someone needs to keep an eye on you."

"And you're volunteering for that detail? Thank you, Detective Quinn, but that isn't necessary. I'll be fine at the hotel."

"Lizzie—"

"I am not going to turn up on your friends' doorstep. Janowitz doesn't even like me. He thinks— I'll be all right at the hotel."

"Janowitz doesn't like anyone until he's gotten inside his or her head and poked around."

"I'm going back to the hotel."

"You're coming with me—"

"Forget it, Quinn."

Cordner said, "John, I did warn you she might not fancy the idea."

"Because she's as stubborn as a Missouri mule?"

"What exactly do you know about mules, Detective Quinn? Did you ever plow with one? And if that was a reference to my home state, I'm from Kentucky."

"You should have stayed there," he said. "Excuse me, Professor Stuart, I'm going outside before I lose my temper."

When I turned from my observation of Quinn's departing back, Cordner said, "Well, shall we go, then? We'll drop you off at the hotel."

"Thank you," I said.

"But I do agree with Detective Quinn. You really must exercise some care until we find this man."

"You also have Dee's killer to find."

"Don't remind me."

"In the meantime, Inspector, I'll lock my bedroom door and keep a stout lamp at the ready to break over the head of any intruder."

"An excellent idea."

Quinn was waiting for us in the corridor outside the waiting room. "My grandfather once owned both a farm and a Missouri mule," he said, directing the comment to me.

"Hence your knowledge?"

"Hence my knowledge. When you saw Donovan in London, did he mention what he'd been doing there?"

"No. I assumed he was there on business."

"But he didn't mention anyone he'd seen? No one that he had spent time with?"

"No, but he wouldn't have. Michael asked me to meet him because he wanted me to be his delivery person—to bring his gift to Tess, that was all. No need to make unnecessary small talk." I hesitated. "He said he'd been following me. I told you that, didn't I?"

"Following you?" Cordner said. "Donovan had been following you?"

"He said that he'd been on his way to my hotel when he saw me leaving. He followed me to see how I would spend my day all alone and anonymous in London. I suppose he thought I'd buy a slinky outfit and head straight for a male strip joint."

Quinn grinned. "Yeah, I can just see you tucking a fifty into some guy's jock strap."

Cordner was smiling too. Quite obviously neither one of them thought I would ever go into a male strip joint. Totally out of character.

Well, it probably was, but still it rankled to have men just naturally assume that I was as dull as a church social.

Not that the last church social I had attended had been dull. The usual sly, but gleeful gossip had passed from lips to ears as the meal was being prepared in the kitchen. Libelous whispers had accompanied the table clearing and dish washing. And as we were leaving, to some people's horror and not a few people's malicious amusement, Deacon Combe's nineteen-year-old daughter had been caught kissing Jennifer Garland's visiting nephew—age twenty-seven—in the minister's study.

"Want to share it?" Quinn said.

I blinked at him. "What?"

"The joke. You were smiling—"

"Oh. I was thinking of—" I shook my head as I looked down the hospital corridor. "I think I was dreaming on my feet. It's time I was in bed."

"You don't say?"

"What?"

Quinn's gray eyes gleamed with laughter. What verbal trap had I stumbled into it? "Nothing," he said. "It's been another long day, we're all getting punchy. Let's get out of here."

I glanced from him to Cordner and then gave up. I was too tired to think. "Yes, let's go."

Chapter Nineteen

THEY DROVE ME BACK TO THE HOTEL. By the time I had gotten myself into my nightgown, washed my face, brushed my teeth, and made a trip to the bathroom, I was wide awake. I punched the pillow, turned over on my side, and closed my eyes. I wanted to sleep. I was going to sleep.

He was standing in the street below with a white mist swirling around him as he looked up at me. I jerked back, stumbling, bruising my toes on the metal door track. From inside the room, I edged forward and peeped out. No one was there. No scarred thug staring up at my balcony. The street was empty except for the parked cars whose tops gleamed with dew. I dragged the balcony doors closed and put the chain lock in place.

The light filtering through the white curtains was more than sufficient to find my way back to my bed. I climbed in and tucked the comforter around my icy feet. I could see everything in the room. No monsters, nothing in the corners.

How long had I been standing on the balcony before I woke up?

I got up again and checked the lock on my bedroom door. The doors downstairs were locked. Edith and Sarah would have checked before they went off to bed. They had been in the lounge when I came in, had invited me to join them, but I had explained that even though it was not quite nine, I was bone-tired.

And then I had looked at their worn faces and felt like an idiot for forgetting even for a moment what they were going through.

After what had happened, they would certainly have checked the front door. The lock was always kept on that door anyway. That was why the guests were given keys. They would have locked the door to the garden as well.

And it had probably been a dream. I had been sleepwalking. When I was a child I used to do that sometimes. My grandfather had taken to putting a chair in front of my bedroom door so that they would hear me if I got up.

Except I had never done that—never sleepwalked—as an adult.

Unless I had done it before and not known. Gone back to bed and never known I had gotten up.

Oh, yes, me and Lady Macbeth. Did I speak a soliloquy while holding my birth certificate?

It had been a dream. No one had been down there in the street. No one.

Go back to sleep.

But I couldn't. I finally gave up. I switched on the reading lamp over the bed and got up. From my tote bag, I pulled out a legal pad and a pen.

Think of it as a research project. First identify the questions that need to be answered, then consider possible sources of information. Be logical, be rational. Stop spooking myself.

Start with what I knew:

a. In London, after I had met Michael inside Madame Tussaud's, an unknown thug had tried to snatch the shopping bag Michael had shoved into my lap.

b. Michael wanted Tess back. Tess was pregnant with Michael's child. Tess was wavering.

c. Michael was a business associate of the Stillmans.

d. According to her husband, Rosalind Stillman was awkward around Michael because she had confided in Michael—told him too much and now regretted it.

e. Michael had done Jeremy a favor—an unnamed favor—for which Jeremy was very grateful.

f. Tess had not been around when Michael and the Stillmans were socializing. Tess had not met the Stillmans until she arrived in Cornwall.

g. Benjamin Stillman had recommended the Gull's Nest Hotel to Michael when Michael came to Cornwall last spring. Benjamin referred to Michael as a "business associate," not as a friend.

h. Benjamin was apparently a creature of habit. He came here to the Gull's Nest Hotel every summer. Because he liked the place. Because he had known the Crump sisters' dead brother. Because he admired the way they had taken in their orphaned niece and provided for her.

Genial Benjamin, with his charming Old World manners. Benjamin chatted bird-watching with Hildegard. Benjamin had stayed behind to care for Sarah while his family took Benjy out after the constable brought the news of Dee's death. Father Benjamin. Son Jeremy.

What about Jeremy? Cool and distant those first couple of days. Snappish with Rosalind and with Dee, the kitchen help. Brooding. Then Dee dies, and Jeremy's suddenly in a much better mood. Or was that the result of finally finding an opportunity to bed his wife?

And what about his wife? Rosalind was nervy, Jeremy had said.

A difficult childhood and three miscarriages before she'd finally given birth to a healthy child. Something had happened when she was at university. Did Jeremy say Rosalind had told Michael what had happened? Yes, when she was babbling on.

Pamela and Rosalind—more than a little tension there. Pamela in the hallway with Benjamin dismissing Rosalind as useless when it came to dealing with her child. Did Pamela find Rosalind equally as inept as her son's wife?

Speaking of wives, how had Pamela ended up as Benjamin's wife? Pamela, the daughter of an Oxford don. Had Benjamin been a student at Oxford? Did she marry a poor boy who was an up-and-comer?

Benjamin had started his own company, been working at it when he first meet the Crump sisters' brother. The brother was the printer with whom he had done business, but he had apparently also considered him a friend. How well had he known Edith and Sarah back then?

All right. What about the present? Benjamin now had a business associate named Michael Donovan who had done a favor for his son Jeremy. What favor? I would have to try to find out about that. It probably had nothing to do with the matters at hand. But still. . . .

And that brought me full circle, back to my thug. As Detective Inspector Cordner had said, Dee's murder was a bit too subtle for said thug. Much too subtle for someone who went around thrusting his hand between women's legs. And he hadn't been the one who had made that call which had gotten Sarah out of the house on Monday afternoon. That had been Sean.

But Sean claimed not to have actually come to the house. He claimed he had seen Dee walking back from the market, argued with her again, then sped off on his motorcycle to Truro. Spent the night with a mate. Got drunk. Came back to St. Regis to find Dee dead. To find Dee lost to him as surely as she would have been if she'd gone off to London. To London and Felicity?

Chain-smoking Felicity, who drank gin and could sit with her legs tucked under her. Felicity who had suggested Dee come to London but had not suggested Dee move in with her.

Aunt Edith had not approved of Felicity and her art. How had Aunt Sarah felt? Aunts who had taken in their motherless niece and raised her as their own. And what had they done before that? Had they worked?

Maybe they had been temps for Hildegard's agency, like Rosalind. Rosalind, the computer consultant recommended by Hildegard, who had married the heir to the family business. But Rosalind had no reason to kill Dee. Unless, of course, Jeremy had been playing games with Dee, and Rosalind was afraid of the competition. Afraid of losing her good catch to a beautiful, younger woman.

An interesting setup that. Three generations of Stillmans sharing a house in London, vacationing together. Gentle patriarch Benjamin helping his grandson to build sandcastles on the beach while hardworking son Jeremy checked in with the office every day. The Stillman family business. Pharmaceuticals—and black market drugs?

But even if that were true, what would it have to do with Dee? Had she been killed because she knew too much? Maybe that was how she had planned to bankroll her move to London—with a little blackmail.

What about Michael as the person Dee was blackmailing? Blackmailing him about something Tess mustn't know—not when he finally had a chance of getting her back. Had he killed Dee to make sure he didn't have to keep paying up, to make sure she never talked?

Michael? Or Rosalind, the threatened wife? Jeremy. Benjamin. Pamela. Hildegard. Which one had motive? Maybe they were all in it together, a conspiracy of silence. A conspiracy to silence Dee.

And then there was the girl with the rose tattoo, the nude girl whom the Sussex schoolboys had found in the field. Cordner might dismiss any connection, but Hildegard had mentioned her.

Hildegard had mentioned the dead girl because she had read about her in the newspapers, had mentioned her as an example of police ineffectiveness. The police stumped by a killer. She had hoped they would have better luck with Dee.

But the thug had said "another dead bitch." Maybe one left naked and dead in a Sussex field, and the next one found and watched. Watched from the street, as he stood looking up at her window and thought of what he would do to her. What a surprise when she sleepwalked out onto her balcony and looked down at him. Had he really been there? Could a dream have been that real? A hallucination brought on by fear and exhaustion?

Sleepwalking. What was it that had set off those episodes when I was a child? They had started one night, had stopped a few months later. According to my grandmother, I had "grown out of them."

Did Benjy ever sleepwalk? Maybe he would after this. Dee had told Benjy that sometimes she felt lost, didn't know where she belonged. Strange thing to tell a child. But maybe a child was the only one she could tell.

But she had talked to Felicity too. I should talk to Felicity again.

Ask her if Dee had mentioned Michael. Ask if Dee had said anything about the Stillmans or Hildegard. Something she might have said in passing.

Cordner would interview Felicity. But would Felicity care to confide in the police? And was Felicity mourning friend or lover?

Presumably two people could actually be both. I had always assumed my grandparents sometimes had sex. *"Behave yourself, Walter Stuart. Don't be messing with me when I got my hands in this dishwater. Don't you see that child sitting there?"* He laughed as he hugged her tighter.

Had John Quinn and his wife ever been both friends and lovers? *"I would have divorced her if she hadn't died."* Quinn the widower who wasn't grieving. Quinn who'd had one helluva of a year.

And had he gone over the edge during that year? Obsessed with his wife, hating her. He kills her instead of divorcing her. He kills her, and he gets away with it. Then he comes to St. Regis. He sees Dee on Sunday evening. Sees her later somewhere else. At a pub. On the street. Maybe she reminds him of his dead wife. Maybe they have a sexual encounter that triggers his homicidal impulses. He needs to kill her too. But it has to be a clean kill. Another perfect crime.

Like Fred MacMurray in *Double Indemnity*, he's a guy who thinks of all the angles. He thinks about how to commit another murder and get away with it. Then Dee hands him the answer. She tells him about her peanut allergy. He arranges to meet her again on Monday evening, and this time he switches the yummy balls and steals her syringe kit.

Then on Tuesday morning, he runs on the beach. He wants to see if Dee will come out for her walk. Instead, he sees me see him. Sees me head for the cliff path. He sits there on the terrace steps and waits. He's there when I run for help. He runs to Dee on the cliff path. Not to help her, but to make sure she dies. Another perfect crime. But, just in case, join the investigation to make sure it stays that way.

Or how about John Quinn, the accomplice? John Quinn, drug-dealing cop, in cahoots with Michael and the thug. Michael went everywhere else. Why not Philadelphia? Maybe it was Michael, not Cordner, who had suggested Quinn call and offer me a sympathetic ear. Keep tabs on Lizzie and don't let her get out of hand. Michael and Quinn. Except Quinn had persuaded Cordner to investigate Michael . . . informally, Cordner had said. What did that mean? Through Quinn's contacts in the States who would be sure to come up with nothing?

Did our Detective Quinn like to kill? First, a soldier, then a cop.

Shoot an enemy or shoot a suspect? Bang, you're dead.

But Dee had been murdered with peanuts. Poisoned, not shot. Enter Hildegard, our confessed peanut lover. Suppose she couldn't resist? Bought some peanut butter yummy balls and sneaked them into the hotel. Decided to share her wealth with Dee. Hildegard, who sucked peppermints when she was drinking. Had Hildegard, the bird-watcher, shot—poisoned—Deirdre Cock Robin?

Or Pamela? Dear Pamela. How had Pamela felt about Dee? Did Pamela have a reason to hate Dee or to fear her? To silence her? If I asked her, would she tell me? Nothing ventured, nothing gained. Ask how she felt about Michael while I was at it.

Ask all of them whatever popped into my head and play human lie detector. Ask why they'd decided to turn my perfectly lovely vacation into a disaster area. Ask them to explain why Dee was never going to see twenty.

Ask and you shall receive—but rarely good answers.

No fast moves, Lizabeth. Drop the pad on the rug, don't worry about the pen rolling away. Reach up and turn off the lamp. Close your eyes and snuggle down. Snuggle under the nice warm comforter and sleep until the birds begin to scream.

Chapter Twenty

I didn't hear the birds. I slept until almost ten.

Edith smiled up at me as I came down the stairs. "Good morning, Lizzie. Did you sleep well, my dear?" The lines about her eyes and mouth indicated she hadn't. But I knew she would probably rather I didn't make that observation. She and Sarah seemed determined to carry on.

"Yes, thank you," I said, returning her smile. I did feel almost refreshed . . . almost as if I were well-rested.

"Come out to the kitchen and I'll fix you some breakfast. And don't say you're not hungry."

"I won't. I am hungry."

"Come along then."

I followed her into the lounge. "Edith, I was wondering about Dee. Do you plan any kind of service?"

"We've scheduled a memorial service for Sunday afternoon. I hope you and Tess can stay to attend."

"We will," I said. I didn't add that the police might have something to say about when we could leave. That did create some practical problems—like what to do about my plane reservation on Monday. Nothing like practical problems. They gave you something to focus on. Better that than simply being swept along by events. "Edith, excuse me—I just need to make a quick phone call—"

"I'll put on the kettle for your tea. Come along when you're ready."

"Thank you." I went back out into the hall. No one else seemed to be around.

Felicity Hollingsworth answered her telephone on the third ring. "Hi, it's Lizzie Stuart. I wonder if you could spare me a few minutes this morning."

"Why?" Dependably straightforward.

"To pick your brain."

"I have to go to the gallery."

"Could I meet you there?"

"Bartlett Street. Up the hill from the wharf. The Artists'

Workshop."

"Yes, I remember seeing it. It's in that group of shops, in a sort of arcade."

"I'll meet you there in an hour." Her receiver clicked in my ear.

Still enough time for a cup of tea and a piece of toast. Edith was coming out of the kitchen with a carrier containing cleaning supplies. With Dee, her housekeeper, gone, she still had guests who needed to be cleaned up after.

"My room's fine," I said. "You needn't bother with me."

"Thank you, dear, but I need to keep busy. But if you wouldn't mind helping yourself to breakfast. If you're looking for anything I forgot to set out, Sarah's out in the vegetable garden."

I was at the Crump sisters' kitchen table eating a peach when the outer door slammed and Sarah came in through the garden room. Hester Rose would have applauded the Crump sisters' knack with vegetable growing. The wicker basket Sarah put down on the work table was filled with ripe red tomatoes and well-grown cukes. Sarah hung her wide-brimmed straw hat on the hook by the door. I tried to think of something to say to her. An observation about the yield from her garden or the sweet, juicy peach I was eating hardly seemed appropriate.

Somehow I felt more awkward with Sarah than with Edith. Maybe because I had seen Sarah's pain raw that morning when I went to her room to wake her. I had seen her without her public mask, and I was still a stranger. She came and stood in the doorway. The hand she brushed across her damp forehead left a smudge of dirt.

"Sarah, what did you and Edith do before you opened the hotel?" So much for tact. Plunge right in, Lizzie.

Sarah limped over to the sink and picked up a bar of soap. "Edith lived in Kent as companion to an elderly relative of ours. I worked in a flower shop in London."

And where had the money come from to buy this house that they had turned into a hotel? "Your relative must have been sorry to lose Edith when you moved here."

"She was dead by then. We used the money she'd left us to buy this place." Question answered.

But Sarah had spoken as if her mind was on something else. The next moment I found out what. "Dee told you that she was going up to London?"

"Yes, that morning when we were talking. She hadn't told you and Edith?"

"She must have planned to wait until she was ready to pack her bags and go."

"Maybe she was concerned about how you and Edith would take it."

"Not well."

"You would have objected?"

"Dee was too young for London. She had no more ability to judge people than a twelve-year-old."

"But maybe being out on her own—"

"Not in London. She wasn't ready to live on her own in a city like London. If living on her own was what she intended. Did she say anything to you about how she intended to support herself?"

I took a hasty sip of my tea. Sarah waited. "I did read in the article in the newspaper . . . hadn't Dee completed computer training?"

"And hated it. That was why she went on working here."

"But even if it wasn't what she really wanted to do, maybe she intended to get a job working with computers until she had a chance to establish herself—"

"To establish herself? Felicity Hollingsworth—did Dee speak of her?"

"No. But I did meet Ms. Hollingsworth yesterday when Edith asked me to return the painting that was in Dee's room."

"We didn't intend Dee for that."

"For that? You mean for—"

"I would rather have seen her with Sean if it came to a choice. But I thought—" Sarah shook her head. "I told Edith that if we tried to stop her from seeing the woman, that would be exactly what she would want to do. Dee was so gentle in her ways, but she did have a rebellious streak. I told Edith we should wait it out." Sarah looked down at her spotless floor. "But maybe I was wrong. Maybe Dee is dead because she was associating with a woman like that."

"You don't think Felicity killed Dee?"

"I think she put ideas into Dee's head, started her thinking . . . got her involved in something that made someone want to kill her."

"What?"

"I don't know what." There was fury in Sarah's voice. "All I know is that my Dee's dead. I should have listened to Edith."

"And talked to Dee about Felicity?"

Sarah's head came up. She looked confused for a moment. "Yes, that's what I meant. I should have—we should have—talked to Dee about that woman."

I stood and reached for my cup and plate. "I have to go. I'm meeting someone."

"I'll take care of clearing up. You go along."

"I can wash—"

"Go on. It's only a moment's work."

I left her there in the kitchen. She should have listened to Edith about what? Not about talking to Dee about Felicity.

I went upstairs to get my backpack. I didn't want to be late for my meeting with the woman whom both Dee's boyfriend and her aunts had suspected of leading Dee astray in one way or another.

Downstairs again, I stopped long enough to call the hospital. When Tess came on the line, I said, "I thought you were getting out this morning."

"I am. I'm just waiting for my doctor to have a look at the results of the blood work they did on me."

"So you should be here by this afternoon, right?"

"Right. And then you can fill me in on everything that's been happening."

I doubted she would really like to hear about everything that had been happening. Especially the part about Michael's lying. "I might be out when you get here, but I'll be back after I run a couple of errands."

I thought of calling Cordner or Quinn and then thought better of it. I wanted to know what they were doing, but I didn't particularly want to tell them that I was meeting Felicity.

Better to check with them later.

Felicity was easy to spot. She was wearing a several-inches-above-the-knees, fire-engine red sundress with no back and a V neckline. She was also wearing black-laced sandals which displayed her matching red toenails.

She was attracting as many glances as the artwork displayed along the rough brick wall of the gallery. When she leaned over a table to pick up a painting, a fifty-something type in Bermuda shorts almost dropped the sunglasses he was twirling between his fingers. Either he hadn't heard about Felicity's preferences or he thought there was no harm in looking.

Felicity turned as I reached her. She held up the small painting she had taken from behind the table. It was of Dee. Dee on a windswept beach, laughing as she held her long black hair away from her face. Dee wearing the black and white polka-dot bikini bottom I'd seen in her backpack. Her bikini top was still missing. "This is what I came for," Felicity said. "I remembered it last night. She told me she wouldn't mind if I offered it for sale. She rather liked the idea. But under the circumstances—"

"Yes," I said. "I think it would probably be better—"

Felicity nodded. "So let's go."

"Where?"

"Out of here. We'll walk. You can walk and talk at the same time, can't you?"

"Usually."

Felicity tucked the painting into her portfolio and slung it over her shoulder. I followed her back through the narrow corridor jammed with art lovers and browsers, back out into the bright St. Regis morning.

She turned up the street as if she had some destination in mind. "Well," she said. In the sunlight, her makeup job was good, but not quite good enough to hide the circles under her eyes. Dee's death was doing no one any good. Except perhaps the person who had killed her.

"Well," I said. "I started thinking last night—actually early this morning when I couldn't sleep. I was going over everything, and it occurred to me that Dee might have said something to you about the guests at the Gull's Nest."

"Are you playing detective now?"

"Speaking of detectives, have you spoken to Inspector Cordner yet?"

"First off this morning. I served him and his American friend tea. They declined the cream cheese and bagels. We had a pleasant chat, which I'm sure they would describe as unproductive."

"Because you had nothing to tell them? Or because you had nothing you *wanted* to tell them?"

Felicity flashed me a look from her blue eyes. "If I had nothing I wanted to tell them, why should I have something I want to tell you?"

"Because we both want to know who killed Dee."

"Are you sure I didn't? I did have opportunity. Dee came to see me Monday evening. She had her backpack."

"Opportunity, yes. But did you have motive?"

"The police aren't sure yet. Lesbians are, however, inherently suspect."

"Felicity . . . I was wondering about Dee's drinking."

Felicity smiled and waved at an elderly couple on the other side of the street. The man waved back. The woman slid her hand through her husband's arm.

"Felicity? About Dee's drinking—"

"Horrors! Dee drank? Alcohol?"

"Dee was drunk when she got back to the hotel on Sunday evening."

"That was the evening she had a nasty row with her erstwhile boyfriend. But you know that."

"Cordner and Quinn mentioned I was there?"

"Yes."

"Did Quinn mention he was there?"

"Hmm . . . if my taste ran in that direction—" Felicity gave me a speculative look.

"Did you see Dee on Sunday? After her fight with Sean?"

"No, I drove out with some friends. We stayed late."

"Do you think it was really over between Dee and Sean?"

"Dee said it was when I saw her on Monday evening. Who knows what was going on in her head? She didn't even know. Care to have your cards read?"

"What?"

We were crossing the street. In front of us was the historic building that served as the town library. "They have a tarot reader," Felicity said. "You can also buy an apple tart or a piece of estate jewelry."

"In the library?"

Felicity pointed. "This way." We rounded the corner. Across the street was a church. "That's where we're going," she said.

"Wait a minute. There are a couple of more questions I want to ask you first. And are you sure you want to go into a church wearing that dress?"

She laughed. "The bazaar is housed in the church basement. By now, they've gotten accustomed to having the notorious Felicity Hollingsworth drop in to buy a jar of honey and paw through their used novels and hand-knit sweaters."

"Okay, if you say so. But first . . . Felicity, did Dee ever mention Michael Donovan?"

"Michael Donovan? He was married to your friend, wasn't he? The one who's staying at the hotel? What's her name?"

"Her name is Tess."

"Why do you want to know if Dee mentioned Michael Donovan?"

"Because Michael stayed at the hotel last spring. Dee said he was a 'lovely gentleman.'"

"And you want to know if that was an impression or something that she'd confirmed at close quarters. Is that it?"

Two guys in their twenties, sporting tans and athletic builds, turned to give Felicity another look as they walked past. We really should move along. A street corner was not the place for a barely there red sundress.

"Lizzie, are you still with me?"

"Sorry. Yes, that's what I want to know. Do you think Dee and Michael had been involved?"

"I would say no. She was too casual when she mentioned him. Dee was still at that age when former lovers matter enough to merit emotion."

So much for that theory. "What about the other people at the hotel? What did she say about them?"

"Let's see. She said one of the guests this week was a black woman from the States. That would be you."

"Yes." I met Felicity's glance and couldn't resist asking, "Is that all she said about me?"

"She also said that you were pretty, nice enough, but a bit of a prude."

"A prude? Dee said—"

Felicity was grinning. "If you'd had a blanket just now, you would have thrown it over me."

"Getting back to what Dee said—"

"In her opinion, you weren't completely hopeless."

"I'm glad to hear it. What did she say about the others?"

"Nothing much. They had all been to the hotel before, so Dee wasn't particularly interested in them." Felicity squinted against the sunlight. "The son and his wife—"

"Jeremy and Rosalind?"

"She said they seemed not to be cooing doves as usual. She thought Jeremy had something on his mind. Wondered if it might be another woman. She was worried about that."

"Why?"

"Because of their son—Benjy? Dee said he was a great little tyke. She thought it would be a shame if his parents were about to call it quits."

A man came out of the church basement carrying a paper sack in one hand and a large cookie in the other.

"Are we done?" Felicity asked.

"Yes. No, wait a minute. Dee's parents—"

"They were killed in a motor accident when she was a child."

"I know. Did Dee ever talk about them?"

"What about them?"

"I don't know. I'm shooting in the dark here."

Felicity put her hand on her hip. "I can tell. What could Dee's parents have to do with this? She was only about five when they died."

"Yes, but when someone's murdered, you ask questions about his or her past."

"You must tell the Detective Inspector that. He and his American friend were more interested in what had been happening in Dee's present. And what I had in mind for her future."

"About Dee's parents—did she talk about them at all?"

"Only tidbits here and there. But from what she said, I gather from a five-year-old's perspective it was a case of 'Daddy loves me and Mummy doesn't.'"

"She thought her mother didn't love her?"

"Her father treated her to pony rides and told her wonderful fairy tales about princesses. Her mother preferred she keep quiet and stay neat."

"But that doesn't mean her mother didn't—"

"Dee's mother was forty-two when she was born."

"Lots of women—"

"These days. Not as much twenty years ago. And Dee seems to have been a surprise package."

"Oh. So the pregnancy wasn't planned—"

"Daddy took the whole thing in his stride, delighted to find himself a father. But Mummy Dearest never quite recovered from the shock."

"'Mummy Dearest'? You aren't saying she was abusive?"

"Not physically. Just unreachable. So little Dee loved her daddy, who loved her back. Then mummy and daddy were both gone. Maybe she had wished mummy gone. But not daddy."

"She said that?"

"I guessed that. I'm getting sunstroke. Blondes are deficient in melanin."

I laughed. "Come on. Let's go browse the church bazaar." I glanced at her dress. "And if they toss you out—"

"You can pretend not to know me."

"Did Dee really say I was a prude?"

"A bit of one. Only a first impression."

No one went into shock as Felicity crossed the threshold of the church basement. The woman who sold us our fifty-pence tickets, the cost of entry, gave us each a smile. The tarot card reader at her corner table waved in greeting.

Actually, Felicity was technically no more unclothed than most of the other summer people strolling around St. Regis. She just managed to look as if she had more bare skin on display. Or maybe it was because I knew she was a lesbian, and I thought people would be more shocked about the combination. Only heterosexuals were allowed to go bare in a summer resort.

I stopped to examine a display of carved animals. Rather eccentric animals. A bear on a unicycle. A fox leaning on a cane a la Fred Astaire. When I glanced across the room, Felicity was browsing used paperbacks and movie posters. I needed to find a rest room. The peach at breakfast was not faring well in my stomach. The tarot reader, white-haired and dimpled, pointed me around the corner. I pointed toward Felicity and said, "Would you tell her where I've gone, if you see her looking for me."

"Certainly. And when you return, I'll read your cards."

Not likely. If more trouble was on the horizon, I didn't want to know about it.

The toilets were down a corridor. Seascapes lined the pale blue walls, a soothing span of hallway. I'd be able to appreciate it after I'd found the toilet.

I was washing my hands when what had been in the back of my mind stepped forward and announced itself. It was an outrageous idea. But maybe it wasn't.

Dee's mother had been forty-two when Dee was born. Maybe she wasn't Dee's mother. What if the brother had agreed to raise his unwed sister's child as his own. His wife reluctantly agreed to go along, resented the child who had been thrust upon her. Then brother and wife die, and the sisters take in the child. Dee, unknowing, comes to live with her aunt and her real mother. Aunt Edith and Mother Sarah.

But that didn't fit. Sarah's affair with the young man in the photograph had happened years before Dee was born. And she'd said after she had injured her leg, she'd been sure no man could want her. But twenty years ago, Sarah would have been in her late thirties, a much more likely prospect for a pregnancy than her older sister Edith.

Or maybe Dee's mother really had been the brother's wife. Maybe she had simply been distant and unloving with her own child. Some mothers were. Heaven knows, mine had taken the concept of distance literally. But she had been seventeen, not forty-two.

I unlocked the toilet door and stepped out into the silent corridor.

Benjamin had known the brother and his wife. I would ask Benjamin. But how to phrase the question?

"Oh!" The exclamation whistled out of me.

"Told you I'd see you again, old girl." His muscled arm had come around me from behind, jerking me back against his hard body. His breath reeked of garlic. I held my breath. Not because of the garlic, but because of the knife which he had at my throat. I didn't dare breathe or scream or move. "Do you like my charming wife, Janey?"

"Your wife?"

"At your smooth brown throat." His knife.

"Please—tell me why you're doing this?"

"You told him, didn't you, Janey? He rung up my Guv and got me sacked."

"Fired? Michael called your boss and—"

"He told Carlyle how I tried to nick your carrier bag. Told him I must be crazy."

"I didn't know Michael was going to do that. If I had known—"

"Shut up!" He urged me back another step. "I got something nice for you, Janey. A nice piece of prime in my rank and riches."

"We can't. Not here. Someone will come."

"We'll bolt the door." He nuzzled my nape. "You smell good. Good like the other one."

"What other one?"

"Shut up, Janey." He twisted us sideways as he reached for the doorknob of the men's room. "You'll like this."

"No!" I stomped on his foot with my walking shoe, slamming my elbow back into his ribs as I pulled away. I felt the knife slash across my shoulder and arm. Blood spurted.

He came after me. I was screaming as I scrambled away from him. He was cursing. He grabbed at my legs and I fell hard on the tile floor. I kicked out at him, and the knife slashed across my calf and ankle. I kicked again, and the knife flew out of his hand. He slammed against me. We fell against the wall, knocking down one of the seascapes. I could hear myself screaming, see myself bleeding, see the hatred in his eyes.

"What are you doing?" a woman yelled. Other voices yelling other questions and exclamations were filling the corridor.

He let me go. He grabbed up his knife and ran toward the exit on the other side of the toilets. No buzzer sounded as he ran out the door. That was obviously the way he had come in, I thought as I sagged against the wall.

"Call emergency," a woman was saying to someone as she knelt down beside me. "Someone get towels."

Then Felicity was there, looking concerned. She shook her head. "Did you say I was going to be the one who caused all the excitement?"

Laughing hurt. "There's a lot of blood, isn't there?"

"Just keep still, young woman." The efficient woman who had taken charge of my first aid pressed a towel to my shoulder. "Help is on the way."

I wasn't going to die. That was the conclusion of the gruff doctor who had examined me, stitched me up, bandaged me, and given me a shot in the arm which wasn't injured. He left the nurse to clean my other assorted cuts and bruises.

That was when Felicity squeezed back into the cubicle. "You're going to live," she said, as she watched the nurse work.

"So I've been told."

"But you might want to try looking as pathetic as possible."

"Why?"

"Because Detective Quinn is outside talking to your doctor, and he is not . . . what is that charming expression you Americans have? Not a happy camper?" Felicity was grinning.

"What's he upset about?"

"Let's see . . . other than the fact that you were wandering around a church bazaar in my company getting yourself knifed when he thought you were safely tucked away at your hotel?"

"I wonder if he actually expected me to stay there until he remembered my existence and came to fetch me?"

"You'll have to ask him that. Although I wouldn't if I were you. When the man came charging through the doors with a constable in tow, he looked ready to rip off a few heads."

The nurse glanced up at Felicity. Then she went back to dabbing her smelly, burning medication on the cuts on my legs. "You'll do," she said as she tossed another cotton square into the waste. "You may leave as soon as you're dressed."

The nurse picked up her tray and turned toward the door as Quinn came through it. She looked as if she were going to object to my second visitor, but apparently she thought better of it. He stepped back to let her out.

Felicity patted me on my uninjured arm and winked. "So long, Detective Quinn," she said as she slid past him.

He didn't respond, but he certainly didn't look as if he were ready to rip off heads. He looked as cool and controlled as he usually did. "Are you certifiable?" he asked. "Are you out of your mind?"

"Not that I'm aware of. But my head does ache."

"You're lucky it's still attached to your body."

"Quinn, I think—I'm really sure—that he killed another woman. He said I smelled as good as the other one."

"Is that all he said?"

"No, he said, 'He told Carlyle how I tried to nick your carrier bag.' He said I got him sacked. But he must have been talking about Michael . . . that Michael had called his boss, this Carlyle. Who else could he have meant?"

Quinn had his arms folded. He unfolded them and pointed at my clothes on the chair. "Get dressed."

"I don't want to put those back on."

"You can't walk out of here in that hospital gown. Put on your clothes. We'll stop at the hotel so you can change."

"And then where are we going?"

"To the police station. Cordner's there supervising the search for your thug." His gray eyes pinned me. "I told him I'd bring you there if the first report was accurate and you were still in one piece."

"All right. I'm ready to get out of here. If you wouldn't mind leaving so I can change—"

He turned toward the door, turned back. He didn't look quite as calm. "Do you know that another few inches and he would have severed your jugular vein?"

"I didn't have any choice. If he'd gotten me into a locked toilet, he would have killed me anyway."

"You had a choice. Why the hell didn't you just stay put?"

"I'm not used to staying put. And I don't remember anyone suggesting I do that."

"We thought we could trust you to exercise some common sense."

"I was at a church bazaar."

"With one of the prime suspects in the case."

"One of the prime— What motive could Felicity possibly have for killing Dee?"

"If we knew that, she'd be in custody right now. Dee was with her on Monday evening."

"Dee was with me on Tuesday morning when she died. Does that mean that I'm a prime suspect too?"

"You don't have a motive. Your friend Felicity might. Get dressed."

He walked out. I angled my way off the examination table and reached for my clothes. I didn't particularly care for the feel of my own still-slightly damp blood against my skin. In fact, it made me nauseated.

And ugly thug, with his garlicky breath, had yet to be taken into custody.

I didn't even ask if Tess was still there in the hospital. The last thing she needed was to see me bandaged and bloody. It would probably send both her and the baby into shock. Besides, if Michael was with her, I might forget myself. Not that I wasn't anxious to have a conversation with Michael. But not in front of Tess.

The constable who had driven Quinn to the hospital held the door for me to get into the backseat of the patrol car. Easier said than done. Especially with Quinn standing there watching. "The station house, sir?" the constable asked when we were all in the car.

"No, the Gull's Nest Hotel. She needs to change her clothes."

I shifted around in the seat, trying to find a position where something didn't hurt. I felt like a punching bag. All I wanted was to go home. Home to Drucilla, Kentucky, where I would climb into my own bed and sleep for a few dozen years.

I managed to get into the hotel and up to my room without running into any of the other guests who seemed to be out. I heard the murmur of voices out in the kitchen as I crept back down the stairs, but if Sarah and Edith had heard me come in, they didn't consider it necessary to rush out and inquire about my comings and goings. I was a guest after all.

"We've got him," Cordner said, when he met us in front of the sergeant's desk. "He's in the back interview room."

"Did he confess?" I asked. "Has he made a statement?"

Cordner shook his head. "He's keeping mute until he has benefit of counsel." Cordner eyed my bandaged arm and shoulder, visible under my short-sleeved blouse. "You look somewhat the worse for wear, Professor."

"I feel it."

"If it's any comfort, our mate in the interview room is nursing a few bruises of his own. He seems particularly concerned about the bite on his hand. One of the constables heard him mumbling something about—forgive me—the bitch probably being rabid."

"A rabid bitch? I wonder if he had a run-in with a female dog." I could feel myself smiling, and it was a ridiculous thing to smile about it. "Did I really bite him?"

"Quite nicely. We'll have to have the doctor in to have a look at it."

"Score one for me."

Behind me, Quinn said, "If you had been killed, a bite mark would have been useful at the trial. A forensics expert could have identified it as yours."

I turned to look at him. "So if I had been killed, at least I would have made sure my killer was convicted. And I told you I didn't have any choice in the matter."

Cordner cleared his throat. "What we need to do, Professor Stuart, is get your statement. And then we'll let you go back to the hotel and get some rest."

"I don't suppose I could just look into the interview room and stick my tongue out at him?"

Cordner smiled. "I don't think that would be a good idea."

I sobered as a thought occurred to me. "There isn't any possible way that he could walk on this?"

"None at all. Unless we do something irregular in handling him. So I would rather you stayed away from him for now."

"And there are lots of other witnesses, aren't there?"

"People who saw him attacking you in the church basement and people who saw him fleeing the scene. We have no problem at all with witnesses."

Quinn said, "And, of course, you had the foresight to leave your teeth marks on him."

"Did you get the knife?" I asked Cordner.

"He's rather attached to that knife. Not only didn't he try to dispose of it, he protested in rather obscene language when it was removed from his pocket."

"He does have a way with obscene language. My ears are still burning."

"Another reason why you don't need to see him again," Quinn said.

Cordner said, "This way, Professor Stuart. Let's go into my office."

Quinn followed us. As Cordner drew out his cassette recorder, Quinn settled into the chair at Cordner's computer table.

When I got to the part about someone calling the thug's boss to tell him about the attempted mugging, Cordner asked me to repeat what I had said.

I did. "It had to have been Michael. What other 'he' besides you and Quinn knew about what happened in London?"

"Yes," Cordner said. "But who is this boss? This Carlyle?"

"He told me to shut up when I tried to ask questions. And I really do think he has killed another woman."

"Or at least raped one," Quinn said.

"Or at least that. But I think if he raped a woman, he would want to hurt her in other ways too. He enjoyed having that knife at my throat and knowing I was terrified."

Cordner turned off the cassette recorder. "If our luck is in, he'll decide to be more forthcoming after he's taken legal advice."

"And if he isn't?"

"Then perhaps we can use the fact that we now have our thug in custody to persuade Mr. Donovan to answer some questions."

"You mean to stop lying?"

"That's what I mean. Do you happen to know where Mr. Donovan is at the moment?"

"With Tess I would think. She's going to be released today. She might already be back at the hotel."

"Then why don't we go round and see if he's there?"

"What about the thug?"

"He'll keep," Quinn said.

A thought occurred me as we were going out the door. "But he must have a record. He was probably strong-arming other children for their candy when he was still in diapers."

"We're checking on his past exploits now," Cordner said.

Had his youthful exploits included molesting his female classmates in schoolyards?

Chapter Twenty-one

EDITH CAME TOWARD US, SMILING. "Lizzie, Tess is—" Her face broke apart. "Oh, no, what happened? What happened?"

I went to her and patted her shoulder. "Nothing to do with Dee."

"But you've been hurt."

"It looks much worse than it is. You should see the other guy."

"But—"

"Were you about to say Tess is back?"

"Yes, she's upstairs. Lizzie, please tell me what—"

"I'll explain later, Edith. I promise. Did Michael bring Tess home? Is he still here?"

Edith looked at Cordner and Quinn standing in her front doorway. "You say this isn't about Dee?"

"It's about another matter, Miss Crump," Cordner said. "Would you mind going upstairs and asking Mr. Donovan to come down to the lounge—if you wouldn't mind our making use of it."

"Edith," I said. "Please don't tell Tess that I've been hurt. Just make up some excuse to get Michael down here."

Edith's glance moved from me to the police officers. Her hands twisted at the skirt of her dress. Then she drew herself up. "Please, go into the lounge, Inspector. I'll ask Michael to help me . . . to help me with a leak in the plumbing." It didn't sound like the kind of task Michael would be adept at, but he would be certain to make a show of coming down to have a look before he suggested Edith call a professional.

Quinn and Cordner went into the lounge. Quinn turned to give me one of his looks as I followed behind them.

"I'm going to stay," I said.

"Why doesn't that surprise me?"

Cordner picked up the newspaper someone had left on the coffee table. He glanced at the front page, then opened the paper. He flipped through the first two or three pages until something caught his eye.

"The other murder," I said. "That's what you're reading, isn't it? The story about the woman in the Sussex field?"

Cordner passed the newspaper over to Quinn. "It would be rather too tidy, wouldn't it?"

Quinn glanced at the article. "You've got the knife the thug used on Lizzie. The body in the field had slash marks—"

Cordner nodded. "The lab can check for a match. But they'll undoubtedly think I'm seeing visions when I request it."

"Do you have that many psychopaths running around England?" I asked.

"No, Professor Stuart, but they rarely make a guest appearance in St. Regis."

"I'm not really an expert." Michael's voice floated into the room as he came down the stairs with Edith. "But I'll be happy to have a look—"

He stopped as he took the last step down into the foyer and saw us waiting there in the lounge. "Lizzie! What happened? Are you all right?" He looked genuinely concerned. He even started toward me with his hands out. He stopped as I took a step back.

"Thank you, Miss Crump," Cordner said. "If you wouldn't mind . . . if we could speak to Mr. Donovan in private—"

Edith nodded and went back up the stairs.

"Speak to me about what? What now? Are you going to accuse me of beating Lizzie up?"

"She was knifed," Quinn said. "Come inside so that we can close the door—unless you want your ex-wife to hear what we're saying."

Michael glanced toward the stairs. Then he strolled into the room and over to the sofa. "Ask your questions."

Cordner took one of the chairs. I sat down on the edge of the other. "He tried to kill me, Michael," I said. "That thug—that would-be mugger from London that you claim not to know—tried to kill me." I expected Cordner or Quinn to intervene. But neither of them said anything.

"Lizzie, how many times do I have to tell you—"

"He said you called his boss—someone named Carlyle—about the mugging. He said he got fired because of that, and that was the reason he came after me. Who is his boss, Michael? What is this all about?"

"Yes, Mr. Donovan," Cordner said. "We would like to know that. I should tell you that the man who attacked Professor Stuart is now in custody—"

"So you might want to get your story in before he does," Quinn said from his position by the sideboard. "We might like your version a whole lot better if you volunteered it now."

Michael looked from Quinn to Cordner. "I might be mistaken, but I think I'm entitled to an attorney before questioning."

"If you would like to invoke that right," Cordner said. "However, at the moment, you are not under arrest. We're merely asking for any information you might be able to provide."

"Do you have something to hide?" Quinn asked.

"Please give him his Miranda warning, or whatever the British version is," I said. "If he's done something, I don't want him to walk because you guys screwed up. He does have enough money to hire a first-rate team of attorneys."

"Hand in glove with the police, Lizzie? I thought you didn't trust cops."

"I trust them a whole lot more than I trust you. In fact, Michael, I've had it with you—right up to the jugular vein I almost got severed this morning. If you don't tell us the truth, I will go upstairs and show my assorted cuts and bruises to Tess and tell her exactly what's been going on."

"You would never do that, Lizzie. You would never risk harming the baby—"

"Your baby, Michael? What makes you think I care about your baby?"

"You care about Tess—"

"Enough not to want to see her with you. Enough to think that she has the right to know what kind of a man you really are. Actually, it is more a matter of reminding her of what she's in danger of forgetting . . . that you can't be trusted . . . that you're a lying—"

"Do you know what you're doing? Do you have any idea what you're doing?"

"What am I doing, Michael?"

He didn't answer. He looked trapped.

"Is there anything you wish to tell us, Mr. Donovan?" Cordner asked.

Michael breathed out an exasperated sigh. "That damn figurine. He thought it was something else—something that his boss could use as leverage. What else would an idiot like Raymond think when he saw a shopping bag passed from one person to another? What else would he think but that it was a drug deal?" Michael glared at me. "When you told me about the mugging— Do you really think I wanted to see you hurt? That I would have asked you to meet me and given you that damn shopping bag if I had known that creep was following me around. He's one of Carlyle's security men. But Carlyle claims he didn't know what he was up to . . . that he had never assigned him to follow me." Michael tugged at the collar of his knit shirt and opened the first two buttons. "I didn't know Carlyle would tell Raymond that I had called. I didn't know Raymond would come after you."

"I told you last night. I told you he had threatened me in the theater parking lot. I told you he had said I was another dead bitch."

"Lizzie, aren't you listening to me? Raymond's one of those musclebound losers who curses women, including his mother, in every second sentence. How was I supposed to know he would go this far? How could I know that he would actually try to hurt you?"

"He intended to kill me, Michael."

"I swear to you I didn't know he was dangerous."

"That didn't even occur to you when he pushed me in front of a bus in London?"

"You said you were trying to hold on to the shopping bag. I assumed your fall had been an accident."

I got out of my chair and walked away before I started screaming in Michael's face. From over by the Chinese screen, as I stared out the window at the street, I heard Cordner say, "Please tell us about Carlyle."

Michael was silent for a moment. Then he said, "Carlyle has various business interests, including some gambling concerns. That was how I met him."

"You're in debt to him?" That question came from Quinn.

"No, not anymore. I paid off what I owed. But Carlyle knows about my family's pharmaceutical company. He's interested in getting in on the ground floor with a new drug that we have in R and D— research and development."

"What kind of drug?" Quinn asked.

"A nuclear pharmaceutical for use in diagnosis. Nothing exotic. Nothing that could go black market. For Carlyle, it would be a legitimate investment."

"What are Mr. Carlyle's illegitimate investments?" Cordner asked.

"He has international interests. I don't know what they are. I'm sure there are people who could tell you about that if you want to know. But neither I personally nor my family's company has had business dealings with him."

Quinn said, "So you write your gambling losses off as entertainment?"

"Carlyle made me a loan when I played at a casino in which he has holdings. I paid off that loan with interest." Michael cleared his throat. "Carlyle spends a part of his time here in England. When he found out I was going to be in the country, he asked for a meeting to discuss his proposed investment in my family's company. I said no, that we weren't interested in selling additional stock."

"And he took your turndown right in stride?" Quinn said.

"I thought he did. I still don't think he set Raymond to follow me. He seemed to be more than a little annoyed when he heard about it."

"Maybe he was annoyed that Raymond had screwed up his assignment," Quinn said.

Cordner said, "Why didn't you tell us this before, Mr. Donovan?"

"I didn't think there was any reason to tell you. I called Carlyle on Tuesday evening—after Lizzie told me what happened—to tell him about the mugging attempt. I demanded to know what was going on. He assured me Raymond had acted on his own and that he would handle the matter. I didn't know that he intended to fire Raymond or that Raymond would be stupid enough to come after Lizzie."

"But you knew he was here in Cornwall," I said. I walked back across the room and faced Michael as he sat there at his ease on the sofa. "You knew that he hates women. You knew he had threatened me."

"Lizzie—"

"I am going to tell Tess about this, Michael."

Michael stood up. We stared into each other's eyes.

Cordner got to his feet too. "Mr. Donovan, if you will keep yourself available for further questioning."

"Are you charging me with anything?" Michael asked.

"Not now. I'm not sure that you have committed any offense that I can charge you with."

"Then if you'll excuse me." In the doorway, he turned. "I'll tell Tess myself, Lizzie. Don't worry, she'll get the whole truth. Better from me than you."

I shook my head. "Why didn't you just admit that you knew who this Raymond was? If you haven't done anything illegal—"

"Knowing that I've been gambling with large sums would hardly impress Tess with my stability. Neither would the fact that I took a loan—even a short-term one—from someone like Carlyle. And it was hardly as if I could trust you not to tell her once you knew."

Michael left the room. I sat back down on the edge of the chair. My shoulder and leg hurt. My stomach burned inside. Maybe I was getting an ulcer.

I couldn't think. Michael was on his way upstairs to tell Tess.

I met Cordner's gaze. "Am I wrong to make him tell her? Did what Michael said make sense to you? Do you think he might honestly not have known how dangerous Raymond is?"

Cordner said, "Whether he knew or not—" Then he shook his head.

Quinn said, "What Inspector Cordner is too tactful to say is that whether he knew or not, Michael Donovan isn't someone your friend Tess needs to be married to again."